Sometimes Moments

Renee,

Life is a cluster
of Sometimes Moments.

Love them. Cherish them.
Live them.
They're more beautiful
when grouped together.
thank you for everything.

x

Sometimes Moments

a novel

LEN WEBSTER
International Bestselling Author

Published: Len Webster 2015
author.lennwebster@hotmail.com
Editing: Mickey Reed
www.mickeyreedediting.com
Proofreading: Jenny Carlsrud Sims
www.editing4indies.com
Cover design: Najla Qamber Designs
www.najlaqamberdesigns.com
Interior designed and formatted by

www.emtippettsbookdesigns.com

For Jaycee Ford and Alex Rosa.
Thank you for walking into my life and fighting dragons with me.
Thank you for being the first to believe in the beauty of sometimes moments.
Our friendship is spelt in the many infinities of this universe.
We are forever.

Sometimes you will never know the value of a moment until it becomes a memory.

~Dr Seuss

Prologue

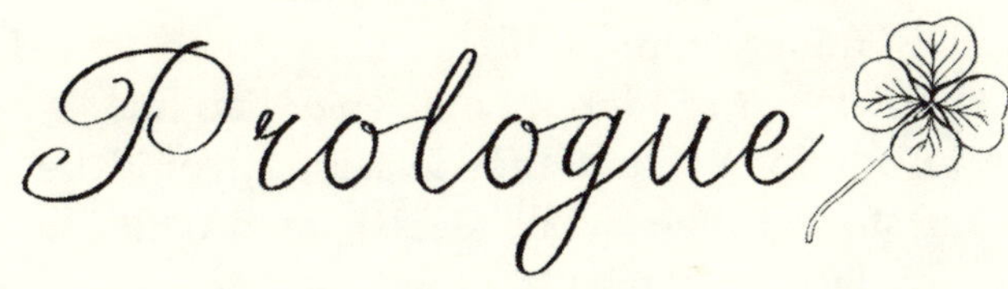

Four years and five months ago.

Infinities exist only when two people believe in them and will for the universe to allow them.

Tap. Tap. Tap.

The taps on the glass window had Peyton's head turning. She sat on her bed, waiting for another sound. Seconds passed.

Tap. Tap.

Silence.

Tap.

Resting her book down, Peyton felt her phone vibrate next to her on the bed. Seeing his name, she picked it up and answered it.

"Tell me it's you outside my window," she said quietly into the phone's speaker.

He didn't answer. Her breathing heaved as she moved the covers off her body and stood from the bed.

"Callum!"

A laugh broke into her ear.

"It's me, Pey. Go to the window."

She smiled at the sound of his voice. Smooth and beautiful. She wasn't sure when it had happened, but when he'd kissed her underneath the cherry blossoms outside her window, Callum Reid was no longer her best friend. That one kiss and their relationship had become *more.*

Hanging up, Peyton stood next to her window and looked back at the bedroom door. If her father caught her with him at such an hour, he'd never let her leave the house again.

But her parents were asleep. What were a few minutes with him? Summer would end soon, and then they'd be attending their final year of high school. They had one last year together before university and life decisions would be made. It was either stay in their small tourist town or leave and go to the city—a decision she hadn't made just yet.

After pushing the curtains back, Peyton lifted the window up and was met with Cullum's lips on hers. Her hands wrapped around his wrists as she kissed him back. Her playful bite of his lower lip had him laughing against hers.

"Easy, tiger," he whispered as he pulled his mouth away.

Her heavy breathing mirrored his, and she smiled up at him. The bedside lamp gave her enough light to see his grey eyes. She had always loved him. All her life, she had. But that one kiss had broken free an unconditional and intimate form of love.

"You have to go," she pleaded.

He brushed her light-brown hair behind her ear before placing his hands on the windowsill. "Just a walk down to the lake together. We'll be back before your father wakes up for work," he promised.

The glint in his eyes had her rolling her own at him. "Let me just change," she sighed, pulling away.

Peyton was surprised when Callum's hand stopped her from leaving.

He tugged her to face him and his eyes ran down her body. "What you're wearing is more than fine."

This was all new to them. They had never gone past their boundaries, and when he did compliment her, she'd blush. Because they'd grown up as neighbours, she knew all there was to know about him.

"Fine!" Peyton said, faking her bothered tone.

Callum grinned as he held out his hands to her and helped her out of her bedroom window. When her feet hit the dry grass, she remembered she had no shoes on. Callum let go of her hands and picked up the basket next to him, taking out a pair of black flats.

"You planned this!" Peyton took the pair of flats she recognised as a pair she had missing.

"I wasn't willing to let you change your mind if you went and changed."

Stepping out of the house, Peyton covered her eyes to the early morning sun. It had been two days since she went to the lake with Callum. The warm wind hit her skin as she sat on the steps of the front porch. Looking across the road, she noticed the moving trucks parked in the driveway of the house across the street. Tucking her hair behind her ear, she stood up and watched men with boxes pack the trucks.

After she walked down the path and crossed the road, she stepped onto the green grass of her neighbour's lawn. She watched as pieces of furniture left the double-story house and was placed in the back of the trucks.

"Peyton?"

She heard her name. When she looked at the door, the grey eyes made her shake her head.

"I don't..." she breathed out.

"I'm sorry," he apologised.

"When were you going to tell me?" The aching in her chest stifled her sob.

He looked away and she felt her heart crumble.

"Callum," she begged.

"I couldn't tell you, Peyton. Had I told you, it would have been difficult to say goodbye," he said and then instructed one of the movers who held a box that was marked 'Callum's room' to place it in the back of the truck.

"This is much worse!" she yelled.

Callum flinched before he breathed out and reached for her hands. Peyton took a step back.

"You're leaving me!" she sobbed.

"Summer's over, Pey. I can't stay in this town. I have to leave. I'm... I'm sorry about everything. It and us... We shouldn't have happened. We should have just stayed friends," Callum said before he turned and walked back into the house.

Friends.

That one word pierced her heart.

Peyton wiped her tears and looked around. More boxes were packed into the trucks, and she tried to process it all.

"Peyton, I didn't think we'd see you today." She heard Mr Reid say.

She lifted her head to see an older version of Callum step out of the house. "I-I," she stuttered, but she couldn't form words.

"Dad, just leave it," Callum said angrily. He didn't look her way as he handed his father another box.

Callum stood in front of her, and the fine line his mouth made was one she never saw.

"You should have told me," she said, hurt and devastated by what was happening around her.

"There was nothing to tell. I'm moving to the city."

"That's it? You're just up and moving to the city. That's all it took? Two days and you changed your mind," she cried.

She had told him that she loved him. He hadn't said it back, but he hadn't pushed her away. That night they'd gone to the lake, she'd given him her innocence and told him that she loved him. Two days later, he was leaving.

"Peyton, it's goodbye," he softly said. The break in his voice didn't match the menacing look in his eyes.

"Then goodbye. But don't you ever come back to this town, Callum. You're dead to me! If what we had meant nothing to you, then good. Go! I never want to see your face again!" Peyton took one more look at those grey eyes before she turned around and walked towards her house.

"Peyton!" he called but she couldn't do it.

She couldn't listen to his voice calling her name. Her heart was too broken to accept any more pain at the hands of him.

One

Present day

Cherry blossoms dancing in the wind caught her eye. Beautifully and gracefully demanding for attention. Sheer, cream-coloured curtains obscured the pink flowers. Breathing out, Peyton parted the curtains and pulled the window open, allowing the cold autumn air to serenade her. The cherry blossom tree outside her window held so many memories, ones she hated and ones she loved. That tree was the reason why her parents had bought the old house in Daylesford, Victoria.

Peyton admired the structure of the tree, taller than the house and older than she. During winter, the cherry blossoms grew vibrant, far more beautiful than in autumn or spring. This one tree strived in showcasing its beauty during a time when snow would sometimes fall. Giving the tree one last appreciative glace, Peyton closed her window and locked the latch.

"Peyton."

She turned around to see her great-aunt Brenda holding a plate of scrambled eggs and toast in her hands.

"Big day today," her aunt said with a proud smile.

After walking over to her oak dresser, Peyton picked up a hair band and tied her brown hair into a low ponytail. With a huff, Peyton made her way to the bed and sat on it.

"I don't know if I can do it, Aunt Brenda," she confessed as she looked down at her hands.

The bed dipped and Peyton turned her head to see her aunty smiling up at her.

"Honey, your mother and father would be proud of you," she said with confidence and placed the plate in Peyton's hand.

"But what if I'm not ready, not skilled—"

"None of that!" her aunty scolded, cutting Peyton off. "Peyton, you worked hard. Your Uncle John and I, we know you can do it. You put yourself through school. You know how to run the hotel. You've run it plenty of times before."

Peyton closed her eyes and took a deep breath. "Yes, but I mean, it's now mine. It's not you and Uncle John running it anymore. It's me. It's mine. I just... I don't want to let Mum and Dad down as well as the town." Picking up a piece of buttered toast, she took a bite to stop her from saying any more.

The fine line Aunt Brenda's mouth made was one Peyton didn't like to see.

"You inherited it, Peyton. It's been yours all this time. We have just been maintaining it until you finished university and decided what you wanted to do with it. Nothing is going to change unless you want it to."

"I know," Peyton said before putting a forkful of scrambled eggs in her mouth and chewing.

"You know, Peyton," her aunt said, taking her hand.

Peyton knew this talk. It was one her aunt had had with her many times before. But the sadness in her light-brown eyes had Peyton's heart aching.

"You don't have to stay here. You can go to the city. You can go anywhere in this world and do what you want. Maybe see Cal—"

"No," Peyton cut her off and handed her aunt the plate.

"But—"

"I will *not* go to the city. I will *not* leave this town. And I will not see *him*. He's dead to me and you know it. He didn't even—" Peyton stopped herself. She felt the tears burn her eyes and swallowed hard, hoping they'd retreat.

Standing up from her bed, Peyton looked at her great-aunt.

The heartbreak was always evident in her eyes. They shared a form of pain. Her aunt had lost a niece and a nephew-in-law, and Peyton had lost a mother and a father.

Aunt Brenda placed the plate on the bed and wrapped her arms around Peyton. "You need to forgive him, love. Your mother wanted you to forgive him," she whispered.

Peyton stood there, letting the tears slide down her face. She had tried to forgive him for leaving her, but the moment that her parents died, the idea of forgiving him had become a thought she couldn't comprehend. Breaking her heart, she'd get over. But not being at her parents' funeral? That, she would never forgive. There was no point in forgiving. He'd left their small town years ago and never once looked back.

Two weeks of no bookings allowed Peyton the time to decide if she'd change what her parents had worked hard to establish. It hadn't been her idea to close the hotel for two weeks. It'd been her aunt and uncle's. Though in their early seventies, they had still managed to run The Spencer-Dayle while she'd finished her last year of high school and then university. But now, the hotel was Peyton's and her aunt and uncle would be enjoying their retirement on the peninsula.

Holding her laptop bag close to her, Peyton walked up the hill until she met the path of trees that led up to the lake. She looked up to see that the leaves had turned into lovely shades of brown and orange. Leaves slowly fell from the branches. She stood there a moment and tried to settle her nerves. It was her first day as owner of her family's hotel.

The moment her parents died in that car accident, Peyton had inherited it all. Her parents' money, the house, and the hotel. They had rebuilt it after the previous owner had let it grow old with time. They'd seen the hotel by the lake as potential, and her parents had chosen right. It had become a popular tourist accommodation and brought income to the family and town.

After making her way through the lane of autumn trees,

Peyton reached the end of the dirt path and glanced over at the fog that blanketed the lake. It didn't matter how many memories she shared with *him* on this lake; she would always love it. The days she had spent with her father sitting on the pier, admiring the hotel were the memories she wished were her reality. But all it had taken was one car crash and she'd lost her parents forever.

Behind a few trees near the edge of the lake was a bench. The first Monday of every month, Graham Scott would meet her there. When she had started her final year of high school, Graham had been one of her best friends, and when graduation came around, he was the only one who stayed in the area. Instead of moving to the city for university, he stayed on his family's lavender farm and enrolled in an online university course just like Peyton. What brought them closer were her parents' deaths. Graham was the only one who could understand after he'd lost his mother to cancer when he was twelve.

Since he'd taken over the farm, she saw less and less of him. But they had stuck to their promise. The first Monday of each month—a morning together by the lake. Peyton smiled, knowing she'd see him next week. Squinting her eyes, she noticed someone sitting on the bench. She knew it was either Mrs Figs on her morning stroll or Mr Tucker feeding the ducks. Peyton walked over to the bench to say good morning.

She stopped just short of the bench when she recognised his baseball cap. Shaking her head, she cleared her throat.

"Think you've got your dates wrong. First Monday of the month is June second," Peyton stated.

A chuckle slipped from Graham's lips as he stood up from the bench, turning to face her. The large grin on his face was one she loved—so was his deep dimple. His blonde hair was just visible from under his hat. Peyton looked down to see a bundle of lavender in his hand. Each time she saw him, he'd bring her lavender from his farm.

"It's a big day for you, Peyton. Couldn't miss it for the world. Plus, it gives me an excuse to see you," he said as he pulled her in for a hug.

The scent of lavender hit her nostrils and she smiled. It was the scent that was forever on his skin.

"Not a big day if you keep me from working!" she scolded before untangling herself from him. Then she let out a laugh as she took the lavender from him.

Turning, she looked out over the still lake and then at her hotel. It daunted her. The idea that she was now the owner of what her parents had once called theirs terrified her.

She didn't want to let her parents down, but she found it would be inevitable. All she could hope for was that she wouldn't destroy the dreams they'd built. She didn't want to tarnish what The Spencer-Dayle meant to her aunt and uncle and the town.

As if he knew that her fears were consuming her, Graham placed his hand on her shoulder and squeezed lightly to reassure her.

"They'd be proud of you, Peyton. We all are."

And that's when she let tears stream down her face. She knew she couldn't let her family's hotel by the lake falter. It was all she had left of her parents.

Two

After they sat on the wooden bench, they walked to the hotel. Peyton opened the main doors and was welcomed with the bright front desk. Once she'd placed her laptop bag on the desk, she followed Graham to the main sitting room.

"What are your plans for this place?" Graham asked as he sank into the dark-grey couch.

Peyton sat next to him and took in the large arched windows that flooded the room with natural light. Though she had been here the day before to check out the last guests, it felt unfamiliar to her. Maybe it was the fact that she now owned it and had to run it. She knew her aunt and uncle would have been happy to run the hotel, but Peyton couldn't do that to them. It was time that she accepted her responsibilities, just as Graham had with the farm.

"Aunt Brenda wants me to make the hotel my own. But I honestly don't think I could do that. I start making changes and it wouldn't be my parents' hotel anymore. This is all that's really left of them."

Peyton looked up at the cream-painted room. She remembered the day that they had painted the ceiling. Her dad had argued over colour choice, that cream was too plain, but her mother had won that argument with a victorious smile. That was true love. No matter the bickering or the arguing,

Peyton knew that her parents loved each other unconditionally. But for her, love was just a concept. She was far from accepting the notion—not after *him.*

"I think your aunt's right on that one, Peyton. Maybe incorporate yourself in it."

She turned her head to see his cheek in his palm. Graham raised his brow at her and then blinked twice.

"How do I do that, Graham? How do I do that and not make a mess of it all? What if I ruin everything that they worked so hard to create? What my aunt and uncle worked so hard to maintain?" Sitting up, she stared at him as he pursed his lips.

"Trial and error," he stated.

"Trial and error? Are you insane?"

Graham straightened his back and let out a short laugh. "I'm the definition of insane."

Shaking her head, Peyton looked down at the lavender that lay on the glass coffee table. For three years, Graham had run the farm, making it one of the most successful in the state. But that was Graham; he knew business and excelled at it. As for Peyton, she lacked the creativity that would make her shine through.

"Change is inevitable. You have to let go and make mistakes and changes. You know your folks would always support you. You just have to try, Peyton. Not trying is never going to get you to move forward with your life. How long do you have till the next guest comes?"

Graham's words burned through her heart.

Change is inevitable.

She didn't want change. She never had. But change kept occurring. Slowly, change had happened around their town. Everyone had started to leave for the city and the inner suburbs. Change had caused too much heartache in her life. She eventually lost everyone she loved. But Graham—she wanted more for him. She knew that he loved the farm, but Peyton knew that he was destined for more.

"What about you, Graham? You should be working for a big marketing agency or something. Not on a farm!"

"I can't leave the farm, Peyton," he said strongly. It was almost like a warning for her to not continue.

"You're a hypocrite. You know that, right? You can't dish out life advice and not take it yourself." Peyton got up off the couch and made her way towards the front desk, annoyed with him.

"Peyton!" Graham called out to her, the irritation in his voice clear.

Upon reaching the desk, Peyton picked up the file that contained reservations and looked at him. She frowned at the sad look in his eye. She was sure he believed that he had hurt her feelings, but it took more to hurt her deeply. She knew what real pain felt like. This was hardly a pinch.

"I'm sorry. You're right. I can't stand here and tell you to make changes when I'm not willing to make them myself. I just think you deserve more than living in the shadow of your parents. Before the accident, you wanted more out of life. You wanted to travel, but now, you can't even step past the town's welcome sign. If this isn't your dream, don't settle for it. Not for the rest of your life. When the farm is settled enough, I'll try the city, okay? I swear I'll try."

Peyton let out a sigh and placed the folder back on the desk, her fingers running over them. Two weeks until her first guest, the Swan's—a young newlywed couple from the suburbs—arrived. And it was a month until the Reynolds' wedding. In the space of a fortnight, Peyton would decide what her plans were for the hotel by the lake. Weddings at The Spencer-Dayle were what made money. Since it was an hour away from the city, most guests stayed overnight and enjoyed the town.

"I shouldn't scold you, either. I'm no closer to leaving this place than you. I knew that I'd always have some connection to the hotel. That I would run it when I was older. I just didn't think that I'd inherit it before high school graduation. For now, I'll run it my parents' way. I'll figure out the rest as I go along. If I don't run it, then Aunt Brenda and Uncle John will, and I don't want them doing that."

Graham approached the desk and leant on it, staring at her.

He gave her an unsure smile before sighing.

"Who'd have thought that you and I would be taking on such responsibility at twenty-one? All our friends are partying it up and having real university experiences, being free. Sometimes I'm jealous that I didn't follow…Krista and attend Deakin with her. Who knows what would have happened to us if I had," Graham said. He looked down at his hands for a moment before looking up at Peyton.

After stepping around the desk, Peyton placed her hand on his arm and gave him a reassuring squeeze. "Maybe if you had just told her that you liked her, it'd be different."

Graham let out an unconvincing laugh. "Wouldn't have helped. She left for Jake. We all know that. And I'm stuck with you, remember?"

Part of being in a small town was that the choices in a romantic partner were always limited. In most cases, partners had chosen themselves before anyone had really made moves. It was just how it had been growing up.

Peyton offered Graham an understanding smile. She knew what it was like to be drawn to and love one person. And how, when they left, it was like nothing made sense, that they were your one true understanding of the world.

"You were too good for her anyway."

"No," Graham said with a sad gleam in his eye, "she was too good for me. Her daddy wouldn't want a farmer dating his daughter."

Peyton leant on the desk next to him. "Any father would be honoured to have their daughter date a guy like you, Graham. I know just what a guy you can be. You're every father's dream."

When Graham fell silent, Peyton glanced up at him. His dimple deepened as he smiled. No doubt he was enjoying the compliment that she'd just given him. Then she slapped his arm and pushed off the desk.

"And any guy would be lucky to be yours, Peyton."

Peyton turned away and stared out the window, the shimmer of the water catching her eye. For four years, she'd blamed herself. She'd done something wrong with him all those years ago. Maybe it had been too quick. Maybe he'd regretted being her first and the 'I love you' that had slipped from her lips. Their friendship had been ruined by one kiss that had led to the events of his leaving.

The sound of a phone had Peyton spinning. She saw Graham staring at his phone before he sighed and put it back into his pocket. His fingers combed his hair and then started to roll up the sleeves of his long shirt.

"That was the old man. I better get going, Peyton. I promised him that I'd go over the sprinkler system on the eastern part of the farm." Graham walked over, pulled her in for a quick hug, and whispered, "You're going to be a great owner of this place, Peyton. I believe in you. Always will," before he kissed the top of her head.

By the time Peyton had settled in and opened the curtains to all of the rooms, it was just after lunch. The regular staff had been put on holiday leave by her aunt and uncle. They had made plans for this fortnight of the hotel's closure for years.

Once she had graduated from high school, Peyton had decided that it was time she took the business for herself and applied for business school. Too afraid to leave Daylesford, she had taken online classes instead. Her bachelor was on display in her living room, above the fireplace. She'd been too afraid to leave town, so Graham and the hotel had hosted her small graduation ceremony and party. It was as close to the real ceremony as she could get. It was a day that she didn't want her aunt and uncle to miss out on. They had made sacrifices for Peyton, and she was determined to never let them down.

Lifting the screen of her MacBook Air, Peyton pressed the power button. As her laptop powered on, she looked over the office that she was sitting in. It had been her father's. The small, gold clock that her mother had given him for their wedding anniversary sat on the right-hand corner of the wooden desk, and a portrait of Peyton and her parents sat on the left. Reaching over, Peyton picked up the frame and stared at the three of them. She was eight when they had taken that photo by the lake. Her blue eyes mirrored her mother's, but her light-brown hair mirrored her father's.

A sadness filled her chest. Being an only child, she had been close to her parents. The moment that the police had told her of their passing, Peyton had felt the world fall beneath her. The pain had made her forget about the hurt that she'd felt when Callum had left town.

She placed the frame back in its original position and logged into her emails. A few business ones would have to be answered today, as well as some from previous guests. After minimising her screen, Peyton logged into her Facebook account and saw a tag notification from one of her best friends, Madilynne Woodside. Clicking on the notification, she tensed at the picture.

"Summer before year twelve! Miss this!"

She swallowed hard at the picture of her group of friends standing by the trees near the hotel and his arm around her waist as they smiled at the camera. Peyton blinked quickly at the picture. Three days later, they had made love under the stars, and then two days after that, he'd broken her heart.

Unable to help herself, Peyton read the comments to see that he had not made one. She hovered her cursor over his face before clicking to close her browser. Then she closed her laptop and took a deep breath in and then out.

He's gone, Peyton. He left. You need to remember that.

"*I really* don't want 'work' in my pub, Peyton."

She set down the guest list for the Reynolds' wedding to see a beer placed on her table. Three hours of going over the wedding plan and she'd been done. She knew one thing: weddings like this one were going to be charged more for such outrageous requirements. Deciding to take a break, Peyton had gone for a walk to go over the list in a new environment. That's how she found herself sitting at a table in the Daylesford Pub.

Squinting her eyes, she stared at the dark-coloured beer in front of her.

"Jay, you know I hate beer," she stated and eyed him, his hand behind his back.

He stroked his short beard before setting another glass on the table. "Yeah, I know. The beer's for me. The Coke's for you. Don't know why you come here if you hate beer. You offend and break my heart every time you walk through my door, Peyton."

Jay sat in the seat next to her, and she reached over for her glass, taking a long sip. The twinkle in his warm, chocolate eyes had her rolling hers. It wasn't that Jay was unattractive—it was the opposite. Any young female who stayed in Daylesford wanted in his bed. But he wasn't the type to use women. He was the settle down type.

Jay was just like Peyton and Graham. He had stayed behind because his family owned the local pub. But, unlike them, Jay liked what he did. Ever since he had graduated from high school two years ahead of Peyton, he had strived to fulfil his role as pub owner.

Putting the glass down, Peyton returned to the Reynolds' wedding list. When one had money, one lavished. And bride-to-be Marissa Reynolds had money—her parents' money, to be exact.

"Ugh, she really chose our town to be the place for her wedding?" Jay asked with much disgust. He sat back in his chair and reached for his beer, almost drinking the entire glass in one pull.

Peyton's eyebrows furrowed, and she tapped her finger on the table. "Don't like Marissa?"

Jay's lips parted and his brows met, bewildered by her question. "You do?"

"I've never met her or her fiancé. Aunt Brenda took the booking a few months ago while I was studying for exams. Should I be worried? Is she a bridezilla?"

She didn't need an uncooperative bride. Peyton knew the importance of the day, but from past experience, the most challenging brides were the ones where money had absolutely no limits.

"She wanted to tear down my pub because it wasn't an ideal backdrop for her wedding pictures. I bloody love the woman! What's she got you doing? Putting fancy Japanese fish in the lake?" Jay set his now empty glass on the table and folded his arms over his chest.

"Just the guest list is substantial. I don't think that I have the staff to cater for so many people. It's meant to be a private wedding, but she's got half of the Collingwood football team coming." Peyton sighed and returned the papers back in the folder and then her folder in her bag.

"Be careful of them, Peyton. I see you near any of them footy boys and I won't make any promises of not breaking their legs."

Jay's tense body had Peyton rolling her eyes.

"Don't go all protective over me, Jay," she said as she got out of her chair and picked up her bag. Her break from the hotel was already long stretched. She needed to return.

She looked down and met Jay's concerned face.

He stared at her for a moment before he closed his eyes and sighed. "Someone has to be, Peyton."

Before she was able to ask him what he meant, Peyton felt her phone vibrate in her pocket. When she pulled it out, she saw a new text message.

> **Marissa Reynolds**: Peyton, since you are now dealing with the wedding and my fiancé doesn't think your hotel is suitable, I will be sending him down tomorrow to have a look over it.

Peyton glared at the message and let her shoulders sag. "Bridezilla's fiancé is coming tomorrow. I better get back and make sure the hotel's of 'suitable' manner for their wedding. I'll see you, Jay."

Three

Marissa Reynolds: Expect my fiancé at around one.

Peyton placed her phone back on the desk and her chin in the palm of her hand. The hotel was quiet—too quiet for her liking. She wished her aunt hadn't sent all the staff on holidays; it would have been nice to spend her days with someone to talk to. A day alone in the hotel and she realised that there wasn't anything physical or structural that she wanted to change about The Spencer-Dayle. Last night, she'd decided that it was the services the hotel provided that she could make her own. She just needed to figure out what those services could be.

Picking up the Reynolds' file, Peyton read over the wedding plan for the fourth time today. She'd spent last night analysing it. Making sure that she made notes on potential issues the fiancé would have, and highlighting any problems she had so they could discuss them together. This wedding would provide enough income to last through the year without any other booking. It was *the* big one.

The sound of the bell rang, alerted Peyton to someone's presence in the hotel. She looked over at the gold clock to see that it had only just ticked 12:21 p.m. She heard footsteps and then it went quiet for a moment before she heard a muffled voice. Upon getting up from the worn, leather desk chair, Peyton walked towards her office door and adjusted her high-waist skirt. With a deep breath, she palmed the handle and opened the door.

Peyton stepped out of her office and closed the door behind her. "I'm sorry, but The Spencer-Dayle is closed due to owner chan—"

She stopped when she looked over at the person standing by the front desk. She felt all breath leave her and her mouth fell open. Her eyes were wide in surprise as she took him in. He stood there with a careful smile on his face and his hands in his dress pants pockets.

"Hello, Peyton," he said.

Blinking didn't take away the image of him standing before her. Not possible. He couldn't.

She stayed quiet as his posture tensed. He used to be so carefree. But now, he was dressed up like he was about to seal a merger with a careful, practised smile on his face. No sincerity to it, there for the sake of it. Glances were exchanged, but Peyton refused to speak, purely due to the fact that words were failing her.

His eyes ran down her body before he looked away and took in the hotel. It was different from how he would have remembered it. Just before her parents' deaths, they had renovated The Spencer-Dayle, adding the old with the new, balancing it out until it was perfect. Little things had stayed, but most things had changed. Peyton followed his line of gaze until it stopped at a photo of the lake. A photo he had taken. For a moment, she watched a regretful smile develop until he shook his head and looked back at her. His smile faded just as quickly as she had blinked.

"It's good to see you," he said.

This time, he sounded like he meant it—which was a ridiculous concept for her to believe. He'd left. Not her. He could have come back but he hadn't.

Peyton let out laugh of disbelief and shook her head, fighting the pain and heat that rose from her heart and up her throat. It was a pressure in her chest that she hadn't felt in years. His eyebrows met and he looked offended by her reaction to him.

"I don't know why you're here, but if I were you, I'd leave. Right now," Peyton warned before spinning on her heel and stalking back to her office door.

"Come on, Peyton. I'm early. I guess *Marissa* didn't tell you that I'd be coming."

Peyton stopped.

Marissa... The wedding...

The constricting pain of her heart, what it felt like, was something she had long forgotten. Her eyes prickled and she mentally cursed herself. Taking a deep breath in, she opened her office door. Once she'd closed it behind her, she leant against the door to stabilise her legs. Uncomfortable heat spread through her body. Emotions she hadn't felt since before she'd turned eighteen. Since the moment she'd found out he was leaving.

Peyton let Marissa's text message play through her mind.

Engaged.

For a moment, she was jealous. Marriage was a concept she could only be a stranger to. She watched weddings, but the thought of her own was something she couldn't conjure. He was engaged, and that was her out. A line had now been drawn.

Peyton let that thought run loops around her head. This was her closure. He'd gotten what he'd wanted out of city life. Though her heart had always wanted a way back to him, it was her head that had told her to let go and move on. It had been easy to forget the pain of him when her parents had died. That pain had been worse. It had taken the life out of her. Only Graham and her aunt and uncle had brought her back to a world of living.

You're acting unprofessional, Peyton. He means nothing in your life now.

With a firm nod, Peyton retrieved the file from her desk. She hadn't connected the dots that it would be *his* wedding. But, then again, she only had Marissa Reynolds' approved guest list, not the fiancé's.

Peyton turned and walked to the door. She drew in another

breath to calm her nerves and reminded herself that he was just a guest.

When she opened the door, she stepped out of her office to find him standing in front of the photograph of the lake. His eyes held a sad glance as he stared at it intently. It had been taken at the small hill just before the lake; the sky was purple and red and the water had sparkled. The memory of watching him take the photograph would always be burned in her memory. It was in that moment, when he'd been unaware that she was staring at him, that she had known she was in love with him.

She pushed that one good memory of them away and cleared her throat. The sad look remained in Callum's eyes, but she ignored the way it pulled her in. The way he had always done so.

"Mr Reid, if you would like to accompany me around the hotel, I can show you how Marissa has planned out the wedding." Peyton gestured to the door and held the file tight.

"Mr Reid? Is that how we are doing this?" he asked raising a brow at her.

The sad eyes were gone. Instead, they looked fascinated by her. She'd have to make sure that twinkle was extinguished. That same twinkle had been persuasive in her losing her virginity to him.

"Yes."

"Well, then. If you wish, Miss Spencer."

His voice had a warmth to it, and she didn't like the way her name on his lips made her heart jump.

Settle down, you stupid vital organ. Remember, he broke you! Shattered you to the point where you thought you might as well be dead. Better not let me down.

Stepping out of the hotel, she guided him out the back and past the conservatory. Then she stopped just by the cleared grass and took out the detailed map of the wedding.

Placing the file under her arm, she held up the map.

"As you can see, Mr Reid, we'll have the post in and the frames up in the next few weeks. Once stained—to the colour your fiancée has chosen—fairy lights will be wrapped around the rafters and lanterns will light the path and around the wooden slates. The dusk will provide enough light to see the lake as you have your first dance together."

Saying it out loud, she realised just how beautiful their wedding would be. She looked out at the lake and let the sadness consume her chest.

Just this one time.

A laugh echoed behind her. She turned around to see him laughing and shaking his head.

"Is there a problem, Mr Reid?" Peyton asked, a little annoyed.

He let out another chuckle before composing himself and returning his hands in his pockets. Then he shrugged at her. "Of course not, Miss Spencer. The wedding sounds beautiful."

That, they could both agree on.

After walking across the grass, she stopped at the end of the cliff and turned to face him. His grey eyes still held beauty to them, and she held the map tight between her fingers, crushing it.

"And the lake's pier and bridge will be the place where the photos will be taken," she said, pointing at both structures.

"I'm sure Marissa will like that."

Peyton ignored the little pang of jealousy she felt and led him towards the guesthouses, though she wasn't sure why she bothered. He'd grown up in this town. He knew it better than anyone else. But still, Peyton showed him around The Spencer-Dayle, ensuring that he wouldn't change his mind when it came to the location of his wedding.

When she finished the tour, she led them back to the hotel lobby. She stood next to the front desk and stared at the amused grin on his face. Callum ran his hand through his hair before he sighed.

"So, Mr Reid?" Peyton said, cutting to the chase.

"Cut the 'Mr Reid' bullshit, Peyton. It's Callum and you know it. I get it. I'm the last person you want to see—"

"You're right about that," Peyton said, interrupting him.

Callum flinched. "But you didn't have to give me a tour of

the hotel. I know it like I know your body, Peyton. And I know it very well."

Peyton tensed. She didn't need a reminder of the only man who had ever seen her naked and the only man who had ever explored her so intimately.

"May I remind you that you're engaged, Mr Reid. And yes, I will continue to address you as Mr Reid, because you are still a client of mine."

His burst of laughter had Peyton taking a step back. The anger within her flamed then coursed through her body. She wanted respect and he was not giving it to her. Peyton pushed the wedding file into Callum's chest.

"You know what, Mr Reid. You and your fiancée can take your wedding elsewhere. I will not be laughed at. *I* am now the owner of The Spencer-Dayle and I will not have my hotel laughed at by you, your pretentious wife-to-be, and your friends." Peyton took her hands off the file just as he held it from falling.

"I don't think Marissa will like that," he stated.

"Well, Mr Reid, I do believe that's *your* problem, not mine. I will refund your deposit first thing tomorrow morning," Peyton seethed, meeting his eyes and ensuring he understood the seriousness of the matter.

"No, Peyton, Marissa will *not* like that. I'm so—"

"I'd like you to leave my hotel, Mr Reid. And I would also like to congratulate you on your upcoming nuptials. It is with regret that I turn away such a wedding. But I have morals and I have some self-respect. Please find another venue to host the wedding." Peyton's heart beat drastically against her chest. She was overreacting, but years of bottled-up emotions had broken free from the confines she'd thought were secure.

"What the fuck did you do, Callum?"

A loud voice had Peyton turning her head to see a man, just taller than Callum, at the door. His nostrils flared and his hands balled tightly.

"Oscar, I—"

"You had one job, man! Marissa is going to kill me!" Oscar

stated through clenched teeth. He approached Peyton and breathed out, "I'm so sorry, Miss Spencer. Please reconsider. I *need* your hotel for my wedding. Please don't let my stupid fuckhead of a friend deter you. I will pay triple. Please."

The desperate tone in his voice had Peyton taking a step back.

"What?" She looked between them both, confused by the situation.

Oscar looked at her before he turned and glared at Callum. "Bloody hell, Callum! I asked you to just meet with her until I got here."

"Me? Dude, she's the one who thought I was marrying Marissa. I just thought it was funny," Callum said. The corners of his lips tugged upwards, the cockiness radiated off him.

Oscar turned to Peyton, who was still stunned and baffled. "I'm sorry, Miss Spencer. It was my mistake to ask Callum to meet with you until I got back from my meeting. I'm Oscar Coulter and *I'm* Marissa's fiancé. Please don't let the actions of my idiot best man cancel our booking. I took one look and I love the hotel. Please let me marry the love of my life at your hotel."

Relief flooded Peyton's chest. Relief that confused her further. She had looked over the file plenty of times but had never come across Marissa's fiancé's name. She had believed it was her client's desire for confidentiality that had prevented his name from being disclosed to her. Callum wasn't engaged, but that didn't mean he wasn't in a serious relationship. Peyton shook her head, clearing her thoughts. He was nothing to her.

Oscar's head fell. "Marissa is going to kill me. Thanks a lot, Callum."

"Shit, man. I'm sorry." Callum put his hand on Oscar's shoulder, but Oscar shrugged it away.

"Forget it. I'll just find somewhere else." Oscar gave her a tight smile. "Thank you, Miss Spencer, for letting us see the hotel. I'm sorry Callum offended you. I assure you, I was very set on your hotel. Please keep the deposit as remuneration for the insult my friend here delivered you. Thank you for your time, Miss Spencer."

Peyton watched as Oscar walked back to the entrance, Callum following him and apologising. "Wait!" she called after them both.

Oscar turned at her voice, the hope sparkling in his eyes. Callum, however, didn't turn.

"I accept your apology, Mr Coulter. You may have your wedding here."

At that, Callum spun around, apparently surprised that she reconsidered.

"Thank you so much, Miss Spencer. You have no idea how much this means to myself and my fiancée," Oscar expressed with a grateful smile before taking Peyton's hand and shaking it.

"Please, call me Peyton." She smiled.

"Then call me Oscar." He stepped back and breathed. His brown eyes flashed with relief and appreciation towards her.

"I'll speak to your fiancée and ensure I have all the paperwork for your wedding in a month's time. However, I do have a condition."

Oscar nodded while Callum tensed. Peyton raised her chin and met eyes with Callum's. Grey and beautiful. She hated his eye colour—hated everything about him. Mostly, she hated him for having broken her heart.

"Anything, Peyton. I'll abide by anything you wish."

The worried look on Callum's face was one that Peyton found pleasure in. He feared her condition, and so he should.

"I'd like it if you ensure that your best man has as little interaction with me as possible. I do not want a repeat of his disrespect throughout this relationship you and Marissa have with me. Your best man is one who I cannot stand to be around. I have some pride, and if you wish to have your wedding here, then you will ensure you control him and his mouth."

Callum raised an eyebrow and then grinned at Peyton.

"Consider it done! Move it, Callum!" Oscar said, pushing him out the door before mouthing, "Thank you," to Peyton.

The moment the door shut, Peyton relaxed her body and rubbed her hand across her right cheek. In the space of an hour, she'd felt so many conflicting emotions that she had no idea what to think. All she knew was that she had to be careful. If he was anything like he had been when he was a teenager, she had to be on her toes. Callum Reid was a persistent bastard.

Four

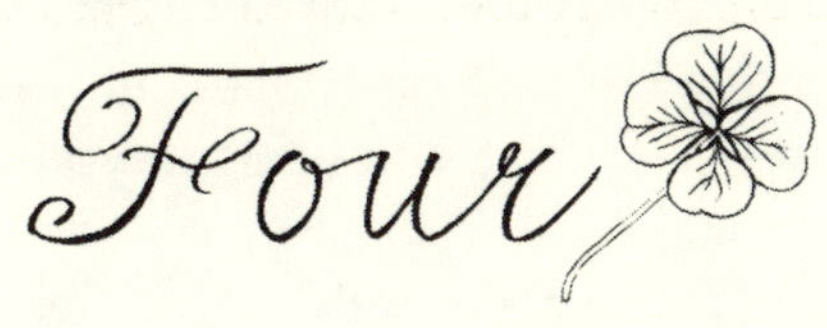

"I can't believe you broke it," Uncle John said.

Peyton leant against the steel bench of the kitchen and placed her palms on the cold top. Then she hung her head in shame. All the years she'd spent helping in the hotel and she had never done any of the hands-on jobs. Instead, she'd done the filing, booking, and anything that required technology. Working the industrial instruments of the kitchen was one of those things that Peyton hadn't done.

"I was just..." Peyton sighed. "I don't know what I was doing. I can't even work a dishwasher!"

A laugh escaped her uncle's lips as he started to adjust the buttons on the machine. "It's all right, Peyton. I don't think you broke it. I think you were just the first to discover the switch problem. Maybe there's a faulty wire or something. How are you going to be able to run this place on your own without your aunt and me?"

Peyton let her head hang low. She had hardly had the job of owner for a week and she had already started to ruin the hotel.

"It would be right for you to break something."

Her head snapped up at the kitchen door to see Jay shaking his head. She definitely didn't want Jay's help. She was meant to be independent, able to run and maintain her hotel on her own.

"What are you supposed to be, my knight in shining armour or something? Thanks, but no, thanks, Jay. I'd rather be in distress," Peyton teased.

She was met with Jay's amused grin.

Jay held up his toolbox and shook it. "Darling, I'm the only kind of knight you need in your life. Step aside, John. I'll take a look."

There was a muffle from her uncle before he stepped away. "Jayden, I think it may be just the switch and the wiring. You sure you don't want me to call your father, see if he's free? You run a busy pub, son."

Peyton crossed her arms over her chest. It was always typical of her uncle to call everyone 'son,' and he was never one to call people by their nicknames. He said that it was because "a mother chose her child's name for a reason. It is the name the child's soul was blessed with." Peyton was never one to argue with her uncle.

"I'm sure I've got this, John. You go back and make your missus a happy woman," Jay charmed.

"All right. Well, then, I'm off. Call me if you need anything, Peyton," her uncle said before he kissed her cheek and left her with Jay.

"I swear to God, if you fix this, Jay, we'll never hear the end of it." Peyton shook her head.

Jay let out a chuckle and placed his toolbox on the kitchen floor. "Actually, Peyton, it's *you* who will never hear the end of it. Would you like to help me?"

Did he just bat his lashes at me?

"I broke the damn thing. Like you need my help. And don't look at me like that." Peyton uncrossed her arms and hugged her cardigan around her tighter. He made her nervous – though she had already been since Callum Reid had walked into her hotel.

"Like what?" Jay asked, taking out a screwdriver from the toolbox. He removed a screw from the front panel of the dishwasher and placed it on the steel bench. "Well?" he said over his shoulder.

Peyton watched his body movements as he pulled apart the dishwasher, fascinated by the way his shirt strained against his muscles. There would be no denying that she didn't find Jay Preston attractive. Every girl did. But he was one of the rare ones who had stayed. The rest of the males had gotten out of Daylesford just before their last year of high school. Most of them had attended private schools in the city—made their résumés look impressive—before they'd attended university.

In such a small town, the pickings of a male companion were slim. Peyton valued Jay's friendship and she'd never cross that line. In fact, she wouldn't even consider dating anyone she knew from her town. Graham was also on her mental 'do not date' list. And Jay happened to be on the top of the list.

You tried the small-town-girl-and-small-town-boy love story. And in reality, it's the worst kind of romance. Be a nun for the rest of your life. Your abstinence has prevented STDs and pregnancy. You just lack a little action…a little intimacy…a little pleas–

"I'm going to ignore that blush on your cheeks, Peyton," Jay said, pulling her from her thoughts and waving the screwdriver in her direction.

She let out a cough. "What blush? I'm not blushing!" she exclaimed, fidgeting with her cardigan.

"Oh, yes, you are. I know a blush when I see one." Jay grinned.

Peyton shot him a dirty look. "Fix my dishwasher."

"How about, 'Please, oh, sir knight. Fix thy dishwasher and release thy maiden's duties from washing thy dishes'?" He dramatically held the screwdriver against his chest as he made Shakespeare roll in his grave. It was like he had sinned against literature. He didn't even have to try.

"How about, 'Please, oh, pub owner. Fix my dishwasher before I go to your pub and break yours with my skill of breaking appliances'?" Peyton said with a smirk.

Jay ignored her and removed the panel of the dishwasher, setting it on the floor. Peyton tried to peer over his shoulder and into the insides of the washer. Jay cranked his face, gave her a wink, and reached for the flashlight.

"Your uncle unplugged this, right?" Jay asked, his back turned to her.

"No, my uncle wanted you to get electrocuted. Of course, he unplugged it," she sassed, untangling her arms and pushing off the bench she'd been leaning on.

He turned around and raised an eyebrow at her. "Got to love them sassy hotel owners."

Peyton sang along to the song that played as she folded the laundry she'd taken out from the dryer. It was a song she knew very well. The artist, June Sinclair, had used the hotel as a writing retreat and would be returning to The Spencer-Dayle in the spring. She was from the city, and pressures from her recording company had had her in a funk. June was someone Peyton admired, and her upbeat music was what was favoured, but when Peyton had heard her acoustic—more country—version, she had fallen in love.

Now, June's music was mixed, and Peyton had even received a mention in June's thank-yous in the album's booklet. Since she'd broken the hotel's dishwasher earlier in the day, Peyton had made sure not to touch anything else in the hotel and opted to call it a day. She had gone home and looked at her plans—she had no plans on her 'plans' paper. So she'd procrastinated and ended up doing housework.

"I can't help but blame myself for thinking we'd make it past all our mistakes," she sang along with June's voice on the speaker.

A loud knock on her front door had Peyton walking over to the speaker her iPod was plugged into and turning down the music.

Peyton stepped barefoot over the cool floorboards until she reached the front door. The stained-glass window panels decorated with Australian birds blocked the view of her visitor. Instead of looking through the peephole or asking who it was, she opened the door.

"Son of a bitch," she said, annoyed by the visitor who stood on her 'Spencer's' doormat.

"Such a warm welcome. Thank you, Peyton," Callum said, sounding almost hurt.

Ignoring whether or not the way she had greeted him was the reason for his hurt tone, Peyton glanced over Callum Reid.

He was wearing dark-blue skinny jeans, and his unzipped hoodie exposed his tight, grey T-shirt. He'd always embraced a casual look. His dark brown—almost black—hair was tousled upwards. She remembered the times that she'd sat under the cherry blossom tree outside her window and run her fingers through it. She had well and truly loved him at seventeen. The heat and tightening of her chest returned from the memories.

Damn it, Peyton. Don't feel. Do not feel anything towards him. Be numb. He broke your heart. Why do you keep forgetting that?

"What do you want?" Peyton asked roughly, wanting him off her property as quickly as possible.

She noticed him wince and felt awful. Though she sassed at Graham and Jay, she was never mean to people. But Callum was an exception. She was a bitter and angry person because of him...and other circumstances. Sometimes, she just hated the world and the cards it had given her. Stupid, unfair cards at that.

"I thought I'd let you know that I'll be in town for a while," he stated, his eyes never leaving hers.

That one sentence stopped her heart and breathing.

Don't show any emotions. Don't give him anything.

"Why?" Her hands clutched the door and she dug her fingernails into the wood.

"Wow, Peyton. Not blunt at all, I see. I deserve that," he said, his body still tense.

If he was looking for a, "No, Callum, you don't," then he was kidding himself.

"Why are you here? I thought you went back to the city. And why are you on my doorstep? And get off my mat," she said, looking down at the customised mat her mother had purchased shortly before her death. It was worn, the 'E' and the 'R' in 'Spencer' hardly able to be made out.

Peyton lifted her chin and scowled at him. Callum looked down at the mat before he took a step back. He wouldn't get why his feet on her surname offended her. It was like another slap in the face for her. He hadn't been there when she'd buried them and seen their last names on their graves. He was literally stepping all over the Spencer name.

When his face met hers, Callum drew out a sigh and placed both hands in his hoodie pockets. Peyton placed her left hand on her hip, waiting, even tempted to tap her foot.

"One, because I need to be here. Two, I did go back to the city, only to get my things. And three, I came here to talk to you," Callum said, answering all of her questions.

Peyton tensed. Frustrated by his vague answers, she straightened her posture and removed her hand from her hip.

Then she cleared her throat. "One, you don't need to be here. I told you to never return. Two, grab your things and go back to the city. And three, I don't want to talk to you. Now get off my veranda and leave!"

Just as she was about to slam the door, Callum stepped forward and pushed it, squashing her attempt at ending their conversation.

"What the hell?" she shrieked.

"Listen to me, Peyton," he panted. His nostrils flared as if he were trying to control his anger.

"Why should I?" she asked as she gave up the attempt at closing the front door. He was stronger than she was; it'd be no use.

"Because."

"Because why, Callum? You never listened to me. You never gave me answers. So, why now?" The anger boiled in her as her throat tightened.

"I had my reasons, Peyton. I'm here now." He pushed off the door and took a step back, ensuring that he didn't stand on the mat.

For a moment, she appreciated where he stood. "Well, I don't want you here or anywhere near me. I made that clear back at the hotel," she stated, crossing her arms over her chest.

In her mind, it was the only way that she could protect herself from him.

"How long have you owned the hotel?" he asked with a sad tone to his voice, deflecting her previous statement.

"Why does it matter to you?"

The wind picked up, tossing his dark hair out of place. Callum's face saddened as he placed his hands in the pockets of his hoodie.

"It matters to me, Peyton."

Peyton met his eyes. Grey and as beautiful as ever. She hated it. Her jaw tensed and she had to battle hard to ignore the heat that took over her chest. First loves were the worst kind—especially when they returned.

"It doesn't matter to me, so leave me alone."

When Callum took a step forward, Peyton raised her hand and placed it on his chest. The way her heartbeat picked up at the feel of it under her fingers made her mentally curse. His chest was far more solid than it had been when he was seventeen. Her breathing heaved as she tried to control the emotions that overtook her. Emotions that had been dormant for over four years.

He stilled under her touch, his eyes firmly staring at hers. The way her heart pained at all their memories together had her eyes stinging. She chanted to herself not to cry and pushed him back. Then she removed her hand from his chest and took a step onto the veranda.

"Fine. Legally, I've owned the hotel for almost four years, but my aunt and uncle have been running it until I graduated—not that you care. But I've officially been the owner for the last four days."

Nope. No mention of my parents. Not a single care.

"So, it was like your first day when I showed up…"

"More or less," she sighed. "Now, seriously, Callum. Why are you here? Why are you back in Daylesford?"

Callum sighed and pulled his hands out of his pockets. His eyes made it down to her lips, staring for a moment before he looked away. Then he turned around and glanced at the house across the street before he stared Peyton in the eyes.

"Peyton Olivia Spencer, I *need* your forgiveness. I'm here for redemption."

The pain of her imploding heart seeped into her veins. "You self-righteous bastard. Get the fuck off my property!"

Five

"Are you sure you'll be all right, love?" Aunt Brenda asked as she handed Peyton her jacket.

"I'll be fine. Jay fixed the dishwasher, and all I have to do is wait for Marissa's email about her wedding and then I can concentrate on my plans for the hotel. I'll be okay. Just have fun on the peninsula." Peyton threaded her arms through her jacket and buttoned it before she faced her great-aunt and gave her a smile.

"But—"

"No buts. You always wanted to be on the beachside in winter. It's my turn to take care of the hotel. It was always my responsibility, not yours," Peyton explained.

"Who will make you breakfast each morning?"

Peyton rolled her eyes at the concern on her aunt's face. And placed both her hands on her aunt's shoulders. "I can make my own breakfast. How many times have I told you not to come over each morning? We talked about this. When I owned the hotel, you and Uncle John would go back to the peninsula. It was a deal."

Aunt Brenda cocked a brow at her. "This eagerness of yours to get your uncle and me out of town isn't just because of our retirement, is it? I'm guessing this is because Callum Reid is back in town?"

Peyton stilled, her mouth dropping. "How'd you know?"

A sad smile etched her aunt's face. "It's a small town, Peyton. You know how this town is. They would have never let this kind of news go unheard of. They won't treat him the same. You know that."

After walking over to the hallway table, Peyton trailed her fingers over the picture of her parents and smiled at their happy faces. It was a photo taken just before Christmas, before Callum had left, and before their accident. Peyton turned to her aunt and sighed.

"I treated him differently, Aunt Brenda. I treated him like..."

Aunt Brenda walked towards Peyton and hugged her. Peyton stood there a moment before she wrapped her arms around her aunty.

After a moment of embrace, Aunt Brenda took a step back and said, "You treated him how he expected you'd treat him, love. I'm sure that he knew what he was walking into. He broke your heart, Peyton. You treat him the way you believe he deserves."

"I called him a self-righteous bastard after he said he came back for my forgiveness. I swear I felt Mum and Dad tossing in their graves, Aunt Brenda. You should have seen his face. I felt awful but...he wasn't here when I needed him. He left me. I gave him everything and he left. I don't think I could ever forgive him."

The way his eyes had clouded and the pained expression on his face had had her almost sobbing. She hadn't needed to see him in agony. He was the one who had delivered her such heartache. He deserved no pardon whatsoever.

Aunt Brenda picked up the house keys and placed them in Peyton's hands. "The ones we love will always hurt us the most, Peyton. You've grown since him, and I'm sure he has, too. If you don't want to forgive him, then don't. It's your life. You choose who deserves to be near your light. And you choose who loves or who hurts you in this world. Remember that forgiveness is always earned and never a right."

Peyton nodded as she picked up her bag and slung it on

her shoulder. "Thanks, Aunt Brenda. Just have a good time enjoying the sea air."

"Remember to call me if you need anything!" Aunt Brenda called after her.

"Love you," Peyton said over her shoulder as she walked out of the house.

The cool wind hit her cheeks and she shivered. It would be winter soon and snow would more than likely fall. Winter brought a good number of visitors. The fog that blanketed the lake was a tourist attraction. Even though Daylesford was small, she loved it. Everything she had ever loved had breathed in the small town she lived in.

Closing the door behind her, Peyton placed her keys in her jacket pocket and looked over at the brick house across the road. It was the first time in years that she took in that house for more than a second. Callum was back, and he lived across the road from her.

The brightness from the lanterns provided enough light to see the cold fog surrounding them. Peyton shivered, but she was held securely against Callum's naked body.

"We can leave, Peyton. It's getting cold," he whispered in her ear.

Peyton turned in his hold and faced him. Callum wrapped the blanket around them tighter.

"I don't want to leave."

"Then we'll stay." He smiled at her before he kissed her forehead.

It was perfect. Everything was perfect. The stars, the sound of the lake, and even the fog made this a memory worth keeping.

Lifting her arm out from under the blanket, Peyton brushed the hair out of his face. But Callum's hand stopped her movements, and he threaded his fingers through hers, bringing their joined hands to his mouth. He kissed the skin just below their thumbs, where their hands joined, and they became one.

"I didn't hurt you, did I?" he asked, his thumb caressing her knuckle.

"No," she breathed. Though the pain was uncomfortable, it passed. She could never have imagined her first time with anyone other than

Callum.

When she'd confessed that she had never had sex, he hadn't laughed or teased her. He'd simply said, "I know," and confessed that he already had. Though it hadn't surprised Peyton, she had been envious that she couldn't be his first.

Callum let go of her hand and wrapped her closer to his body, his chin resting on her head. They lay there as the night slowly turned into day, the air getting cooler.

She closed her eyes once he rubbed her back before he whispered, "I have to go to the city tomorrow, Peyton, but just know that I'll be back on Monday."

"Callum, just know that I love you," she whispered back.

He'd never said it back. Three simple words that he had kept to himself. Peyton had spent years trying to figure out if he'd ever loved her. She'd always come to the conclusion that he hadn't. He'd chosen the city over her. Taken her virginity and then left her.

Shaking her head, she cleared that 'perfect' night from her head. She walked down the steps and onto the path. When she reached the mailbox, she stopped and glanced at the house. Then she felt something wet against her cheek. Reaching up, she pressed her fingers to it and realised it was a tear. Though they always prickled, they had never breached her waterline over their memories. She had refused to.

Ignoring that it was because of the memory of the first and last time she'd had sex, Peyton took a step on the footpath and started to walk to the hotel, chanting to herself to stop remembering.

Tapping her pencil against her lip, Peyton observed the lake from the cliff. The hotel was built on a slope next to the lake, and the cliff overlooked the entire lake. It was a popular place for guests to watch the sunrise or sunset, and one of the main reasons that her parents had packed their bags and moved to Daylesford.

When they died, Peyton's aunt and uncle had moved from the ranges to be with her, even buying a house of their own a few streets away. Hence, breakfast being made every morning.

By the time Peyton had brought a notepad and a pencil to the cliff, it was just after eleven a.m. She sat near the edge as she thought about how to make the Reynolds' wedding memorable. As she did a sweep of the horizon, her eyes landed on the pier, then the small feeding bridge, then the middle of the lake, and an idea sparked.

A floating dance floor!

Just as she started to draw the lake on the piece of paper, she heard the sound of leaves crunching. Turning her head, she saw Callum standing just next to the path outside of the hotel, looking at her. He didn't say anything. His eyes were on hers as if he were waiting for the go-ahead to approach her. Without a word, Peyton turned her attention back to the lake and then continued the drawing she had started.

She didn't hear him leave, so she assumed that he was still standing there. She fought an internal battle with herself over whether or not to invite him to sit with her. The memory of their last night together had barely left her—as much as she'd tried to forget.

You never forget the first and last time you have sex.

After drawing a rectangle to symbolise the pier, Peyton sighed and placed the notepad down.

"What do you want, Callum? I'm busy," she said, not looking over her shoulder.

She heard nothing but the sound of the ducks *quacking* in the distance. But just as she started to relax, she heard his footsteps and let out a groan. From the corner of her eye, she watched as he sat down next to her. Not what she wanted.

"I want your forgiveness, Peyton. I made that clear last night before you called me a bastard and slammed the door."

Her nostrils flared. He didn't get it, and it made the anger rise in her throat. Peyton took a deep breath and said, "Self-righteous bastard," correcting him.

Turning her head, she saw him staring out at the lake in the direction of the trees just near the boathouse—the exact area where they'd spent their last night together tangled under a blanket after what she believed had been a passionate memory they shared together.

"Why can't you give me your forgiveness, Peyton?" he asked, still staring out at the trees.

"Because you don't deserve it," she stated. It was no lie.

Callum looked down at his hands. "I know I don't. But I want to earn it. I want to redeem myself," he said before he faced her.

The vulnerability in his eyes had her wall strengthening. No. She would not break for him. He had already broken her before. She wasn't willing to go for round two.

"Well, you can't, Callum. Let it go. Just go back to the city already." Peyton collected her notebook and pencil and stood up.

"But why can't I redeem myself?"

The begging in his voice had her throat straining. Heat overtook her body. Not something she wanted either.

"The fact that you just asked me proves that you can never redeem yourself to me. Go home, Callum. Stay in the city until you have to be at your best friend's wedding." Her eyes never left his.

"But—"

"But nothing. Nothing you say or do will ever be redeeming in my book. Redemption is just something you don't deserve."

"Peyton," he tried.

"Go fuck yourself, Callum," Peyton snarled over her shoulder as she stormed back to the hotel.

Sometimes the F-word is necessary.

Six

Floating dance floor.

Peyton rubbed out the penciled design of the floating dance floor. It wasn't a stupid idea; it just wasn't very smart. There was a lot to consider: whether the dock would be bracketed onto a pier or if it would freely float. There was also insurance; no doubt someone would fall off, so clauses and waivers would have to be drawn. It involved a lot of risk management, and in the end, Peyton decided against the idea. Instead, she'd figure out another 'wow' that was cemented to the ground, avoiding the possibility of drowning her guests.

Letting out a sigh, she screwed up her grade-three kind of diagram of the lake and placed it at arm's length from her. While she was rummaging through piles of paper to her left, she spotted the wedding menu Marissa had emailed her that morning. Once she'd gotten into her office, she'd printed the menu and the groom's guest list and walked to the pub. She'd been tired of the silence that engulfed The Spencer-Dayle. She'd needed to hear more than just her own voice. And when she'd noticed Callum's name on the groom's guest list, Peyton had wanted to throw the glass vase that was to her right.

She didn't want him back in her town. He had run off and made the city his home. It had been two days since he'd asked for her forgiveness, and during those two nights, Peyton had stared at the ceiling of her bedroom, wishing that God hadn't put him back on her path. He had already taken so much. She didn't want anything more than to live a simple life.

Shaking her mind to clear the thoughts of him, she picked up the menu.

You don't owe Callum Reid anything, Peyton.

"What did I tell you, Peyton? Can you help me out here? Just once, I want to see your beautiful face in this establishment without some kind of paperwork in your hands. I run a pub."

Peyton looked up from the wedding menu and rolled her eyes at Jay.

"Darling, I'm pretty sure that hotel of yours has an office," Jay stated as he picked up her empty glass.

"It does," Peyton confirmed and placed the sheet of paper on the table.

"Then what are you doing bringing work in here?" he asked with a raised brow.

"Fine. It gets lonely." Peyton deeply sighed and leant back into her chair, her eyes avoiding Jay's.

When his silence reached an uncomfortable level, she peeked to see a frown on his face. Jay's shoulders sagged before he walked over to the bar counter and placed her empty glass on it. Moments later, he took the seat next to her.

"I like to hear everyone's voices, Jay. That's why I like being here. It reminds me that this town had my back when I lost everything. I know I can be annoying and I take up too much room in your pub, but sometimes…it's all I need," Peyton explained before he spoke first.

Before she could even react, Jay took her hands and leant forward, his eyes staring into hers.

"Peyton, my pub doors are always open for you. Every time I see you, you have papers in your hands. I say these little remarks hoping that you'll tell me that you're either getting them done early so you can hit a party or go to the next town or something. Anything other than the hotel. I keep waiting for you to tell me that you're about to live your life."

Peyton sighed. He was right. It was always work. She never

went to the pub to just drink or hang out. She went to hear the voices of others who were living.

"Maybe one day when you ask me what I'm up to, I'll have a more entertaining answer for you, Jay. One day, I'll have one." Peyton smiled before taking her hands back from his.

He gave her an honest—yet concerned—smile before he stood up and returned to his position behind the bar.

Peyton listened until Jay's familiar laugh rang high and then she breathed out. His laugh was a form of remedy for her. Though he was so much like Peyton and Graham, he was far different from them. Jay was comfortable with his life. For Peyton, she was just managing.

Shaking her head, Peyton looked down at the papers sprawled on the table. The sound of a chair scratching caught her attention. When she lifted her gaze, she was irritated to see none other than Callum Reid sitting in front of her, his arms crossed over his chest.

Peyton closed her eyes tight and sat properly in her chair. It was a talk Callum wanted, and Peyton had thoroughly avoided it since his return.

"Peyton," Callum acknowledged in a dull tone.

"Callum," she said, mimicking the lifeless pitch in his voice.

His lips pursed and he eyed her. Silence was exchanged between them, suffocating her. When it reached an unbearable quota, Peyton started to collect her work.

"Why does everyone in this town love you so much but hate me? I grew up here, too."

His question startled her, causing Peyton to lift her head and glance at him. His eyes swept over the pub, filled with disbelief.

He really doesn't get it.

"Because you left, Callum," Peyton stated.

He slowly turned his head until his eyes met hers. Callum's jaw locked as if he were attempting to control his emotions around her.

"So did everyone else," he pointed out.

"Everyone had their reasons."

Callum's eyes flashed and he abruptly leant forward. "And

I didn't, Peyton?"

"Yes, you did. But you didn't give *me* a reason. They all left because they gave a reason. They told the town. They let people know. But you? You just up and left, Callum. You didn't tell me."

Callum flinched like her words had hurt him, which Peyton found ridiculous. "I had my reasons, Peyton," he said through clenched teeth. "But that doesn't explain why these people I've grown up with can't even look at me."

This time, it was Peyton who flinched. Her eyes burned. He still didn't get it.

"Because you didn't come back!" she shouted, tears running down her cheeks. That façade she hid behind crumbled. She no longer used a fake smile. For Peyton, this was as raw and as naked as it got for her.

His eyes grew sadder, but she didn't care. Around them, the voices had started to hush until the pub had silenced around them.

"Look around you, Peyton. Nobody else came back!" Callum raised his voice.

Her heart clenched at the truth he spoke.

"But they did," she sobbed.

Callum shook his head. "No, they didn't."

"But they did when I needed them the most!" Peyton cried before she wiped the tears from her cheeks, hating the weakness she was showing.

"What?" he breathed.

"They all came back—every single one of them. The town hates you because you didn't come back. Everyone came back, Callum. My parents' funeral—they were all there…except for you!" Her lips trembled as the heat burned through her chest.

"Peyton," he said almost apologetically.

"No! That one day. Their funeral. That was the day you could have redeemed yourself, Callum. I don't care if you couldn't love me. I needed you then. I lost them and you didn't show. It was their funeral, Callum. They died. My parents, they loved you. Don't you get that? They loved you! They wanted me to forgive you, but I couldn't, and when they died, I knew that I could never forgive you. You didn't have to be there for me. You could have been there to pay your respects or to say goodbye, but you didn't. The moment that I buried them, I also buried any hope of you redeeming yourself."

"I'm—"

Peyton shook her head. "Save it. If you had just come back, I would have forgiven you for breaking my heart. I don't care if you couldn't love me back. I just needed your support and for you to acknowledge their deaths. They all came back. The only person who didn't show was you." Peyton sniffed and tucked her hair behind her ear.

She had vowed that day never to let him back into her life. The last glint of hope had died with the very last breath her parents had breathed that day all those years ago.

"Get the fuck out of my pub, Reid." Jay's growl had Peyton lifting her eyes to meet his. The vein on his neck protruded as he balled his fist.

"Look, I don't want any trouble," Callum said.

From the corner of her eye, Peyton could see him holding his hands up.

"Well, you chose the wrong town to return to…and the wrong pub. Get your sorry ass up and leave. If I see you ever make Peyton that upset again, I'll have my fist to your jaw. Got it?" Jay took a step forward.

Peyton shot up from her chair and stepped between them. "Enough, Jay," Peyton said, but he kept his eyes on Callum.

"You tell Graham that he's back in town?"

"No," she replied.

Jay's eyes met hers. Disbelief took hold of his face. His eyes darkened and his face tensed. "Then you better tell him before he finds out from someone else, Peyton."

"What are you, Jay, her protector?" Mr Preston asked and placed his hand on his son's shoulder.

Mr Preston was just like Jay—chocolate eyes and a strong jaw. She imagined he was what Jay would look like once he aged. The way his lips curved tightly indicated that he would calm down his son.

"I'm more than what that little fucker ever did. I'm her friend. He couldn't even—"

"Jay, it's not your place to have a say. This is between Peyton and Callum. For far too long, this town has had an opinion on what happened. We don't get a say," Mr Preston said before holding his hand out to Callum. "It's good to have you home, Callum."

Callum stepped around Peyton and shook hands with Jay's father. "Thanks, Mr Preston."

Jay snorted. "This ain't your home, Reid. Hasn't been for a long time."

Peyton kept quiet, staring among the three of them. No one in the pub spoke. It seemed like they were all holding their breaths.

"He's a boy from Daylesford. Just like you, Jay. He's one of us." Mr Preston's fingers dug into Jay's shoulder, but Jay didn't flinch.

"Then he should have been there when she buried Cindy and Stuart," Jay growled and shrugged his father's hand off his shoulder. He took a step and put his face as close to Callum's as possible—to the point where their foreheads were almost touching. "You hurt her or even make her cry, you answer to me. Don't think that I'm afraid to hurt a city boy like you. Don't think for a minute that you're one of us. You spoilt son of a bitch left behind something special. You weren't there to see her cry. You weren't there when she found out they'd died."

Peyton winced. She had never seen Jay so forceful or terrifying. But she knew that he was protecting her. He had been there when she'd found out that her parents had died. They had been walking down Main Street when Sergeant Downs parked his police car next to them and told her the news. Hit and run. Her parents had died instantly an hour outside of the town's limits.

"Stop it, Jay," Peyton said sternly.

His eyes locked on hers and she shook her head at him—a warning to lay it to bed. It was the single worst moment in her life and he was digging it back up for the whole pub to hear. Peyton hadn't just lost her parents. The town had lost their friends.

Peyton stepped towards her table and collected her work. She was stacking the files when she heard Jay say her name. That's when she stuck her hand up at him to stop him from saying any more.

"You've said enough, Jay. I don't need your protection or for you to make a statement on my behalf. Leave it. And you, Callum, are leaving with me before Jay does something that I'm going to hate him for." Peyton reached over and took Callum's wrist in her hand.

He tensed under her touch, but she ignored him, dragging him away.

As she walked towards the pub doors, she heard Jay say, "Don't you fall in love with him, Peyton. Don't you do that to me."

Seven

With a heavy sigh, Peyton placed her work papers on her desk and slipped out of her jacket, resting it on her the chair. She searched through the bundle of papers until she came across the Reynolds' menu. Smoothing it out, she separated it from the other documents.

"I remember when this place used to be so…"

Callum's voice stopped, and she turned around to see him looking around the office. It was far different than what he'd known when he was seventeen.

"Alive?" Peyton deadpanned.

She noticed his quick flinch at her words and smiled to herself.

"Not the word I was going for," Callum said as he walked towards the bookcase.

"Well, things die. The heart of this place died along with my parents." Her eyes followed his movements as he inspected the wall before facing her.

"It's gone," Callum breathed.

The way his mouth formed a frown had her feeling guilty.

Turning to her left, she looked out at the lake. Since his return, she'd spoken more about her parents than she had at any other time in the last four years. The burning sensation in her eyes had her trying to blink it away.

"I had to take it down. I couldn't see their faces every day," Peyton explained. When the burning left her, she faced him.

"I'm sorry," he said softy.

Peyton tensed. "For what?"

"Everything. I was a kid, Peyton. I was seventeen. I didn't know what I was doing. I just knew that I had to leave. I couldn't stay."

He couldn't stay. Peyton let that simmer in her thoughts. Couldn't and wouldn't were two different words with two different meanings. Just like Callum. He used different words that didn't match their actual meaning.

"How do you know Oscar?" Peyton asked, dodging the question of the past and reaching for the menu.

When he didn't reply straight away, she glanced at him with a 'go on' expression on her face.

"He was one of the first people I met once I got to the city. We went to high school together and then uni… Where's the staff…the guests? Where is everyone?"

Peyton placed the menu down and walked around her desk, sitting in the large leather chair. "The hotel's under a blackout period. No guests or staff for two weeks until I figure out how I want to run and own it."

"It's funny," Callum said before he reached the desk and leant forward until his face was close to hers. "This is the most we've spoken since I got back. You haven't told me to fuck myself or get the fuck off your property." He gave her a smirk but his eyes were laced with regret, almost like he was sad to see her.

Her eyes squinted. "Go fuck yourself, Callum, and get off my property," she slowly drawled out.

"Like the time you told me that you didn't want me to kiss you—nothing but a lie. I know you, Peyton. When you drag out your sentences like that, it's a challenge. But that's not what I want with you." Callum pulled back and stood straight, his hands in the pockets of his jeans.

Before Peyton could even speak, he stopped her when he let out a deep sigh. Then he pulled his hand out of his pocket, combing his fingers through his hair.

"How long have you and Jay been together?"

She flinched in her seat. They had all grown up together. Jay and his friends were a few years older, but when Jay had graduated high school, he'd stayed behind. And when Callum had left, she and Jay had gotten closer, just like how she and Graham had.

"I'm not with Jay," she bit back more defensively than she would have liked.

"Seems like he's in love with you, Peyton."

"Don't you fall in love with him, Peyton. Don't you do that to me."

Jay's words had been hard to ignore. The walk from the pub to the hotel had had her constantly replaying it. He had never said anything so deep before. He'd sounded desperate, and it left an ache in her chest. She loved Jay, but only in the most platonic of ways.

"He isn't. Your friend's wedding isn't for another month," Peyton said, reaching for the papers on her desk. She opened the right drawer of the desk and placed them inside. When she closed the drawer, she noticed Callum staring at her, as if he were trying to figure out the cogs of her mind.

"I'm here for you, Peyton. I came back for you."

The way his voice softened had her heart beating faster. Words that would have been perfect…four years ago. So instead of letting him see the effect those two sentences had, she let out a short laugh. His jaw clenched as well as his fist.

"You loved me once, Peyton… You fell in love with me. Why don't you believe me when I say I'm back here for you?"

The hurt in his grey eyes made it hard for her to breathe.

He never told me he loved me. He never said it back.

"So what, Callum? I'm just meant to fall in love with you? Is that it?"

Callum's eyes glistened and he shook his head. "I wouldn't let you, Peyton. It would be the last thing I'd let you do… I'm not that cruel."

What?

The unsaid apology swept his eyes. His words made no sense to her. Callum looked to his left, not saying any more. His faraway stare was one she didn't understand.

Just as she was about to ask him what he'd meant, Callum turned around and made his way to the door.

"Wait," she said, getting up from the chair.

Callum stopped just steps away from the exit.

"What do you mean you wouldn't let me?" she asked.

He didn't face her. Peyton stared at his back, hoping he would look at her.

"I wouldn't let you fall in love with me. That's not why I'm here. I don't ever want you falling in love with me, Peyton Spencer. I'll make sure that you don't. I'm just here for forgiveness for not being there for their funeral. I don't want your love. I don't need it. I just need to know that you forgive me and then I'm done. I'll be satisfied with the choices I made."

With that, Callum walked out the door, leaving her with tears in her eyes.

"I'm sorry for your loss, Peyton. If you need anything, just give me a call."

The voice sounded like Father Mitchell, but Peyton didn't say anything. Instead, she kept staring at the plaques that marked her parents' graves.

"They were good people," another voice said.

"No daughter should be left alone in this world. It's a shame."

Tears fell down her cheeks as she read their names again and again. More voices of people giving her condolences surrounded her. Callum had left her, and now, both of her parents had, too. It became difficult to breathe as she remembered the last thing her parents had said before they'd driven to the city for a tourism convention. It was about getting over Callum. Her mother had told her to "forgive and forget," and now, Peyton couldn't. Not anymore. There wouldn't be forgiving. He hadn't shown. The one time she believed he'd come back, and he hadn't.

She let out a sob. He hadn't even said goodbye to her parents. She'd called his phone to tell him about the funeral, but he never called back. Her voice message hadn't been much. She'd just told him that her parents' funeral would be in Daylesford and that she'd like it if he could make it. Let the past be the past. But as she stood there on the soft ground, she knew she'd made a mistake by calling him. He didn't care. She hated him more than she could have ever thought.

Ignoring the person offering their condolences, Peyton walked towards the exit, past the old graves, past the office and the sign that read 'Daylesford Public cemetery.' For a moment, she heard Graham call after her, but Peyton ran. She didn't care that her lungs were burning. She kept running.

She didn't stop when she reached the lake. Instead, she kept going down the lane of bare trees and the small hill that led to her street. When Peyton reached her house, she heaved, trying to regain air in her lungs. She paused for a moment as she stood in the middle of the street. On her left was her parents' home, and on her right, Callum's. His parents had shown, but he hadn't.

She looked back and forth as tears continued to fall and memories flashed in her mind. The moments she'd run across the road and into his arms, her parents telling her to be home by ten. The moments she'd snuck out of her bedroom window to be with him. The moment they'd kissed under the cherry blossom tree.

Wiping her face, Peyton walked towards the backyard. She opened the gate and kept walking until she was staring at the cherry blossom tree. She had so many memories of this one tree. Callum had once breathed, "Be with me, Peyton," in her ear as they'd sat underneath it.

She shook her head to rid herself of the memories and took one more glimpse at the tree before she headed over to the shed. Peyton paused before she opened the door and was greeted with dust. The light illuminated at the flicker of the switch and she looked around until her eyes found the axe. She picked it up and felt its weight. Turning around, she gazed over at the house, realising that she was now alone in this world.

With each step Peyton took, leaving the shed behind, another tear ran down her face. She stood two steps away from the tree and held the axe tight in her hands, ready to chop it down. After she'd picked a spot where she'd let the axe blade enter the bark, she took a deep breath, held the axe so tight that her knuckles turned white, and drew it back before swinging the blade into the tree.

Cherry blossoms fell from the tree as she removed the blade and readied it for another swing.

"Peyton, stop!" Graham cried as he ran to her. When he reached her, he tried to take the axe from her.

"No! Stop it, Graham! Just stop." Peyton fought back, but it was no use.

He removed the axe from her hands and threw it away from her.

Before Peyton could yell at him, Graham wrapped his arms around her and held her. Sobs escaped her as she realised what she'd been about to do. As a way to get rid of the memories of Callum, she had almost destroyed her mother's favourite tree. The tree that had convinced her father to buy the house they'd lived in.

"Oh my God. I almost – "

"I know, Peyton. I know," Graham said as he stroked the back of her head. "You're not alone. I'm always here. You're never alone."

Peyton looked up to see the small smile that Graham offered. "Promise you won't leave me."

"I promise."

Peyton opened the front door to find him there with a less-than-impressed expression on his face.

"He's back?" Graham asked as he put his phone in his pocket.

"He's back, Graham." She took a step back and let him into the house.

Graham walked to the hallway table and put his ute keys on it before heading towards the living room. Peyton followed behind him after she shut the door.

She didn't have to look to know that Graham was on her couch, scratching into the arm of the chair—something he did when he was frustrated. Peyton went to the fridge and grabbed a beer and can of Coke. After approaching the couch, she sat next to him, handing over the beer. Then she raised her legs and tucked them underneath her as she opened her can and took a sip.

"I was going to call you," she said, staring at the red can.

"I'm sure you were, Peyton." Graham let out a sigh before taking a long pull of his beer.

"Jay told you?"

"Yeah," he replied as he placed the bottle on her coffee table.

"He told me to tell you. Why did he call you?" Peyton asked as she mirrored Graham and put her Coke down.

Graham lifted his feet and rested them on the glass table. "He's worried about you."

"He doesn't have to be. Callum made his intentions clear. He just wants my forgiveness for not showing up to Mum and Dad's funeral."

Graham's eyebrows shot up. When he turned his head to meet her eyes, his blue eyes had darkened. "Is that it? He's not sorry that he left you or played with your feelings?"

She shook her head. "I don't think he actually cares. He just wants my forgiveness and that's it. I could just say that I do forgive him and make him leave, but he'll be back for his best friend's wedding."

Graham took his feet off the coffee table and placed them on the carpet. His eyebrows furrowed. "Wedding?"

Peyton sighed. "That last-minute booking Aunt Brenda made was Marissa Reynolds' wedding and Callum's the best man," she revealed.

"Wow," Graham breathed.

"Yeah, wow," she agreed and rested her head against the back of the couch. "I never expected this, Graham. I never thought he'd come back. Why did he have to?" she asked softly, staring at the couch cushion that separated them.

"Come here," Graham said as he took her hand and brought her closer.

Peyton smiled as she settled her head in his lap, Graham's hand stroking her head. It was too much for her. She hadn't anticipated Callum's return. She had only just got her life together since his departure and her parents' deaths.

"I don't think that I'll be strong enough to face him again. I have to just ignore his being back. I didn't go to the hotel today because I was scared I might run into him in town," she said, staring at their beverages on the table.

"You don't have to be scared, Peyton. You didn't do anything wrong. It was him."

Graham's right. Callum's the one who left me. I didn't. I wanted to be with him. I wanted to be his.

Peyton turned her body until she was facing Graham. He gave her a sincere smile, his dimple deepening. She smiled back at him. If she'd ever loved someone unconditionally, it was Graham. Not Callum or Jay. Just Graham. They had a friendship no one could ever understand. They shared so much pain. If it hadn't been for him, she would have lost herself right after the funeral. He had healed her.

"Sometimes…"

"Yeah?"

"Sometimes I wish I'd never fallen in love with him. Never kissed him. Never told him that I loved him. I wish it hadn't been him," Peyton confessed.

Graham wiped the tear off her cheek. "I sometimes wish that, too. Then I wouldn't have seen you on that bench crying. But if it hadn't been for him, I would have never been as close as I am with you. Never forget that I love you, Peyton."

She blinked away her tears. Graham was never one to show his emotions around people. Peyton had been one of a few who Graham let close. But in this moment, Graham had shown a vulnerable side to himself.

Sitting up, Peyton placed her hand on Graham's chest, leant forward, and kissed his cheek. "I love you, too, Graham."

It wasn't a love that had blossomed overnight. It was unconditional. It was a friendship bonded by an undeniable connection. He came first in her life. Not Callum. And not even the hotel mattered more than Graham Scott.

Eight

The morning sun hitting her eyelids caused Peyton to let out a soft groan. Slowly, she opened her eyes to find herself staring at Graham's naked chest, his hand on her hip. Peyton watched him, the calm expression on his face as he slept. She smiled knowing that this was only one of the rare times where he wasn't worrying over the family farm.

She looked down to see her palms on his chest. It wasn't uncommon for them to fall asleep while watching a movie, but Graham's partially naked chest was a first for her. She had spilt red wine on his shirt before they'd slept. So it wouldn't stain, Peyton had placed it in the tub and let it soak in stain solution.

A knock on the door echoed through the quiet house. As silently as she could, Peyton slipped away from Graham's hold. He stirred for a moment before his breathing evened. Peyton scratched her head and let out a yawn. The cold hardwood floors made her wince as she walked towards the front door. After unbolting the chain and the lock on the handle, Peyton opened the door and was startled.

"Callum," she said, shocked.

His eyes stared at the pyjama shorts and tank she wore before meeting her startled glance. "Good morning, Peyton," he said with a tight smile.

"Why are you on my doorstep so early in the morning? Can I help you with something?" Peyton asked.

"Marissa called me last—"

"Peyton, is someone at the door?" Graham asked, stopping Callum from continuing.

Peyton stilled at Graham's question and watched Callum's eyes widen in surprise. She heard Graham's footsteps move closer until he stood next to her. Callum stared at Graham—no doubt taking in his naked chest and making assumptions—before he looked back at Peyton.

She ignored the way his jaw tensed and turned to Graham. Then she smiled before saying, "Morning."

"Morning, Peyton," he said sweetly before he placed a kiss on her cheek.

She felt Callum's eyes on her, but she didn't care. She knew what Graham was playing at. But she did, however, blush at him. If this was how Graham treated women, then they were lucky.

Callum let out a cough, interrupting them.

"Callum, I heard you were back in town. How are you?" Graham asked.

Peyton turned and met eyes with Callum. She couldn't decipher the almost angry look in his eyes.

"I'm good, mate. How's the farm?"

Their small talk just adds to the awkwardness of this morning.

"Good," Graham said, placing an arm around Peyton's waist. "Have you had breakfast, Callum? I'm just about to make us some. You're welcome to join."

Both Peyton and Callum flinched in surprise. Callum shifted uncomfortably in his place. Looking down, Peyton noticed that he was standing on the veranda rather than the doormat, and that made her smile for a moment.

"Thanks for the offer, but I'll pass. Listen, Peyton, could I talk to you for a moment?" Callum asked.

"Okay. I'll get breakfast ready before I grab a shower," Graham said. Then he squeezed her waist and left her alone with Callum.

"So, it's you *and* lavender boy," Callum said blankly. It was a nickname Callum had given Graham when they were kids. It was a nickname Peyton had never really liked.

"None of your business," she stated firmly. Though there was nothing between Graham and her, Callum had no right to question it.

"You're right. It isn't."

Peyton tucked her hair behind her ear and then crossed her arms, waiting for an explanation to his early morning visit. "Again, can I help you with something, Callum?" she asked with an irritated tone to her voice.

"Will you be at the hotel today? I stopped by yesterday but you weren't there. Marissa called and sent over some drafts of the dance floor, some selections on silverware, and other ideas," he said.

"Wait." Peyton uncrossed her arms. "Why didn't she just email them to me? Why is she going through you?" she asked, slightly offended.

"I almost lost them The Spencer-Dayle, so I owe it to them to make sure everything is ready. And Marissa wants constant updates and having Oscar up my ass will get her them. So, will you be at the hotel today?"

This time, it was Callum who folded his arms over his chest. She noticed that he was wearing a green, long-sleeved shirt. It was cool out, but she wasn't sure if it really warranted a long top.

Peyton closed her eyes, knowing that what she said next would affect the next few weeks of her life. She would be working close with the man who had broken her heart and betrayed her trust.

"Yeah. I'll be there at around eleven," she answered.

Callum's lips curved upwards. "Sure. I'll see—"

"Peyton, where'd you put the bread?" Graham yelled, making Callum stop.

His smile faded. "I'll see you at the hotel at eleven," Callum said before she watched him walk down the steps towards the house across the road.

"See you then," Peyton whispered to herself.

When Callum entered his house, Peyton closed her front door, her forehead pressing on the stained glass. She closed her eyes and reminded her heart to stop the achy throbs it was doing. It was business between them. But she couldn't help but feel dejected by the events that had occurred over the past couple of days.

He'd said that he'd never let her fall in love with him, that love wasn't on the table between them. The seventeen-year-old in her died inside. In a perfect world, Callum Reid wouldn't have left her on that early Monday morning.

"He's gone?" Graham's voice had a layer of concern in it.

Peyton took a deep breath before she turned and smiled at him. He was still shirtless. "Quite the performance you gave there, Graham."

Graham nodded with a victorious smile. "I could do a whole lot better. You tell me when I need to go another level and I'll have you on a wall, kissing me."

She burst out laughing.

"What? You don't think we'd make him jealous if he saw us kissing?" Graham cocked a brow.

She chuckled at his confusion. "I don't think we'd make him jealous, Graham. Not when he doesn't care. This is all just for my forgiveness. He doesn't want me. Now, did you actually make me breakfast or was that part of the performance, too?" Peyton took a step forward and gave him her best puppy-dog eyes.

His hands cradled her face. "Froot Loops are in a bowl, waiting for you, and your tea with lemon is there, too." Then he kissed the top of her head.

"God, you are perfect! I'm going to marry you," Peyton said once he let her go.

"You'd make me a really happy man, Peyton Spencer."

"At least I'd make someone happy to be with me. We still on with that promise of ours?" She looked down at the promise ring on her left hand. A ring he'd given her a year after Callum had left town.

Graham took her left hand and bent down on one knee. "Peyton Spencer, do you still agree to marry me if we both go unwedded by the time we're forty?"

She let out a laugh as the excitement twinkled in his blue eyes. Then she tilted her head and smiled at him. "You did put a ring on it…so I'm still kinda promised to be married to you." He got up off his knee and wrapped his arms around her. The feeling of Graham's solid and strong heartbeat against her ear was one that made her chest warm.

"No Jay and no Callum. It's us, Peyton. You and me."

She smiled because it was always just them. No one could ever out-love the love she had for Graham.

"Always."

Peyton checked the time on her watch. She still had twenty minutes before she had to meet Callum at the hotel. She would get there before him and work through a game plan on how to deal with him. Life could not alter in any way since he had returned. This town was no longer his to call home and her heart was no longer his to claim. She shivered against the cold wind as she walked through the lane of trees and up the hill that led to the lake.

When she reached the top, she overlooked the entire lake and smiled at the hotel. She made it down the hill and towards the lake. Then she passed the bench and went down the path to the water's edge. Just as she reached the old pier, she noticed someone sitting at the end with their legs dangling over the water.

Before she could stop herself, Peyton stepped on the wooden pier and continued towards him. She didn't say anything while she observed him as he stared at the forest just near the hotel. Her chest constricted as she realised what spot he was looking at—the same spot they'd spent their last night together and the same part of the forest where she had given herself up to him. The part of the world where she had confessed that she loved him.

Peyton swallowed the large lump in her throat and started to walk off the pier, trying to stop the memories of that night from resurfacing in her consciousness.

"Peyton?" he called out.

She stopped. She was halfway off but halfway to him.

Taking a deep breath, she turned to face him. He gave her a tight smile—one she had seen many times since he had returned. Her chest heaved as she stared into those grey eyes.

"Want to sit with me for a bit? Before we go through Marissa's plans?" Callum carefully scooted over and patted a spot for her.

She remembered the many summers they had spent sitting on the edge, watching the world go by. Simple times. Before everything in her life had changed. Inhaling a deep breath to settle her heart, Peyton treaded cautiously towards the end of the pier and sat down, her legs dangling over the edge.

They sat there in silence, staring at the lake and the people who pedalled their small boats across the water. Though Daylesford offered little in extravagance, it did offer simplicity and peace. Closing her eyes, Peyton let the feeling of the wind consume her. Peace. That was what she loved about this town.

"I always knew you'd marry lavender boy," Callum said softly, almost in a whisper.

Peyton slowly opened her eyes and looked at him. "What?"

"Though it's not on the right finger, I know an engagement ring when I see one. I thought it wasn't, but seeing you with him this morning… It makes sense that you two got together," Callum explained, still eyeing the trees behind her hotel.

"It's a promise ring," Peyton stated as she played with the white-gold ring on her middle finger. She wasn't sure why she was clarifying herself to him, but she felt the need to.

Callum stared at his hands in his lap. "That you'll marry him?"

Peyton moved the hair that blew in her face and tucked it behind her ear. As her eyes scanned over at the trees, her heart ached at the memory of them at seventeen. From the way Callum had looked at her in the lantern light, she'd believed he had loved her, too, in some way.

"I'm not here to discuss my relationship with—"

"Lavender boy," Callum said, interrupting her. His eyes met hers.

"No. His name is Graham, not lavender boy. Don't call him that!" she said, raising her voice.

"You love him, not Jay."

Peyton shook her head in disbelief. Then she stood up and looked down at Callum. The dejected expression in his eyes caused her to flinch.

"I don't love Jay. Get that through your head. I love Graham."

Truth.

"Like you loved me?" he asked.

Peyton didn't blink. "More," she said without reserve.

Callum stilled and looked like he had lost his breath for a moment. Then he stood up and glanced down at her almost as if he were relieved.

"Then marry him, Peyton."

His answer surprised her. It wasn't the answer that she had expected.

"How does loving someone more than I loved you warrant marriage?" she asked, bewildered.

Callum—for the first time—gave her an honest smile. "Because I know how much you loved me. And if you love him more than you loved me, it says something. Now, let's go talk about my best friend's wedding." Callum stepped around her and began to walk off the pier.

Turning around, she watched him make his way towards the hotel. The emptiness inside her began to widen. Her heart had dropped at what he'd said. Until they were seventeen, she'd been his best friend. What she'd said hadn't been a lie. She did love Graham more. He knew her pain and had been there, loved her through the weakest points in her life.

No one could ever come close to being as important as Graham was to her. But Callum...he was her first love, and she'd believed that he would be her last love. And for the last four years, she'd forgotten what it was like to love him. Somewhere deep inside, she feared that she would remember soon enough.

Nine

"Two dance floors on two different parts of the hotel? Is she insane?" Peyton looked at the sheets of paper and then at Callum. When she'd unfolded them, she hadn't expected what she saw.

Callum laughed, took the papers out of her hand, and returned them to her desk. "She hasn't been formally diagnosed, but I suspect she is."

Peyton glared at him. "This is not a joke, Callum. I don't have the resources for this. You've seen this hotel. It's not in its prime. My parents were the ones who had the big ideas for it, not me." She let out a sigh and covered her face with her hands. Then she noted that she would never allow last-minute wedding bookings ever again, no matter the price.

"Hey," Callum said as his hands touched hers, pulling hers away from her face.

The way her heart throbbed at his contact surprised her.

He held her hands for a moment, staring at them. Peyton watched as he got lost in the moment.

"Callum," she breathed out, gaining his attention.

He slowly looked up until their eyes met. "Want to walk around the grounds? Maybe we can come up with a location for a second dance floor together," he suggested.

He squeezed her hand once before she pulled back. The

way her heart had leapt from that one squeeze was too much.

Peyton stood up and nodded. "Let's go."

Stepping out of the hotel and onto the path that led to the cliff, Peyton felt like she was a teenager all over again. The days she used to spend holding his hand as they'd roamed the hotel's grounds. He'd let go at one stage and kiss her or she'd run down to the cliff and he'd chase her. But now, years later, they stood some distance apart as they searched for the perfect location of a second dance floor.

Her heart missed when he used to reach for her hand as they walked together. But she knew it wouldn't happen between them. Yet she couldn't help but want it to happen, to confirm whether or not she still felt the same.

The vibrating of her phone had Peyton stopping. Callum stopped, too, turning to see why she had. When she pulled out her phone from her pants pocket, she saw that she had a new message.

Graham: Sprinklers have faulted again. I'm gonna have to go into the city and pick up some new ones or find a whole new system. I'll see you in a couple days. Be good!
Peyton: You be careful driving.
Graham: Yes, wife.
Peyton: IF I have no other options.
Graham: Someday you will.
Peyton: Is this sudden need to fulfil our promise because of you-know-who?
Graham: Yes. I'm about to leave your place. Be careful around him, Peyton. If he hurts you and I'm in the city, I will never forgive him. And Jay wouldn't either.
Peyton: He's not going to hurt me. I'm not going to fall in love with him.
Graham: Peyton, I think we're well past fall. We both know you're still in love with him.

Still in love with him.

Peyton stared at Graham's message. Her chest constricted at the thought. Still being love with Callum Reid would bring problems. And she didn't need them. No, she'd gotten over Callum a long time ago.

"You okay?" Callum asked, his voice was as sweet as she remembered.

Dammit!

"Fine," she said, returning her phone to her pocket. "Now, do you have any ideas for a spot?"

Callum looked at her and gave her a small smile. "I have an idea," he said, turning around and leading her down a path.

She followed him as they walked away from the hotel and to a path that led to the forest. Peyton hesitated as she realised just where he was leading her.

Just as she was about to tell him no, Callum reached over and took her hand.

"Trust me," he said.

Peyton looked at him and her eyebrows furrowed. "Like I trusted you not to break my heart, Callum Reid?"

He let out a sigh but never let go of her hand. "I had my reasons, Peyton. You wouldn't understand."

"Try me," she said firmly.

"In time. Now, come on," he said, pulling her into the forest.

Each step they took, her breathing heaved. She hadn't been this far into the forest in years. Peyton noticed a round rock that was almost perfectly smooth. She knew what that rock meant; it was a marker. They'd only have to walk a few more metres, take a turn at the broken tree, pass the small embankment, and they'd find their spot.

Peyton stopped next to the round rock, yanking her hand from Callum. The loss of his hand left her confused with old emotions. His touch was one she used to crave, but she couldn't anymore.

"What's the matter, Peyton?" he asked, a worried look consuming his face.

"I can't go there with you. I'm sorry, but I can't. I can't let strangers see *our* spot. I'd rather give up the wedding than let them all see," she confessed only loud enough for them to hear.

Callum's face went blank as he stared at the round rock. He took a step forward and held her hand again. Peyton's heart raced, and the aching heat filled her entire chest. When she looked in his eyes, she thought that they meant more than he had led her to believe for a moment. That he loved her more. But she knew otherwise. At the end of the day, he had been her first love. And Graham was her unconditional love. She had said that she loved Graham more, but maybe she loved him more than she had loved Callum only when they had been best friends.

"It's not for them, Peyton. It's for me." There was an unquestionable layer of regret in his voice, and it rendered her breathless.

"Why for you?"

He squeezed her hand. "Because you're the mistake I got right and all I'll have are those moments. I won't make you go down there. Just give me a few minutes, okay?"

The vulnerable glint in his grey eyes had Peyton's breathing falter. Her head told her that what she was about to say was stupid, to just let go of the past. But her heart wanted more.

"I'm a mistake to you?" she uttered.

"Yes," he said without hesitation.

"Then going down there will mean nothing." Peyton took her hand back and left him as she walked towards the end of the ridge. She ignored the burning that consumed her chest.

She heard his footsteps follow her as they went deeper into the forest. The fallen leaves crunched under her shoes as she held her head high and ignored the fact that Callum Reid had labelled her a mistake.

The moment that she arrived at the small spot of clear forest, Peyton tightly balled her hands. She forced herself to forget what had happened in this spot over four years ago. Her eyes roamed around the trees that made a circle clearing. It had gone unchanged. She could just see their initials carved into the tree in front of her from some distance away. Instinct had her wanting to walk over and feel the carving under her fingertips, but her pride won. Peyton crossed her arms over her chest as she watched Callum walk to the exact spot where they had made love for the first time.

He stood there, staring at the autumn leaves on the ground, seemingly lost in the past. Though she tried not to, she remembered them sneaking away from her house until they were far enough to run past the lake. He had pulled out a blanket from the basket and placed it on the ground before he'd lit the lanterns. Then they'd watched the stars until she'd asked for more than just a goodnight kiss.

"It was right here, wasn't it?" Callum asked, pulling her out of her memories.

Peyton gave him a shrug.

"You told me that you loved me in this exact spot," he said, meeting her stare.

Peyton tensed. It was definitely not what she wanted to talk about. "And it's the exact spot where you didn't tell me that you loved me. Such a sentimental spot, isn't it?" She looked away, afraid to cry. So she stared at the tree next to her, her eyes following the natural pattern of the bark.

"Peyton…"

She met his darkening, grey eyes.

"I never said it because the first time I told you those three words, I wanted them to be true and I wanted you to believe me."

Another blow.

This time, tears started to form and Peyton let out a hard laugh. "I'm glad we've cleared the air, then. God, did I waste those years. Guess mistakes are a two-way street then."

Callum flinched and surprise crept on his face. He took two steps until he was face to face with her. "I'm a mistake to you?"

"The biggest one I've ever made," she said, ensuring that her voice sounded strong.

"Then I guess we both did something right in our lives," Callum said as he walked past her.

She listened to his footsteps as he made his way farther

from their spot.

Peyton quickly turned around, her tears skimming her face. "Why am I a mistake to you?" she cried.

Stupid question, Peyton. You should have left it.

Callum stopped for a moment before he turned around. Pain filled his face, and his eyes were shiny with unshed tears. The sight was a first for her.

"Why am I a mistake to you?" he roared, startling her.

"I asked you first!" she cried.

He rushed back to her, his body close to Peyton's. The absolute grief in his eyes made her regret her decision to ask.

"My mistake was walking away, leaving this town. But it was a mistake I got right. You stayed here, Peyton. You didn't… You… You were saved from me!"

Peyton silently gasped. Anger and resentment boiled through her. She took a step forward and inhaled a deep breath before drawing her palm back and slapping his cheek. Instantaneously, she felt the sting in her hand.

"Saved from you?" she asked unbelievably.

Callum placed a hand on his cheek and rubbed her assault. He wasn't angry. He seemed relieved as his features softened.

"Yes."

"That is the biggest pile of bullshit I have ever heard. Saved from you? How in God's name does that even make sense? I loved you, Callum. In that exact spot, I gave you everything. What did you keep from me? Why did you walk away?" she cried.

Four years of bottled emotions had exploded and tarnished the one place in the world that meant everything to her.

"You wouldn't understand. But what I did saved you. I stand by that. I will never regret what I did to us. You were happy here," he said with as much emotion as he did when he had once asked her to be his.

"Happy?" She shook her head. "My parents died and I buried them! Staying in this town, I've been far from happy. Everything here is a constant reminder of my parents and of you! You did a great job saving me, then, Callum."

She didn't wait for him to reply. Instead, she turned around and walked up the steep slope. When she reached flat ground, she quickened her steps. She hoped they could just get back to the hotel in peace. And if she were lucky enough, he'd go home.

"Peyton. Peyton, wait!" The desperation could be heard in his shouts.

She stopped and looked up at the sky through the gaps in the branches. Taking a deep breath in, Peyton spun around.

"No! No more waiting. I've waited four years and I'm done. I'm over you. You should have never returned. You should have begged your friend for a new venue, because I can't do this. I don't want you here. When Oscar's wedding is over, just leave, Callum. Just leave! Do what you're so good at and walk away. I didn't need this in my life. I called you, for God's sakes. I shouldn't have. But I needed you then. I don't want or need you in my life—not when you proved that you didn't want or need me."

Silence. The best form of goodbye.

Ten

Aunt Brenda: A lovely young woman taught me how to message you. I hope you're doing well, Peyton. You call me if you need anything and we'll come straight away. Don't forget everyone comes back from leave on Monday. I love you and don't forget your breakfast.

Peyton laughed at the text message her aunt had left her. Aunt Brenda wasn't one for anything tech-savvy. As long as it called, she was good. Her uncle was one who could do it all with technology. After giving her aunty a quick reply, Peyton placed her phone back on her desk and picked up the piece of paper with her design on it. Once the first dance of the Reynolds' wedding was done, the guests would move from the hill to the lake, where the dance floor would expand out on the water almost like a jetty.

It wasn't much of an idea, but she needed to get a plan on paper to show Callum and then Marissa. It had been just over a day since she'd last seen him. Now, she sat in the hotel's office, still pissed off that the universe had brought him back to Daylesford.

A crack of thunder had Peyton almost jumping out of her skin. Pushing the leather chair back, she got up and walked to the window. She looked at the grey sky and sighed. She hoped it was only thunder, but in this part of the state, she knew a storm was to be expected.

One winter, the sky had been clear, and then, a few hours later, snow had fallen. Most of the town had stood on top of Wombat hill and looked at the town blanketed with white. It had been beautiful and it was a moment that made her appreciate the town she called home.

Another loud crash of thunder and lightning confirmed her suspicion. Upon walking back to the desk, Peyton placed all her work and her laptop into her bag. Then she grabbed her keys and started to lock up the hotel. As she took a step outside, she prayed that the storm wasn't like the one in '06. Windows had been broken and a tree had fallen on top of one of the outer guest cabins. If Peyton was left with the same kind of aftermath, she knew she couldn't afford to rebuild another cabin—not if she wanted to expand and redesign the hotel to her liking.

After taking a few steps down the path, she turned around and looked at the old Victorian hotel. She noticed that the worn hotel sign needed repainting; the flaking paint wasn't particularly flattering to the eye.

"You better be standing when I get back. We've been through a lot more than a storm. You're all I have left, so don't go falling over," Peyton warned the building, knowing she was being ridiculous. But in truth, she felt a connection to the hotel. She had grown up in it and around it.

The hotel was the keeper of her memories.

A strong gust of wind hit her, almost making her stumble back. As she turned to walk the path back home, the local pub caught her attention through the trees. Not wanting to go home anytime soon, Peyton made her way up the hill and to town.

"Peyton!" the pub cheered as she took a step inside.

She was used to it. It was how the town treated people. And if they didn't know your name, they'd scream "Stranger!" and welcome you to Daylesford.

She smiled and nodded as she walked past all the patrons and towards the counter. Placing her bag on top of the oak, Peyton took a seat on a barstool. She looked over at Mr Preston, who came over to her.

"Coke, Miss Peyton?" he asked as he reached for a glass.

"That'd be nice. You don't normally work the counter, Mr Preston," Peyton said, rubbing her hands together. The temperature had dropped on her walk to town.

"Jay's gone down to the Wilcox farm to help them get ready for the storm. Have you checked on your house? Do you need me to go down there to help you tie down anything?" he asked as he placed her beverage in front of her.

Wilcox farm... Daisy Wilcox.

"No, I'm fine. I'll just move what I can into the shed." She took a sip of Coke as she looked up at Jay's father. "Jay isn't mad at me for walking out of the pub with Callum, is he?"

Mr Preston gave her a tight smile. "No, darling. He realised that you were doing it to prevent the coppers from being called in. He isn't mad."

Peyton placed her glass down. "Is that why he went to the Wilcox farm? Because he's *not* mad at me? Not after Daisy Wilcox called me a sook after my parents died and claimed I was after the town's attention. She slapped me in this pub and Jay banned her."

"She was intoxicated, Peyton," Mr Preston tried to reason.

Peyton pulled out her phone from her pocket and brought up Jay's contact to send him a message.

Peyton: Traitor!

"Explains why she goes out of her way to make me trip or have something thrown at me every time she's in town. Your son deserves better than Daisy Wilcox and you know it." Peyton got off the barstool, put her phone in her pocket, and picked up her bag.

Mr Preston sighed. "It would take Callum and Graham

hurting you before he got the girl."

Her eyes quickly met his. "Why would you even put your son third on that ridiculous list?"

"Because we all know he's third on *your* list, Peyton. My son is a good kid, but he'd never measure up to Callum or Graham. The town saw how you looked at Callum as a teenager. You were completely in love with that boy. And Graham you've already promised to marry. Jay knows all of this, yet he's still at your beck and call."

There was no anger in his tone or hint of humour on Mr Preston's face.

Peyton stood there, astonished. She had no comeback. The pub had gone quiet around them, and she cursed her need to mention Daisy Wilcox. Instead of saying another word, Peyton turned around and walked towards the exit. When she opened the door, cold air and rain hit her.

"Peyton, let me get you an umbrella. Or you could stay here until it passes," Mr Preston said behind her.

It was typical small-town-folk behaviour. Insult a person then offer them shelter from the rain. The buzz of her phone against her thigh had her pulling it out. She had a new message.

Jay: I could say the same thing about you, traitor.

Pulling her wavy, light-brown hair through the elastic band, Peyton tied it up into a high ponytail. She walked to the kitchen window to see the trees branches in the backyard start to sway violently. In the middle of the garden, the rotary clothesline spun and the pegs flew out of the small plastic basket, landing on the wet grass. The rain fell heavily, and she let out a sigh as she fed her arms through her rain jacket.

As Peyton zipped it, the sound of her phone echoed through the kitchen. Looking around, she spotted it on the small buffet that leaned against the wall. She walked over and answered it the moment she saw a picture of a blonde with bright red lipstick on the screen.

"I'm guessing your hibernation is over. Exams done and dusted?" Peyton asked as she walked towards the door that led to the backyard.

"Finally. Ugh, I just need to graduate already. I really shouldn't have failed a few of those units back in first year. I could have been done by now like you, Peyton," Madilynne Woodside, her best friend, said.

"You were too busy loving city life," Peyton stated as she turned the knob and opened the door, feeling the instant hit of the harsh wind.

"What can I say? I loved being in proper clubs in Toorak rather than Jay Preston's pub that was turned into a 'club' on the weekends. It's so much better than Daylesford," Madilynne bragged with a gleam in her voice.

"I know. You tell me every time we chat, Mads," Peyton pointed out as she took a step onto the back porch.

"Well, get your ass here and we can celebrate anything and every—what is that sound? It sounds like a wind tunnel or something."

A crash of thunder made Peyton jump.

"Jesus, Peyton, are you in that storm? Dude, get inside!"

The worry in Madilynne's voice had Peyton letting out a chuckle.

"It's a little rain. I'm just going to move what I can into the shed. Is it bad in the city?" Peyton asked as she walked over to a fallen patio chair.

"It's not *just* raining. Seriously, I heard thunder. You're outside, aren't you? That's why I can hear it so clear. I don't think you should be on your phone while you're out in that weather. You could get hit by lightning or something!" Madilynne's voice hitched a little higher.

"The odds of that happening are low. And who cares if I do? Means I don't have to deal with you coming home," Peyton teased.

"Hey! I can't believe you said that. You know that I need your reference for when I apply for management positions."

Madilynne let out a huff.

"Relax, Mads. Just make sure you're here by the end of next week. This'll be fun. It'll be good to have you back in Daylesford," Peyton said as she picked up the fallen chair. Another deafening rumble filled the air, much closer to where Peyton stood.

"You are the only reason why I'm looking forward to coming home. Mum and Dad complaining that I didn't become a doctor or a lawyer—or even worse, a politician—is not one of them. Seriously, Peyton, I'm going to hang up now. I will not be an accessory to your death by natural elements. I'll see you soon and please hurry up and get inside. Don't think I won't call someone to make you," Madilynne warned.

"You're so dramatic. I'll see you when you come home. Don't forget to call me when you've passed Ryder's spot."

A loud crash had Peyton looking over to see that the gate had flown open.

"I'll call you from Ryder's," Madilynne confirmed before they both hung up.

Ryder's spot was a short pole on the side of the highway that marked the exact spot where Daniel Ryder had walked almost ten kilometres—drunk—before passing out. The next day, his friends had placed a pole and the exact beer can he had held in his hand to mark the spot. Ryder was famous in town for it, but he had no recollection of it. It was the night he'd drunk away the memory of his girlfriend leaving him. It also became a saying: "Do a Ryder, walk a tenner."

Turning around, Peyton walked back into the kitchen and placed her phone on the bench. Another bang of the gate had her sighing. If the latch was broken, it would be a sleepless night with the noise.

Leaving the house, she walked towards one of the chairs and picked it up before going down the steps to the shed. Rain drenched her and the wind hit her hard. By the time Peyton placed the chair inside the shed, she had to wipe her face with her cold hands. She panted, trying to get her breath back.

After another roll of thunder, she ran back to the porch to

retrieve another chair. She continued to do this until all six chairs were stacked away. In the end, her ponytail was dripping wet and her body started to shiver. Exiting the shed, Peyton looked over at the swinging gate. She debated, deciding to leave it and get back inside the warm house. The gate could be fixed later when the rain had lightened.

A glimpse of a shadow caught her eye and Peyton stopped. Glaring, she saw a black cat sitting on the grass. It was Mrs West's cat, Mr Lucky. He was a strange cat, hated the sun but loved the rain. Peyton knew Mrs West would be looking for him and decided to return him.

While approaching the gate, Peyton didn't take her eyes off the cat. She walked slowly, ensuring she didn't startle it.

Then she raised her hands up and said ever so slowly, "Hey, Mr Lucky. You're far from home. Let me take you back so you can get warm."

The cat lifted its head before it meowed at her. She ignored her shivers and slowly walked towards Mr Lucky, smiling when he didn't immediately run from her. Peyton carefully stopped in front of him then placed her hands on her knees and bent down.

"Who's the good cat? Come here," Peyton said and started to reach for him.

Mr Lucky let out another meow before he bolted past Peyton and into her backyard.

"Damn cat!" she cursed. "You get back here, you little shit!"

Peyton quickly turned around and saw Mr Lucky sitting in the middle of her garden—smirking—before she just caught a glimpse of the gate swinging towards her and then saw black.

Eleven

"You two have never kissed before? Like, never?" Martha asked, disbelieving. She sculled back her beer and placed it on the ground, next to her feet.

Martha Downs was the daughter of the town's sergeant. Her being invited to their bonfire parties was mainly because she could get anyone off the hook if they were caught drinking underage. However, most things in town were overlooked or ignored. If you stirred up trouble, then the law book would be handed to you.

Peyton turned her head and stared at Callum, who was watching the fire intently. She looked back at Martha and shook her head.

"No. We're best friends," Peyton simply stated.

Martha's mouth gaped and her forehead creased as she looked at Peyton in disbelief before she pointed at a couple near a tree. "See, Taylor and Kenny are just friends and they're making out. You guys are constantly around each other. The way you both act… You're like a couple."

Peyton let out a nervous laugh. Sometimes she believed they could be a couple. She'd had that belief since she was thirteen, when he'd held her hand as they walked down Main Street, but she had thought too much into it.

"We're just – "

"Why don't you both just kiss? Show us all that you're both just friends," Martha said, cocking her brow and interrupting Peyton.

"I... Uhh..." Peyton mumbled and picked up her cup of Coke from the ground. She took a long sip as the party around them silenced and all eyes focused on her.

"Come on," Martha said as she smirked and played with her curly ponytail.

"Yeah! Do it!" someone behind Peyton yelled.

"Knock it off, Martha. You get stupid when you drink," Madilynne said, taking a seat next to Peyton.

"Please, Mads. I'm just as curious about these two as the rest of the town. I can speak my mind. My Daddy's the sergeant, remember?"

Madilynne let out a short laugh. "Yeah, and you never let us forget it. If we're going by social status, then I should remind you whose daddy is the mayor who employs your daddy."

Madilynne hated to use her father's title, but when Martha talked, Madilynne always had the urge to shut her down. It made for some interesting fights between the two.

"Come on, Pey. We're getting out of here," Callum said, getting up from his chair.

She looked up at him and he continued to stare at the fire, waiting for her.

"Callum, Martha's just being a teasing bitch. Stay and party with us," Madilynne said.

But Peyton knew otherwise. The tensing in his jaw told her that something was worrying him.

Standing up, Peyton looked at Madilynne. "I'll see you later."

"But it's not even one yet," her best friend argued.

"I have to get her home before her dad realises she snuck out, Mads. We'll see you later," Callum said and started to walk away.

Peyton gave Madilynne an apologetic shrug before chasing after Callum. He didn't say anything as they walked away from the forest near the boathouse, past her parents' hotel, and towards their street.

Peyton had always wondered what it would be like to kiss Callum, but she knew better. They were friends. Though it had hurt seeing him kiss Tasha Morecombe at Peyton's sixteenth birthday party, it was the realisation she'd needed. So she'd buried her feelings deep.

When they arrived at their street, he surprisingly took her hand and led her quietly to the side gate of her house. Her heartbeat sped up at the feel of his touch, but she swallowed hard to ignore the bliss she felt.

Callum let go of her hand the moment they made it to her bedroom window. She leant on the tree and watched as he lifted it up. The brightness of the moon gave her the light needed to see him and the cherry blossoms that fell on the shirt he was wearing.

A girl could only dream of the day when Callum Reid asked her to be his. For Peyton, she wouldn't be that lucky girl. She'd rather be his friend than nothing at all. It was a sacrifice her heart hated making.

Callum moved the curtains, and she watched as he looked into her room. When he glanced over at Peyton, he gave her a restrained smile.

"It's clear. Doesn't look like your parents noticed. The house is quiet," he stated and leant against the weatherboards of her house.

The worry in his eyes had her frowning. "Callum, does it annoy you that people in town think more of what we actually are?"

He tensed. "Peyton…"

"Are you embarrassed at the thought of kissing me?" she asked, a little hurt.

"No," he whispered.

Her heart threw itself against her ribcage. Not the answer she had been expecting.

So she pushed off the tree and took a step forward. "Then kiss me."

He looked at her, surprised. "I don't think – "

"Prove to me that we're just friends. What are you afraid of? It's just a kiss."

"It's not, Peyton."

"It is. What are you so afraid of?" she asked, tilting her head up at him.

He let out a sigh and said, "Of falling further for you than I already am."

Callum said it so softly that she almost missed it. She looked at him in shock at his confession. Before she could even comment or reply, he grabbed her and crashed his lips onto hers, searing her heart as his for eternity.

Warmth surrounded her. It wasn't just a sensation that lasted mere seconds; it was prolonging. She snuggled into it and smelt wood burning. Then she opened her eyes to see the glass coffee table of her lounge room in front of her. She bunched her eyebrows at the sight. Not what she had expected to see. Her eyes wandered as she started to slowly remember her last memory before the darkness.

"That damn cat," she mumbled as she tried to move, a blanket tight around her restricting her attempt to sit up.

"Careful, Peyton. Slowly," a voice instructed.

She lifted her eyes up from the coffee table to see Callum walking into the room. He checked on the fireplace before he kneeled and set a cup on the table.

"Why are you in my house, Callum?" Peyton asked, groggy.

She pulled her arms from under the blanket and then sat up too quickly. Her head pounded heavily and she placed a hand on her forehead, trying to soothe the ache away.

Callum sat beside her and cradled her cheeks in his hands, steadying her face as he looked over her.

"What are you doing?"

"Making sure that you're okay. I think you should be fine. Do you need me to take you to a doctor or the local hospital?" Callum dropped his hands from her face and adjusted the blanket to cover her up more.

"I... Uhh, what?" she asked, confused.

"I found you near the gate unconscious in the storm, Peyton. What were you thinking? I found your phone on the bench once I brought you inside. Your last call was to Mads eight hour ago. I found you two hours ago. That means you were unconscious out there for almost six hours. Lucky you had that jacket on."

"There was a cat," she explained as she pulled the blanket off her. Then her eyes widened and she quickly covered herself, her cheeks heating instantly. "Umm, care to explain?"

Callum looked down and then back at her, his cheeks turning a rosy red. "Your jeans were soaked, so I had to pull them off you. You were out cold. I tried to wake you, but it was no use. So I, ahh, took the initiative and took your pants off."

"Wow. Makes me glad that I wear underwear. So when sexual deviants like Callum Reid take off your pants when you're unconscious, nothing is on show. Please tell me you didn't do it on my lawn."

"No, Peyton. I brought you into the house and put you on the couch. I made sure you were okay and had the fire going before I removed your pants," Callum explained with a slight smirk on his face.

Peyton wrapped the cream blanket around her tighter and stood up from the couch. "I feel very violated right now." Then she looked down at Callum, the colour in his cheeks fading.

"You're upset that I took your pants off but you're not even gonna thank me for bringing you in. Peyton, you were unconscious. What happened to you?"

She let out an irritated huff. "I was trying to get Mrs West's cat and then I guess I didn't see the gate swing forward from the wind. You know you could have just left me there. I don't need saving."

Callum stood up and looked down at her. "I wasn't going to leave you out there. Do you really think I could live with myself if I just saw you on the ground and walked away?"

Her heart leapt. That wasn't something she'd wanted to hear. Her heart wanted to be saved, but she knew Callum Reid wouldn't save her. If anything, he'd ruin her...further.

"Thank you," she said softly. "I feel really uncomfortable knowing that you've seen me in my underwear. I might go shower, scrub off the humiliation, and then change."

"Peyton, I've seen you in far less than underwear. Grab a shower. I'll make you a new cuppa and then I'll check out that bump you have." His voice had softened, almost echoing the same way he'd spoken at seventeen.

She had believed him then. Now, standing wrapped in a blanket and with her hair slightly damp, she still believed him.

"Callum, that's nice of you, but—"

He took a step forward and cupped her face in his hands. Just the feel of his fingers on her skin had Peyton biting the inside of her cheek and trying to control the tension in her chest. Callum turned her head slightly and inspected the side of her face.

"What are you doing?" she asked.

"You said I was nice. I gotta make sure you don't have a concussion. There's no way that you'd say anything so pleasant about me," he teased. Then his lips tugged upwards and Peyton saw the seventeen-year-old in him.

Back before the universe had tested her, she would always kiss him once that sweet smile appeared. Now, she had to be cautious of it to keep her heart safe.

She took a step back. "You're right. Concussion has me rambling lies."

His smile quickly faded and that glimmer of the past left his eyes. Instead, the cold version of the boy she'd once loved stood in front of her. The want for the past to be reality was hitting her. If she could have the past, she'd have him and her parents back in her life.

But that wasn't how the universe worked. Because even when you'd lost it all, the world continued around you. It continued to create and take away. Continued to give beauty and inflict pain. Life was the never-ending journey of air and breaths. To live and to die. A domino effect of decisions and outcomes, each affecting each other. For Peyton, Callum and her parents' deaths were just that. One after the other, she'd lost them.

"How about you take a bath, instead, and I'll make you something to eat," Callum offered.

She flinched, taken aback by his suggestion. "Thanks, but you should go home."

He closed his eyes and breathed in heavily before he looked back at her. "Peyton, if I hadn't found you, who would?"

Her shoulders sagged. He'd just won the argument she hadn't wanted to have. She wanted him out of her house and to draw up a plan on him staying away.

"Someone would have…eventually."

"Exactly. *Eventually.* Maybe the next day or the day after that. What if it had been worse than it really was? Peyton, you could have died from natural exposure or brain swelling… Anything for Christ's sake."

The straining vein in his neck caught her attention. This was too much involvement for someone who had left her to grow up in the small town they'd promised to leave behind.

"God! Why can't you be like other men in this world?" she asked as she held the blanket securely around her.

Callum let out a sigh and his muscles and posture loosened. "And what do *other* men in this world do?"

She glared at him, noticing his pupils dilating. "They break up with a girl and never call or see her again. Why can't you do that?"

He mirrored her glare. "I did do that, but I can't continue to do it. Now stop arguing with me and just go have a bath!"

Peyton looked up at the ceiling and mumbled a curse before she marched past him towards the bathroom. "May God let me get hit by lightning while I'm in that tub!" she yelled angrily to him.

When she reached the bathroom door, she looked up at the ceiling. "God, if you're listening to me, then you should know you made the wrong decision. You had to go and make that son of a bitch save me. Should have let me die, Big Man. It'd be less painful and I would have appreciated it more."

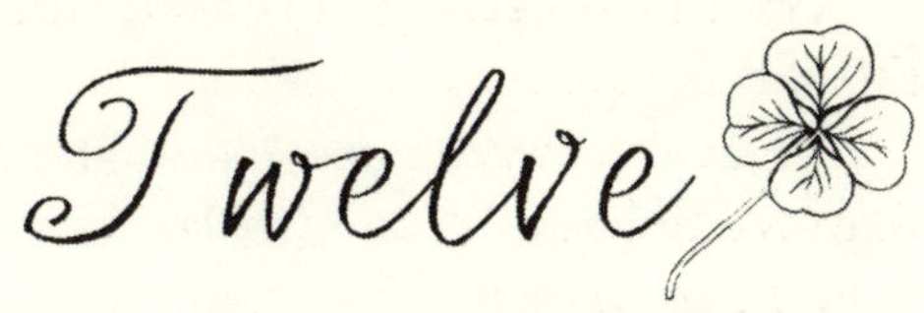

Twelve

Peyton sat in the tub with her arms crossed over her breasts and murmured her displeasure. Though she enjoyed the warm water relieving her achy muscles, she was still bitter about her *saviour*. It killed her inside that he had been the one to find her. If she hadn't tried to get Mrs West's cat, she'd have avoided all of this.

"Fucking Mr Lucky!" she cursed as she untangled her arms and placed them on the sides of the porcelain freestanding bathtub. "I'm going to kill that cat!" she promised before she submerged herself under the water.

Opening her eyes, she saw the cream-coloured ceiling all blurry under the water. She counted in her head as she continued to stare. Being submerged, she enjoyed the quietness of the water, the thunder almost silenced. If she weren't so afraid of drowning, she'd try to reach longer than a minute without air.

Peyton sat up, quickly taking in oxygen and wiping the hair away from her face. She hung her arms over the bathtub, letting water droplets slip off her fingertips and onto the tiled floor. Another crash of thunder had her turning her head and staring out the window. It was close. She smiled at the thought of how ironic it would be if she were to actually be struck by lightning.

Just then, lightning beautifully and terrifyingly lit up the dark sky. Another flash and thunder cracked in unison. Peyton looked up at the pendant to see it continue to flicker before her.

Footsteps rushed to the bathroom door. Peyton stilled before three bangs were made against the door.

"Peyton, are you all right?" Callum shouted over the sound of thunder.

Her eyebrows furrowed and she groaned. "I'm just waiting to be struck by lightning. It shouldn't be long now!" she yelled as she tipped her head back and closed her eyes.

"I swear to God, Peyton. If you have a window open, I'm coming in there!"

Her fingers tapped against the tub. Then she turned her head and stared at the wooden door. "Anything to see me naked. You're such a pervert, Callum."

She sat quietly, waiting for him to reply, but he didn't. She didn't hear his footsteps disappearing either, so she knew that he was still there. More minutes passed as the water in the tub started to cool.

Pulling her leg up from the water, she noticed that her toes had wrinkled, but she didn't mind. She submerged her leg back in the water and waited. It seemed she had always being waiting for Callum.

"I almost came back, you know," Callum said from behind the bathroom door.

Peyton kept quiet and looked at the soapy water.

"I got to the wooden 'welcome' sign and I parked my car on the side of the road. I sat there for an hour deciding whether or not I should see you. I've done that almost trip about six times, Peyton. And each of those trips, I turned around and went back to the city. At least once a year, I came back to that part of the highway. Why it's so different now is because I made it past the sign. This time, the need to see you outweighed the consequences I'd be facing."

The sadness in his voice caused the ache in her heart to rise to her throat. Tears silently slid down her face. Because she, too, had made it to that sign. She had parked her Volkswagen Golf in the middle of the highway and stared out in the direction of the city. But in the end, she had always done a U-turn back to town.

Peyton silently got out of the tub and reached for the towel on the counter. Not wiping the bubbles that slid down her body, she wrapped the cotton towel around her. She knew what she had to do next.

Ignoring the flung blanket on the bathroom floor, Peyton walked towards the door. She took a deep breath in attempt to settle her anxious heart. With a hard swallow, she turned the knob and pulled the door open. Then she looked down to see Callum sitting on the carpet, his back to her.

"You're forgiven," she whispered.

Callum quickly looked up, his sad voice from before mirroring the sorrow that consumed his eyes. He looked at her in bewilderment, and Peyton gave him a restrained smile. If he really had almost come back, then she had to send him away.

"I'm what?" Callum asked, quickly getting on his feet.

Her eyes met his, hoping he'd believe her and hoping what she'd say would be enough for him to leave town. "I forgive you, Callum. I'm not angry at you anymore."

"Just like that?"

Peyton nodded. "Just like that," she said before she pushed past him and walked down the hallway, towards her bedroom.

"Bullshit," he said, stopping her.

Peyton balled her fists tight before she turned around.

Callum's facial features tensed and his nose flared. "I call bullshit."

"You got what you wanted, Callum. You have my forgiveness. You can go home now. I'll see you at the wedding," she said casually.

Her hopes of him believing what she said were dashed when he marched towards her and stared her down.

"No, you're lying. I don't have your forgiveness. I can see it. You're still hurt. I haven't earned it. I want to earn it, Peyton. I *need* to redeem myself. Nothing I have done has been worthy enough of you."

In that one moment, she saw it. A flash of the first night he'd kissed her, the same unsure and afraid eyes. Somehow, she was stuck between the past and present, and it completely terrified her.

"Do you want my forgiveness or not?" she asked, tired.

Callum sighed and he shook his head. "Not like this, Peyton."

"Then how?" she asked desperately.

"Spend some time together. Have moments together... I don't know, Peyton. I just need to be around you. I need to make it all up to you," Callum revealed.

Before she could tell him how absurd it sounded, a loud crash of thunder violently thrashed and the hallway light flickered once before the house darkened. The moment she couldn't see Callum's face, she let out a heavy sigh.

"I'll find candles," he said.

She felt him walk past her, his arm grazing hers. "They're—"

"Last drawer in the kitchen," he said, cutting her off.

"How'd you know that?" she asked, turning around.

"Your house hasn't changed, Peyton. Everything is in the same spot. It's like you preserved this house to be the exactly how your parents left it. Get dressed and I'll make you something to eat," Callum said. His footsteps could be heard in the kitchen.

"Let it contain rat poison, please," she softly begged.

Peyton pulled open a drawer and rummaged through it. The almost black room made it difficult for her to find anything. After raking around, she pulled out a pair of lacy underwear. Peyton held them up to the small amount of light coming from the window and the sight confirmed what she held.

Lace.

"Yeah, I'm gonna have to find something in the grandmother department—especially with that pervert in the kitchen."

With a reassuring nod to herself, Peyton put the lace back in the drawer and felt around until cotton hit her fingertips. It was a comforting feeling. Cotton wasn't as daring as lace. Why she had that sort of underwear, she didn't know. But she never wore it. Lingerie was not her expertise. She wasn't even sure when she'd last worn a matching set. She'd always felt it was a symbol for her life. Nothing ever matched and different pieces never fit. Instead, they always had to adjust.

Realising the extent of thought she had put into underwear, Peyton quickly slipped the pair on and rummaged in the next drawer until she found flannelette pyjama bottoms. Then she silently dressed herself. Once she was satisfied with the articles of clothing on her body, she began to towel-dry her hair. After a few minutes, she placed the damp towel over the railing of her bed and walked out of her room.

Each step that she took she ensured was long and slow. Taking time away from being with Callum was better than actually spending those minutes with him. She had offered him forgiveness. She had given him an out, and he still hadn't taken it. He was stubborn as ever, much to her displeasure.

The flicking of ember flames caught her eye as she stepped into the darkened kitchen. The entire room was filled with lit candles. For a moment, she let herself enjoy the thoughtfulness of the extravagant use of wax. And as quickly as she enjoyed it, she forced herself to hate it. She walked towards the kitchen table and was just able to see the length of it—with the help of two lit vanilla candles.

Peyton pulled out a chair and sat down, ensuring that he heard the groan she let out. She blamed the storm, but she knew it was higher than that. She had to direct her hatred for such circumstances to Fate. And Fate was a sinister bitch when it came to Peyton. Let's not forget Divine Intervention; she was even worse. Or he. Whatever gender, Peyton hated Divine Intervention as much as she hated Fate...and Death, too. All those bastards were working hand-in-hand against her.

A plate was placed in front of her and she looked at it. A sandwich. Perfectly cut into triangles with the crusts removed. Her heart was the first to react, becoming heavy and uncomfortable. And then her mouth formed a frown. Memory Lane was becoming an allying bastard, too.

"I'm hoping you still like Vegemite and cheese sandwiches. You had it all there, so I assumed," Callum said as he sat in the chair in front of Peyton.

He gave her a faint smile before he stared at the candle; the flame reflected in his eyes. Not liking the circumstances she was in and the pressure on her chest, Peyton leant forward and blew out the flame that he was looking at intently.

"What was that for?" he asked. The light from the other candle on the table made his cheek visible.

Peyton sat back and gave him a shrug. "I'm not one for romance, and these candles are a red alert for me. I'd rather we eat in the dark since my first request of you to leave my house isn't happening."

"Fine," Callum said before he moved closer to the last candle on the table and blew it out. Only the light from the candles behind him made some things visible. "I'm not trying to romance you, Peyton. I don't want that."

She rolled her eyes, not caring if he could see or not. "Me, either."

"You don't?"

She smirked at the curiosity in his voice. She didn't want him to seduce her, purely because she knew her heart couldn't withstand him for much longer.

"No, Callum Reid. You are the last man who I want *romancing* me."

She was just able to see a smile on his face. And that didn't make her feel satisfied with her response at all. She couldn't figure him out. She had given him what he wanted, yet he wouldn't take it. He was far too much of a mystery. A challenge her heart wanted to conquer and claim.

A tremble coursed through her. She blamed it on those feelings the seventeen-year-old she had been had harboured for him. Not the twenty-one-year-old. No, that Peyton hated the man who sat in front of her.

"Glad we can agree on something. You know you can be pretty stubborn, Peyton. Always have been. Guess with time it's gone from pretty stubborn to definitely and proudly stubborn,"

Callum pointed out.

Crossing her arms over her chest, she glared at him. "I'm not stubborn. You're a challenge not worth my time. Been there, done that. I'm over you."

There was no quick reply like she had expected. Instead, she heard the sound of a matchstick. Then the candle to her right was lit and then the one to her left. Callum blew the matchstick out and placed it on the table.

Peyton missed the darkness that had consumed him. The light provided a detailed look of anguish on his face. Her breathing became shallow, hardly reaching her lungs.

"How'd you get over me, Peyton?"

She heard the break in his voice. He hadn't seemed to notice it, but she had. That vulnerability made her heart leap, filling it with useless hope.

"It was easy."

"How easy?" he asked.

Peyton sensed the hurt in his question. "It was a completely and utterly simple task," she stated as she sat up and uncrossed her arms. Then she picked up the sandwich and took a large bite, internally cursing him for having remembered one of her favourite foods.

"Do tell," he said with a raised brow.

"What's to tell, Callum? It's simple. You ripped out my heart, crushed it in your hands, and forced it back in my chest. You left me with a gripping ache for four years. That's how I got over you—because I had to. Because life made me."

Her throat tightened and she found it difficult to hold back a sob, but she'd be damned if he saw her like he had in the forest. Never again.

"How did life *make* you get over me?"

Peyton put the sandwich back on the plate and stood up, looking down at him. He had grown since they were together. He'd experienced more and seen things she hadn't. She closed her eyes for a moment before she stared at him. The regret in his eyes was something she winced at.

"Because life...God...the universe...any higher power out

there killed my parents and broke me more than you could have. Grieving their deaths made it easier to forget you. I didn't just get over you. I forgot you. I had to."

Lie. Death made me remember you more.

"Can we stop this?" he asked softly.

"Stop what?"

"This back and forth. I know that I hurt you and betrayed your trust. It's not like I forgot, Peyton. I had to live with it for the last four and a half years. I wasn't there when I needed to be. But I am *now*. I came here seeking your *true* forgiveness. So that when you're old and married, you don't think back and hate me for the rest of your life. Can we just be friends…or at least something along those lines?"

He didn't turn away and his voice rang with certainty. Hope was also recognisable. And Hope was a close friend to Fate and her arsenal of bastards—probably more like sick lovers.

For once, she appreciated the darkness around her. The hurt inside would no doubt be plastered on her face. The lack of light gave her a comforting veil to hide behind.

"We can be whatever you want, Callum. Frankly, I don't really care or understand. Since you have my whole life figured out for me, you should know that I would say get the hell out of my house… But I'm not. Stay until morning. The storm will be finished by then. Blankets are where you think they are. I'm going to bed. The couch is yours, 'friend or at least something along those lines,'" Peyton said.

Then she walked towards her room, not waiting for him to reply, allowing her pride to win and accept that she'd gotten the last word.

Thirteen

"Don't cry, Peyton. Just don't cry," *she told herself.*

It was pointless. Her quick blinks couldn't stop the tears. Peyton looked up at the willow tree branches and squeezed her eyes closed. She kept them shut as she tried to compose herself. After she walked back into the house, she ran into her room and sat on her bed, unable to stop the sobs that escaped.

The moment she heard the sound of the trucks reversing, she stilled. When she couldn't hear the engines driving away, Peyton got off her bed and walked out of the house. Unsure of where she was going, she continued to take steps until she reached the lake path. She could either turn right and go up the hill to town or continue to her parents' hotel. Going into town wasn't an option as the tourists and locals would fill the streets. And her mother would know something had happened the moment that she saw Peyton.

To her left, the bench under the willows caught her eye. She sat on it and looked out onto the lake. It was still early. No one would be by the lake for a while. Those who lived in Daylesford always had a routine, never changing or altering what they did on a daily basis. But now, Callum was gone. And the comfort of a routine had been taken away. Everything had changed.

She never sat on this bench. Normally, if she were around the lake, she'd run into the forest with Callum and stay there until she had to go home. But now, it was all over. He was on his way to the city, leaving her behind.

"Peyton?"

She opened her eyes and quickly wiped her cheeks before she turned her head. The first thing that caught her eye was a bundle of lavender tied together with a purple ribbon. She looked up to see a concerned frown on Graham Scott's face.

He had always been nice to her, and she'd always liked the dimple that graced his smile. Peyton sniffed before she sat up properly.

"Are you okay?" Graham asked before he took a seat next to her, placing the lavender in his lap.

"You're normally not in town on Mondays," she said. Then she gave him a fake smile, hoping he'd ignore the state she was in.

"Dad couldn't do the deliveries, so I told him that I'd do them," he replied. The concern look on his face didn't go away and that made Peyton uncomfortable.

"Oh. Did you already drop off the hotel's order?"

"Yeah. Jenny took them off me."

Jenny Fields was the manager of The Spencer-Dayle. If there were any problems with the guests or the hotel, they went through her before Peyton's parents found out. Jenny had been the one to cover for Peyton when she used to sneak away from her desk duties to be with Callum.

"I've never seen you around the lake this early," Graham pointed out.

Peyton turned her head and looked out at the water. With a deep breath, she ignored the searing heat that had settled in her chest. She'd have to find a way to move on from Callum Reid. He had left her in their small town alone while he escaped to the city. Peyton didn't have the heart to leave this small place that held so many of their memories. Even though the moments she shared with him were painful to remember, she'd treasure them and their town. The sight of the boathouse and the flag being raised brought a sad smile to her face. Daylesford was officially awake for the day.

"Just out for a walk."

"Here," Graham said.

She looked over to see him holding the flowers out to her. The bright-purple colour was truly beautiful. His family's farm was famous for having the best lavender in the area. That's why the town was so loyal to the Scott family business – The Spencer-Dayle being one of their biggest clients.

Peyton shook her head and gave him half a smile. She appreciated the gesture. "I can't take them from you, Graham. Don't you have to deliver them to someone?"

He shook his head. "There's no one more important than you right now, Peyton, and I'm done with my deliveries," he stated, his mouth tugging upwards, revealing his dimple.

Not wanting to hurt his feelings, Peyton took them from him. Then she brought them to her nose and inhaled the scent. Fresh and beautiful. It smelt exactly like her parents' hotel.

"Thank you. I appreciate this," she said, placing the bundle on her lap and admiring them.

"Where's Callum? I don't normally see you without him these days."

Just his name made Peyton tremble. For a moment, Graham had made her forget. Now, uncomfortable aches filled her body.

"Gone," she choked out. She didn't meet his eyes, instead staring and playing with the ribbon that held the lavender together.

Suddenly, she felt an arm around her. Graham pulled her closer to him, and she rested her head on his shoulder and sobbed.

"I'm sorry, Peyton," Graham whispered.

That's when she cried harder. They both knew that Callum Reid was never coming back. People who left had the tendency of never returning.

The memory of her first Monday on that bench with Graham left her unsettled. Peyton rolled onto her back and stared at the ceiling, listening to the sound of the whistling wind outside. She lay in the darkness, reliving the memory of the day she had become best friends with Graham Scott. As the years had passed, he'd become more than just another friend. He'd become someone who she needed in her life. He was the peace and her sense of direction.

"Peyton?"

Her name was said softly before she heard a faint knock.

Peyton eyed the door and was just able to make out the knob turning and then opening. At the sight of Callum stepping into her room, she quickly sat up.

"Everything okay, Callum?" she asked.

"Your phone vibrated," he said as he walked towards her bed carrying a lit candle and her phone. Then he sat on the edge of her mattress and handed over the phone.

Peyton took it and noticed that she had a missed call and a text from Graham. She drew her knees up from under the cover, unlocked her phone, and read his text message.

> **Graham**: God, Peyton, please tell me that you're okay. Dad says the weather's gone to shit. Let me know you're all right. I'll call you first thing in the morning.
> **Peyton**: I'm fine. It's just windy. Stop worrying about me.

She locked her phone and placed it on the bedside table. Then she reached for the candle, took it off Callum, and put it next to her phone.

It had been years since he'd last sat on this bed with her. Years since he last held her in his arms until she fell asleep. The light seeping through the gap the curtains had made allowed her to see Callum in the dark. He turned his head and stared out the window. After a long moment, he blinked and looked back at her, meeting her gaze.

"How many times did we sneak you out of that window?" he asked softly.

Peyton crossed her legs and sighed. "Too many times. I'm surprised my parents didn't catch us."

Callum let out a low chuckle. "Actually, your dad caught me at the gate once."

Her eyes widened and her lips parted. "He did not?"

He nodded before he brought his legs up on the bed and crossed them like hers. "He was standing there with his arms crossed, shaking his head at me. They had known for a long time before we told them we were together."

"What did he say?" Peyton asked, curious.

"Give me your hand," he instructed.

She huffed and then shook her head. "What did my dad say, Callum?"

"First, your hand," he said as he held out his, waiting for her.

She knew what he was about to do and she'd rather he didn't. It was something he had done back when they were together. He would lean against the cherry blossom tree outside her window while she sat in the space his legs made. He'd rest his chin on her shoulder as his finger traced up and down her palm, whispering promises in her ear. Those were the days that she hated to remember the most. The days when she had loved him the most.

Her heart throbbed with cherished memories only they knew about. While people they knew had had meaningless sex with each other, they had been building what Peyton had thought was forever. She could almost remember the feel of the cool air on her skin and every trace that had sent shivers down her spin.

The light from the candle touched his palm, flickering. Peyton took a deep breath and moved her hand over his. Every fear told her no, but she was struggling to keep him away. Just inches from contact, he pulled his hand back and left Peyton to stare at his lap.

"You're a tease," she whispered, pulling her arm back closer to her.

"I'm doing this right," he said.

She looked up to see a hint of confusion in his eyes, like he wasn't sure of his next move.

But before she could reply, Callum crawled across the bed and sat next to her, his back leant against the headboard. He looked up at the ceiling for a moment before he turned his head to her and held out his arms.

She stared at him and then breathed out.

"There's only one way we do this, Peyton, and it's the only

way I want to do it," he said.

She tilted her head, trying to understand why she wanted to be near someone who'd broken her heart. But first loves were the ones that couldn't be let go. Every poet and writer was right. First loves defined the person you became. They became memorable.

Breathing in deeply, she removed the blanket and moved into his arms, shifting before pressing her back into his chest. The tilt of her head allowed his chin to perfectly rest on her shoulder. After a moment of being still, Callum wrapped his arms around her. Just the feel of him holding her caused an immediate pang in her heart.

He turned her left hand over. "Your dad said we were terrible liars and I was a bad influence. He always knew when I snuck you out. As long as I got you home, he was okay with us. He said you were happy being with me," he murmured.

She closed her eyes to stop the tears from flowing at the memory of her father and savoured this moment. Her time with Callum had seemed limited and she'd wanted to keep it, never having admitted that to him. This was a form of closure. Sometime soon, she'd find the goodbye that he'd neglected to give her. One she hoped had an explanation.

Callum's fingertips trailed along her index finger and over her promise ring before tracing circles along her palm. Over and over again, he continued. She was slipping from her stance, her heart heating and throbbing. Peyton kept her eyes closed tight, enjoying the sensation of being lost in him.

"I was happy being yours, Peyton. I really was. I promised your father that I'd never hurt you and I failed him… I failed you and I failed us."

The tracing stopped, and Peyton opened her eyes.

Callum rested their hands on her stomach, and she didn't take her eyes away from the dresser that leant against the wall. The way his breathing hit her skin caused her to shiver unwillingly. Her attempts to conceal her shiver had been a lost cause.

"Are you cold?" he asked, wrapping her tight in his arms.

She ignored his question, resting her head against the side of his face. She was getting too lost in this moment with him. But she couldn't pry herself away. She wanted his body against hers, like old times. Seventeen-year-old Peyton was winning. And she was a naïve girl caught up in the illusion of forever.

"Why am I letting you in my bed…or my life, Callum?" she asked, studying his large hands against hers.

He sighed. "I don't even know. I'm surprised that you haven't fought me like you did in the forest. That bump must be more serious than I thought."

She was surprised at the honest chuckle that escaped her. The aching thumps in her head didn't deter her from smiling. It all felt too familiar, and for tonight, she'd enjoy this. She'd forget it like she'd forget the storm.

Closing her eyes, she turned and moulded herself to his body. With a deep inhale, she breathed in his familiar smell, but this time, it was mixed with the hint of rain and candle wax. The scent of him, combined with her exhaustion, and sleep was winning. No longer wanting to fight against her tiredness, Peyton placed her hand on his chest. Then he hugged her tighter. Relaxing the muscles of her body, Peyton lay listening to the sound of his fast heartbeat and breathing.

Nuzzling into Callum's hard and warm body, Peyton sighed and gave sleep its inevitable victory. Her fingers grazed his chest as she breathed in deeply, finding a familiar comfort and security in his arms. "What is this between us, Callum?" she asked, slipping into unconsciousness.

Somewhere far away, she felt a squeeze of her hand and then heard a voice whispering, "A sometimes moment."

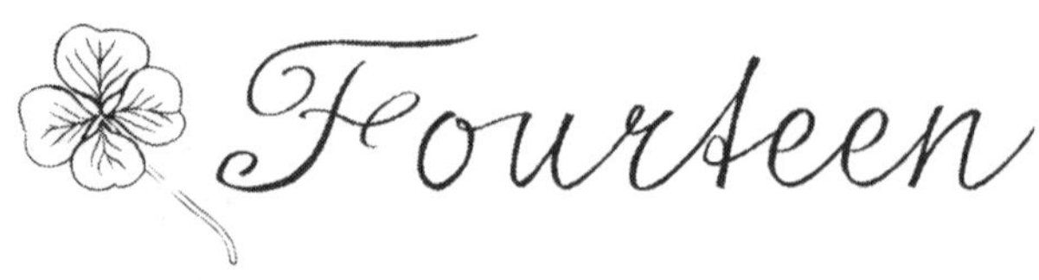

Fourteen

Bang!

Peyton gasped as she sat up from her sleep. She looked around her room, disorientated. When a sudden pain hit her head, she quickly placed her hand over her forehead to relieve it, but it was pointless. It came in thumps, one after the other.

Another *bang* led her to find that her bedroom door was open.

"What happened last night?" she groaned.

After throwing the blanket off her body, she slipped out of bed and walked over to the door. When she noticed that the curtains had been pushed aside slightly, her feet automatically took her to the window. Peyton moved the curtains farther apart and saw cherry blossoms falling from the tree as branches swayed with the wind. She stared at the way the light broke through and touched the petals of the pink flower.

"Good morning, Peyton."

Oh God, it wasn't a horrible dream.

Closing her eyes, Peyton sighed before she turned around to see him by the bedroom door. His eyes were a bright grey, but they couldn't mask the hint of regret she saw—one that deserved to be there. In the light, he was beautiful. Last night, the darkness had kept him in the shadows, allowing her some sort of shield from him. But now, visibility was clear. She officially hated last night's storm…and Mrs West's cat, Mr Lucky.

Peyton leant against the windowsill and looked at Callum. Her eyes travelled down to see him holding a plate.

"What do you have there?" she asked.

"French toast is still your favourite, right?" Callum glanced at the bread and then at her, appearing unsure of himself.

Peyton pushed off the sill and wandered towards him. The smile Callum had made seemed to seek her approval. She took in the two pieces of toast that had berries placed on top of them. And then she saw it—cream and chocolate chips. Two ingredients her mother had placed on Peyton's Sunday French toast. When her parents had died, Peyton had decided that Sunday breakfast at the hotel was no longer a tradition. Instead, she ate a bowl of Froot Loops and the occasional English breakfast made by her aunt.

"It was. Is that where all that noise was coming from? You struggling to make French toast?" Peyton watched his blush turn from a subtle pink to a vibrant red.

"I'm not much of a cook. It's no longer your favourite?" His smile quickly faded and the disappointment could be seen on his face.

Feeling guilty, Peyton took the plate from Callum and sat on the bed, inspecting the breakfast. It resembled her mother's. For someone who wasn't much of a cook, Callum had outdone himself. It was presented exactly how she used to like it. Cream and chocolate chips sandwiched between the two pieces of bread with berries on top.

Callum walked over and sat next to her, the mattress moving under the weight of him. Peyton took the cutlery in her hand and began to cut a piece. Once she had a strawberry on the fork with the toast, she stared at it, afraid of all the memories that would flood back.

She missed her mother's smile and her father's laughter. She missed their Sunday breakfasts and she missed them telling her to let go of her anger towards the man who was sitting next to her. That holding grudges would leave her unhappy with life... And they'd been right. It was a shame they weren't alive to tell her so.

Peyton placed the fork down and put her hands on the mattress.

"It can't be that bad. Can it?" he asked nervously.

The worry in his voice had her internally smiling.

Peyton shook her head. "I'm sure it tastes wonderful, Callum. But I haven't had this in a long time. The last time was... was the day before my parents died. Please don't be offended if I don't eat it. I honestly appreciate the gesture." She turned her head and offered him the sincerest smile she could.

Callum nodded and took the plate from her. "Do you think I could make this for you every Sunday while I'm in town? Maybe one Sunday you may want to try?"

"Tomorrow's Sunday," Peyton stated.

"Can I make you breakfast tomorrow, Peyton?" The way he asked in such a low voice was beautiful. She'd be lying if she said that her heart didn't explode within her.

What's happening to me?

"Why would you want to do that, Callum?" she asked, still wondering why that wall wasn't blocking it all—the feelings, the curiosity, and the memories.

"Like I said last night. I want *moments* together," he answered.

Peyton stilled.

Sometimes moments.

He'd said that last night. She was sure that he had. Just before she'd fallen asleep, she heard those two words. And she was also sure that, in her dream, she'd heard them being whispered again. Something along the lines of, *"I want sometimes moments with you, Peyton. Ones I'll remember...before I say goodbye."*

What in God's name is a 'sometimes moment'?

She'd never heard of that phrase. Never heard someone use it in a sentence or ever defined it. And it was definitely a phrase Peyton herself wouldn't have used or made up. So it had to have been Callum. She should have asked him. But for some reason, she believed the worst in sometimes moments. She'd rather be oblivious to its meaning.

"Peyton?"

She caught it—the slight shakiness in his voice. She loved the sound of concern in his voice. Just like she had when they were teenagers.

"Did we sleep in the same bed?" she asked, turning her body to inspect her mattress.

"We *didn't* have sex," he quickly clarified.

Peyton rolled her eyes. She wasn't an idiot. She'd know if she'd had sex last night. She'd *feel* it. She pushed his arm, Callum holding on to the plate so it wouldn't fall.

"I know that. I was just asking if you left during the night. I think I heard you say something."

He froze. "What did you hear?"

Caution. That's what she'd heard in his voice.

"Was I supposed to hear something in particular?" she asked, cocking her brow at him.

"I heard something, too," he stated.

The hell he did.

Peyton took the plate out of his hands and placed it on her bedside table, next to the remains of the half-melted candle.

She lifted her legs and crossed them on the bed. "What did you hear?"

Callum mirrored her sitting position on the bed. "What did *you* hear?"

"I asked you first."

"Then you answer first," he retorted.

She huffed out. "Fine. I heard nothing. I was bluffing."

Lie. I heard you call us a sometimes moment.

Callum glared at her. Then he closed his eyes for a long moment and let out a hum. Rolling her eyes, Peyton leaned back against the headboard. Waiting.

The sunlight that passed through the window hit the side of his face, and she mentally noted just how beautiful he was in this moment. He looked peaceful and unworried. A version of the boy she had fallen in love with. Peyton clenched her fists. It was happening. And she hated herself for it. Somewhere within him was the person she loved—had loved.

He slowly opened his eyes. No smile or frown. He seemed restrained, not wanting to show his emotions to her.

"You mumbled that you still loved me," he said.

Did I say that last night? Christ, Peyton!

Peyton let out a hard laugh. "Me? *Still* love you? That's such a lie. I did not," she downplayed.

Still was a very strong word. Though, in the back of her mind, she knew that word was a representation of her current status towards him... She just didn't want to admit it.

Callum rubbed his arm, his long-sleeved top riding up. Peyton quickly sat up, staring. She was sure she'd seen something on his skin. So she grabbed his wrist, feeling him wince in her hold.

"What are you doing, Peyton?"

Ignoring his question, she stared at the black on his wrist. After a moment, Peyton looked up at him and raised her brow in disbelief. If it was what she thought she saw, then she was in the presence of the world's greatest hypocrite.

Callum struggled to pull back and free himself, but had been met with Peyton clutching him tighter. She looked at him, hoping her face expressed her seriousness before she eyed the sleeve that covered up the questionable mark on his wrist. When she thought back, she realised that everything he'd worn since he'd had returned covered his arms and it only made her even more curious. Unable to help herself, Peyton loosened her hold and let her thumbs caress the mark.

"Peyton," he warned and jerked back. "I got one, okay?"

Her hands fell in her lap. "You said you'd never."

He got off the bed and shook his head. "Well, I did. I don't need to explain myself to you."

Too curious to care about the harsh tone in his voice, Peyton rose to her feet. She placed her hands firmly on his hard chest and pushed him into the wall. He let out an, "Oomph," and before she could take a step back, he held her arms, trapping her.

"Let go of me," she said sternly.

"Not unless you say that you won't look."

She shook her head.

"Then I don't want you to see," he stated.

Peyton looked him dead in the eye. "You walked out on me."

His hold on her loosened before his arms fell by her side. Then he turned away from her and said, "Fine."

She took a deep breath and readied herself. When she was growing up, it had always been a pissing contest with the boys when it came to tattoos. Callum had straight up said that he'd never, promising her that he wouldn't.

Peyton held his left wrist, traced his skin, and slowly pushed up his grey sleeve. When she was able to see his entire forearm, she stopped and stared. Reddish-pink colour against the black tattoos caught her eye. She held her breath as her fingers traced the inked cherry blossoms on Callum's arm. As he turned his arm over and she looked at his wrist, she immediately stepped back.

Her eyes never left his wrist. The throbbing in her chest and the lump in her throat rendered her speechless.

"I got it when I turned eighteen, a few months after I left," he said in a soft voice.

"But why?" she managed out.

"It seemed necessary," he replied.

Peyton shook her head in disbelief. "My-my name... necessary on...your wrist." She looked up at him, confused.

He'd left her the weekend after she'd given him her virginity and told him that she loved him, yet he had tattooed her name on his wrist.

"I don't understand. You left me and then got a tattoo of my name? That's crazy!" she exclaimed.

Callum ran a finger over each letter on his wrist before meeting her eyes. "It reminds me every day of why I did what I did. It's a constant reminder of what I gave up for you."

"What did you give up for me?" she asked, a little hurt.

"A horrible future with me," he confessed in a small voice.

"No," she whispered, staring at the way her name marked

his skin in permanent ink. The useless hope that had filled her heart now consumed it.

Peyton quickly brushed the tear that was running down her left cheek. She walked towards her dresser and pulled open the drawer. After rummaging through her jumpers, she found a bundle of Polaroids. She stared at them for a moment before she turned and walked back to him, placing them in his hands.

"We were happy together, Callum. We could have had *this,* but you decided to walk away instead of fighting dragons with me. You turned your back on me and a future together. We were going to leave this town, go to Deakin, and live together. You went and did that all without me. Do you know how much it hurt me to hear that you went to Deakin while I was stuck here, grieving my parents?"

He sifted through the Polaroids of their time together and swallowed hard. She hadn't touched them since the day after her parents' funeral. She had been stupid to believe that he'd attend. Never answering her call should have been a clear indicator. But she'd been hopeful.

"You think it was easy going to Deakin without you? Going to classes and thinking maybe you had applied, too? That maybe I'd see you walking to class and we'd bump into each other? It didn't happen. I waited for you, hoping you'd show up. That you didn't let what I had done to you stand in the way of your dream school." There was an it's-not-my-fault stance in his voice.

Peyton sat back on her bed, rubbing her forehead. It was too early to be arguing with him. But there was so much that had gone unexplained between them. They were imploding.

"How do we move on from this? You're adamant that you won't leave until after the wedding. How do we coexist in this town?" she asked, defeated.

Callum sighed and crouched in front of her. She noticed his sleeve still pushed up and was able to see that her name had visibly branded him. He placed the photographs on her unmade bed and then rested his palms on her knees.

"I'm not saying that you should forgive me so easily,

because I don't want that. Just let me in your life, Peyton, even if it's only for a little while. We keep taking too many steps back. I don't know if you'll ever forgive me, but I won't stop trying to get you to. Can we just have a start fresh? Actually become friends or at least something along those lines?"

Peyton blinked once.

She turned her head and looked at the Polaroid picture of them sitting on the pier together. It had been a good memory of them—one she had reflected on throughout the years. He might have not loved her, but he cared—his tattoo proved it.

"Okay," she said, her eyes still on the picture. Her mother would be proud about that one word. She turned and met his stare. "But can I ask you a favour?"

"Anything."

While staring at his tattooed arm, Peyton smiled at the way the letters of her name joined together perfectly. For whatever reason, it was sentimental to him. And the thought had her breathing out as she kept her eyes on his hands across her knees.

He can't keep my name tattooed on his wrist... I don't want to be a reminder.

"When you leave, can you get my name removed? That reason behind it isn't necessary anymore. I shouldn't be a reminder for you."

His hands left her for a moment before he placed a finger under her chin, lifting her head to meet his. Then he gave her sorrowful smile and nodded.

"Okay. It'll be the first thing I do when I leave town. I promise, Peyton." His voice was wrapped in a delicate and painfully beautiful whisper.

Her heart ripped wide open. Callum Reid would wind up breaking her heart all over again. And for some reason, Peyton was willing to once again feel the pain he'd inflict once goodbye had left his lips.

Fifteen

Callum didn't say anything else. Instead, he kept his eyes planted on various parts of her face. First, it was her eyes, then her nose, and then finally her mouth. That's when her breathing decided—in that very moment—that it was an unnecessary function. Peyton wished her lungs would work. Just enough to say that his gaze didn't leave her breathless... and hopeless...and *desperate.*

Air. Shit. I need air.

"Can I ask you a favour, Peyton?" he asked, his eyes still locked on her mouth. She couldn't deny the fact that she, too, was staring.

Afraid of the possible shakiness and betrayal in her voice, Peyton nodded.

Callum's fingers slowly trailed from under her chin to her cheek, lightly brushing against her skin and almost giving her a heart attack. The sigh he had exhaled echoed in the air before he cupped her face firmly in his palms, his actions requiring her attention. It was then that her lips instantly parted as she took in the features of his face.

She used to stare at his chin dimple when he smiled. She thought back to the days he'd sat next to her in class. When he'd brush his chin as he worked on his questions and she'd stare until he'd look over at her with a raised eyebrow. She'd laugh in the middle of the lesson and the rest of the class would gawk at them. In this moment with him, she wished they were back there, in that classroom. Back to simple times.

"Peyton," he breathed, and she quickly met those grey pools of conflicted and frustrating emotions.

She swallowed hard, trying to regain some form of composure. "What's your favour?"

He didn't turn away or blink. He kept his gaze hard on her. "Promise me that you won't let me kiss you? I can't lose focus on *why* I'm here. And I can't let anything happen between us. You can't let me kiss you, okay?"

Her heart plunged, leaving a sick and tight knot in the pit of her stomach. No kissing. She shouldn't be so disappointed. If anything, she should be relieved. She wouldn't travel down that path, but deep down, she wanted to know what his lips felt like…for one last time.

Straightening her back, she gave him a firm nod and said, "Scout's honour, Callum Reid," before sticking up her pinkie.

His lips curved upwards, and then he entwined his pinkie with hers. "Scout's honour, Peyton Spencer."

They both laughed, acknowledging the time they were Cubs in Scouts Victoria. The only reason why she quit the Scouts was because she hadn't liked one of the older Venturer girls—the one who'd dunked her in the mud pit of the obstacle course. Callum was the one who had pulled her out and quit Scouts the next day with her.

He gently pushed on her knees and stood up properly. When he took her hand and helped her up, Peyton tried to ignore the tingles that his touch ignited.

"What's *our* plan today, Scout Peyton?" he asked and let go of her hand.

She was sure that he could feel the sweat of her hand. He made her nervous and uncomfortable. As discreetly as she could, she wiped her hand on her pyjama bottoms.

Then she let out a sigh and picked up the plate of untouched food. "I have to go check on the hotel and make sure the storm damage isn't too bad."

"Can I come with you?" he asked.

Peyton walked out of her room and into the kitchen. She was surprised when she saw that it was clean. From the noise he'd made, she'd been sure she would have been standing in the middle of a bombsite. The kitchen was immaculate, more so than when she had gone to bed. She set the plate on the counter and faced him.

"I'm just going to survey the hotel and then pick up some paperwork that I left behind. I have to get everything ready for when the staff return on Monday. Sure you want to come?" Peyton asked, reaching for an apple in the fruit bowl. She shined it against her tank top and took a big bite, staring at him.

"I'd love to," he said. Then he winked.

Peyton rolled her eyes. "Well, I guess I can show you my plans for Oscar and Marissa's wedding."

"Sounds good. Meet you here in fifteen? I'll just go back to my parents' place and shower. That's enough time for you?"

Peyton took another bite and shook her head, placing the apple on the bench. She raised three fingers of her left hand and formed an 'O' with her right.

"Thirty?"

She swallowed and nodded. "Thirty."

Peyton hugged the towel as she opened her bedroom door. She hummed along to the song that played through the speakers of her phone. It was June's song. One that had been Peyton's favourite. She remembered June singing it by the lake, strumming her guitar. Peyton had been on her way to town when June had called her over. The moment she'd heard it, Peyton had felt like it had been written about her. But what heartbreaking song wasn't?

She walked to her bed and stared at the Polaroids that sat on the covers. Then she picked up the picture of them sitting on the pier. Callum looked happy, and that's what was so deceiving about him. He *looked* happy to be with her, but she wasn't sure if he really had been. Staring at her former self, Peyton could see the differences from then and now. Seventeen-year-old Peyton had had a twinkle in her eye and a smile that twenty-one-year-old Peyton had forgotten how to make. The teenager had looked carefree and happy and...*in* love. Present Peyton didn't know how to be any of those. Slowly, one by one, all of those things had disappeared. Death had become her.

What she missed most was the glow on her face. That was something she'd lacked since Callum had left.

After placing the Polaroid back down with the others, Peyton took a deep breath and walked to the wardrobe. When she set her fingers on the knob, she stared at the promise ring that Graham had given her. She knew deep down that it was a promise they'd break, but in that moment, she wanted the possibility of being someone's future. But Peyton knew the truth; one woman would make Graham fall desperately in love. It was just a matter of time.

Turning around, she leant on the wooden wardrobe and looked at the diamond. It was beautiful. If she weren't a backup plan, she'd love it more than she did. She lifted her left hand up and ran the thumb of her right hand over it. Then she stopped her movements and held her breath. She always knew the day would come when she'd take it off, but she hadn't thought it would be for a long time to come. It was constantly in the back of her mind, but today, it felt right to do so.

A knock on the bedroom door didn't distract her from the way the ring glittered in the light.

"Peyton, it's been thirty minutes," Callum said from the other side of the door.

"Callum," she called out, her eyes still on the diamond.

"Yeah, Peyton?" The hint of uncertainty in his voice made her heart tense. It was Callum's being back in town that made her unsure of the decisions she had made since she'd last seen him.

"I'm Graham's backup plan," she announced.

Silence.

Peyton counted the seconds that ticked by. When Callum

said nothing, she turned her attention away from the ring and looked at her bedroom door. A small intake of air had been taken before she walked towards it. Her footsteps echoed and she had no doubt that Callum could hear them, too. Once she got to the door, she turned around and placed her back against it. The faint sounds of his breathing reached her ears.

"Then he's an idiot," Callum said.

Forty-three seconds.

The sadness in his voice made her tense, and she stared at the bedroom window she used to sneak out of.

The neediness in her heart nagged her, wanting to know what kind of choice she was to him. Peyton leant her head back and glared at the ceiling before she turned her head to the side.

"If circumstances were different. If I made you happy and if you loved me back, would I have been your first choice?" she asked into the wood of the door.

There was a slight *thump* against the door and a sharp inhale of oxygen. "You would have been my only choice, Peyton."

Peyton shut her eyes and softly said, "If only."

"If only," Callum agreed, and that's when a tear ran down her face. Because those were the two words she had continuously wondered for the last four years. "I'll wait by the couch for you."

The sound of retreating footsteps made her heart clench harder. Tears continued to skim down her face, and she wiped them away as quickly as they fell.

"You've only ever been my choice, Callum," she whispered to herself.

And there it was. The truth she had been denying all these years. Her one and only choice. And by July, she'd say goodbye. There was no future with Callum Reid. His return was purely to dust off their hands and move on with their lives.

Peyton pushed off the door and walked over to her bed before sitting on it. She picked up the Polaroids as water dripped from the ends of her hair and onto the towel. Reaching out, she took the almost four-and-a-half-year-old memories in her hands and sifted through them.

During their last summer together, she hadn't seen him not snapping pictures of their time together with his Polaroid camera. They would halve the pile of photographs between them, and just moments before she fell asleep, she'd look at them before tucking the photos under her pillow.

After stopping on the last picture, Peyton set the others back on the bed and stared at the one in her hand. Madilynne had captured this particular moment. It was of Peyton smiling at the camera and Callum staring at her, oblivious to anyone around him. This was when she'd felt his love—if it had been real and not a figment of her imagination. Hope was a sadistic bitch and Peyton would rather they not cross paths. But this one picture filled her with just that. With a bittersweet smile, she leant the picture against the half-melted candle on her bedside table.

Standing, she placed her fingers on her promise ring and slipped it off. There was no regret or doubt in her mind. Just sheer relief to have it off. Once she'd opened the drawer of the table, she placed the ring inside and closed it before staring at the Polaroid.

I want sometimes moments.

Sixteen

"This is good," Callum said, staring at her design for the dance floor by the lake.

Peyton sat behind her desk, her chin in her palms as she watched him mull over the idea to make the Reynolds' wedding a success.

"You mind if I go over it, though?" he asked as he sat in the chair in front of her.

She let out a sigh. "So, it's terrible then."

Callum shook his head. "It's not. It just needs an architect's look at it."

"How am I going to afford one?" she asked.

A smug look overcame Callum's face. "You're looking at one."

Her eyes widened. "You did not become an architect."

He nodded. "I'm practically Ted Mosby."

She laughed at his *How I Met Your Mother* reference. It surprised her that Callum had become an architect considering he had grown up complaining about his father's property development business and how he wanted nothing to do with it. But architecture wasn't property developing.

"Well, *Ted,* how does my terrific design look in comparison to all the architect-y things you've seen?"

"It's not hor—"

"Peyton!"

The roar had Callum stopping and stilling. Peyton quickly stood up just as Jay burst through the office doors.

"I knew it!" he growled as he stalked towards the desk.

"Jay, what the hell?" she asked.

"You slept with him?" he asked in disbelief mixed with pain.

Callum put the paper back on the desk. "Jay, you have the wrong idea."

"Shut the fuck up, Reid," Jay said firmly before he looked at Peyton. "What's the matter with you, Peyton? You're better than that. How could you do this to *me*?" The torment in Jay's eyes confused Peyton.

"What are you talking about, Jay? We haven't slept together. We're working on the Reynolds' wedding," Peyton explained.

Jay's nostrils flared and he banged his fists on the desk before sweeping everything onto the floor. Peyton watched, horrified, as her father's clock hit the wall. A gut-wrenching pain she had never known attacked her stomach at the sight of broken clock.

"Callum, I need you to leave," she said, not sure how her voice sounded.

"Peyton—"

She raised her voice. "Get out!"

Callum nodded once before he walked towards the door.

"You're going to give up everything for *him*?" Jay asked, unaware that he'd just torn out her heart with his previous action.

"You don't understand. Nothing's—"

"The whole town's talking. Someone saw him leave your house this morning!"

She noticed Callum stop just near the door, his body strung up tight.

"They have the wrong impression of what—"

"But he spent the night?" The anger in Jay's eyes was something that she hated seeing. He was meant to be her friend, but he wasn't listening.

"You're not letting me finish!" Her breathing came in gasps as she raised her voice higher, demanding his attention.

Jay looked at her hand. "You took off Graham's ring."

Callum winced before he walked out of the office. Then the front bell rang, signalling that he had left the hotel.

Peyton stared at the door, ignoring Jay's presence.

"Look at me, Peyton," Jay demanded. With each interaction they had, she was beginning to see a new side of Jay. "You. Took. It. Off."

"And?" she asked, shaking her head and stepping towards the mess Jay had made. She bent down and picked up her father's clock. The sight of the mangled pieces caused her eyes to water as she took in the broken hands and the lack of ticking.

"Shit, Peyton. I'm sorry."

"Get out, Jay," she said, trying to control the hot emotions working up her throat.

"Peyton—"

She stood up and looked at him hard. "He spent the night, okay? But nothing happened. You were at Daisy's farm and I'm not even mad that you went against me for her. Keeping me safe from stuff like a storm was your thing. I never obligated you to it. But when I needed someone, Callum was there. And yes, I took Graham's ring off. Not for Callum, but for *me*. You won't understand, but Graham will. I'm not giving up anything for Callum. He's leaving soon."

She wasn't sure when she'd lied, but somewhere in what she'd said, there were a few. Right now, though, she didn't care. She decided that in order to save their friendship, Jay would have to leave. Peyton placed the clock down on the wooden desk and fought the tears from falling.

"Get out, Jay. Before I say something that I'll regret."

Jay clenched his fists tight. "I'm sorry, Peyton. The clock—"

"Just leave," she instructed, not looking at him.

When the door slammed shut, she breathed out exhaustedly. That wasn't what she'd expected. Rumours spread like wildfire, but Jay had believed them.

Peyton looked at the papers, the pen, and the frame on the

floor. Then she bent down, picked up the picture of her and her parents, and placed it back where it belonged. The glass had smashed, and the sight of the fragments angered and destroyed her. After she examined the frame, she saw the pier design on the floor.

"Callum," she uttered and raced out the door of the office.

Her heart was beating wildly as she ran out of the hotel. She needed to find him, explain, and apologise for her harsh ways. She just hadn't wanted him to see Jay in such a way.

Peyton stood on the path outside the door of The Spencer-Dayle. She wasn't sure where he'd be or how she would contact him. Desperation bled into her chest as she scanned the area, her eyes landing on the pier across the lake. The achiness in her chest relieved the moment she saw him sitting on the edge, staring at either her or the hotel. She wasn't sure.

When Peyton turned her head, she saw Jay stalking towards town. He didn't get it, but she understood where he was coming from. Jay felt a need to protect her; she had sensed it in the years since they'd become friends. Sometimes, protection induced suffocation. And that was how Peyton felt when she was around him.

She looked back at the pier and then to the path—two choices, and whichever direction she chose meant consequences.

She squeezed her eyes shut before she started to run down the path. She was sure she saw Callum's head dip from the corner of her eye. But all she did was run. Hard and fast. Her breathing had become heavy gasps.

Peyton heaved as she reached where her head told her to go. She stopped for a moment to regain herself before she walked towards him.

"You should go after him, Peyton."

I am.

She lowered herself down next to Callum and let her legs fall over the edge. "What good would that do?" she asked, her eyes sweeping the view. This spot would always be her favourite. A lot of good times outweighed the bad. And Callum was a bit of both.

He let out a bothered sigh. Peyton turned her head to see him also staring out at the lake.

"Peyton, you're losing people who you love because of my return. It's my fault that he did that to your father's clock. And I assume it's my fault that you've taken off Graham's ring."

A handful of emotions filled Callum's face. First, it was anger, then anguish, and finally regret. His eyes lightened instead of darkening. He was remorseful.

"I'm making your life worse. I wanted to come back because I owe you a lot of apologies. I'm trying to make up for a lot of wrongs that I should have made right four and a half years ago. Instead, I'm getting in the way of your friendships and causing the town to talk about you. This wasn't part of the plan. It's only going to get worse from here if we stay friends, *Pey*."

All breath fled her. It had been a long time since he'd called her that. He was the only one to ever call her Pey. She was his when he breathed it out.

She blinked quickly at him, letting everything about him sear into her memory. She'd only get what little time he was willing to give to her. But she'd take it. All of it.

"Look at me," she softly demanded.

Callum turned, his eyes meeting hers. So much filled them that she couldn't tell what they held anymore. It was a mixture, but his pain hit her first.

"This is my fault. I'll talk to Jay and get this sorted. I can't let this town hate you the way they hate me just because we spend time together," he said before his eyes left her.

Peyton stared at the side of his face.

"I never, ever wanted to hurt you, Pey," he whispered.

And that's when it all came crumbling down. Her supposed stance weakened and she was exposed.

I'm sorry, heart. I am so sorry.

Peyton lifted her legs up on the pier then leant closer to him. Once Callum turned to face her, she reached up and cupped his face in her hands. Wonder and surprise filled his eyes. Peyton loved it more than the pain and hurt that had been there earlier.

"I'm so sorry, Callum," she said.

He opened his mouth to speak, but Peyton let her lips crash into his, stopping anything vocal from escaping him. Her heart stopped and then dipped. And then it did something that surprised her—it expanded in relief.

He kissed her with as much desperation as Peyton gave. *This*. His lips and just the feel of his hands on her hips bringing her closer had her eyes welling. She tingled all over. The memory of just how much she'd loved the way that he kissed her was like a crash of water against rocks—hard and painful.

Callum groaned and Peyton tangled her fingers in his hair. Something she always loved doing and wanted to do since this morning. He squeezed his fingers into the side of her body, causing Peyton to gasp. Then he automatically stopped, his fingers loosened—to her disappointment—and he pulled back. He looked stunned, and Peyton couldn't help but feel disheartened by the displeasure on his face.

"You promised me that you wouldn't let anything like this happen between us, Peyton," Callum said.

Her hands still cradled his face. She took the opportunity and let her thumbs stroke his cheeks. He shivered under her touch, which was a win for her. It didn't matter if he didn't love her. She still had an effect on him.

"I promised that I wouldn't let *you* kiss me. *I* kissed you," she stated. This was what she had missed. Having him in her arms and in her hands. She knew what the end spelt, and for now, she wouldn't care.

Callum shuffled backwards once, Peyton still holding his face in her hands as he tugged her towards him. She placed her legs over his laps and straddled him—just like all the times they had spent during their last summer.

His eyes showed her the terrified side of him. Peyton moved her hands and brushed his hair back. Then Callum took a sharp breath and squeezed her hips.

"I can't offer you forever," he said, breaking the fantasy she was in.

But she wouldn't let him see that. Her chest ached, but she ignored the pain. She wanted him. That, she was sure of.

"Then give me *now*. For as long as you can," she whispered before letting her fingers trail down the side of his face.

"I can only give you sometimes," he said.

Peyton gave him a smile. It was all she was going to get. "Then I'll take your sometimes."

"And then it's goodbye," he said.

Peyton nodded. "Then it's goodbye to you, Callum Reid."

Callum pulled her closer to him. "And to you, Peyton Spencer."

She didn't reply. Instead, she let her lips slowly make their way to his, sealing what she had already known. That they had just agreed on the end of their story.

We just planned our demise.

The moment his lips met hers, it was an implosion of relief and satisfaction. This was an undeniable want. *He* was an undeniable want. Unlike before, this was slow and savoured. Callum's lip guided her to a pattern of open and closed movements. Again and again, it continued, never bordering on too soft or too hard. They found a rhythm and speed in which time became a word and not a force. The same force that would drive them apart soon enough. It was just a matter of when. The thought had Peyton missing a beat in their kiss. But pushing the thought of the inevitable away, she quickly found her way.

Callum wrapped his arms around her lower back and brought her closer. The surprise of his willingness evoked a silent moan, allowing his tongue to find hers. If there were a way to beautifully explore her mouth, then Callum had found it. The gentle stroke of his tongue against hers caused her heart to pound insanely hard. Though years had passed, it was familiar, like he hadn't forgotten the way they kissed. Each movement and moment of the way his mouth worked her into a frenzy was memorised. *Time.* It kept looming over her.

"Peyton," Callum breathed against her, and he slowed their kiss until they mutually stopped. Then he pulled back, brushing her hair away from her face. "Not like this. Please."

"Like what?" she asked, looking anywhere other than his eyes.

"Like you can change the ending. I can't give you happily ever after. I can't give you anything." He sighed.

Peyton removed her hands from his hair and let them fall in her lap. The need to get off him became desperation. She was ashamed. Her stance and willpower had weakened and she had let her pathetic heart win. Now, it sat uncomfortably behind her ribcage, throbbing and twisting.

"I don't want a happily ever after, Callum. I need an ending. No spin-offs or sequels. Just a standalone. And maybe someday, I'll get to hear your epilogue."

Then she placed her hands on his shoulders and pushed herself up. The stinging of her lips reminded her that she had let desire win. She took a step away from him, leant on the railing, turned her head to the left, and stared at the shimmering water of the lake. She felt his eyes on her, but right now, her mind wasn't in a good place. She didn't trust her decision-making abilities at the moment.

Callum, standing up, caught her attention. When her eyes met his, the controlled Callum was before her.

"My epilogue?" he asked.

Peyton nodded. "Yes. A conclusion to all of this. I want to hear it someday."

He scratched his arm, thinking. Hints of his sleeve tattoo poked out. "What do you want to hear in it?"

She relaxed her body and let the uncomfortable heat spread from her chest to the rest of her body. Then she gave him a tight smile, knowing that what she was about to say came hand-in-hand with their upcoming goodbye.

"Everything. Write it down one day and send it to me. I want to hear about you meeting the love of your life. I want to hear about how you proposed to her. I want to hear where you said 'I do.'" Peyton stopped and quickly wiped her tears away. She hadn't thought it would be so hard to talk about his future. "And I want to hear about your firstborn and all the children you have after. I want to hear their names. I want to hear how happy you are with your life."

God, Peyton, you're being ridiculous. Cut that shit out!

She looked up at him. His red and swollen lips appeared to tremble before his jaw locked. Callum turned away as his nostrils flared. Whether it was anger or hurt, she didn't know but the way his eyes flashed in pain didn't go unmasked. He had fallen silent until he finally faced her.

"And that's something that you'd want me to send you?" he asked. There was nothing in his voice that suggested he wouldn't.

"It's something I'd love."

"But what if you move houses or something?"

Peyton let out a short laugh. "You'll find me right here in Daylesford, Callum. Just like you did before."

"And what about you, Peyton?" he asked.

She swallowed hard and shook her head. "I don't have one to write. Some stories don't need one. And I'm afraid this is kind of the end of the line for me. Just the hotel and this town."

Callum stepped towards her and placed his arms on the railing, trapping her. "There's more out there than just Daylesford."

Her heart pounded against her chest, threatening to squeeze through her ribcage. She looked up and nodded. "I know there is. There's nothing out there for *me*."

He tilted his head at her. "How do you know? I've seen what's out there."

She gave him a fine smile before saying, "Because everything I have left is here. Memories are more important to me than the city. I'm content with my life here."

Callum exhaled heavily before resting his forehead on hers. "There's so much more outside of the town's limit, Peyton. You belong out there, experiencing more than what Daylesford offers you."

Her heart felt like it was being tugged in different directions simultaneously. She peeked up at him through her lashes, Callum's grey eyes meeting hers.

"I belong here," she said.

I always thought I belonged to you. Not this town.

He pulled away and nodded. "Then let's give Oscar and

Marissa a wedding they'll never forget and get the hotel the recognition it deserves." Then Callum dropped his hands from the pier, turned, and made his way off it.

"Callum," she called out as she watched him leave.

He stopped and, without hesitation, faced her. Peyton stood at one end of the pier and Callum at the other, separated by planks of nailed wood.

"Yeah?" he asked, digging his hands into his pants pockets.

"I'm sorry that I kissed you."

He looked at the ground that met the first plank of the pier before he looked back up at her. "Don't be, because I'm not. We just can't let it happen again, Peyton. Want to head back to the hotel and go through those plans?"

She didn't feel anything. Finally, years of hoping and wishing had finally paid off—Peyton no longer felt. And to her disappointment, it wasn't as satisfying as she had imagined. Rather, it left her longing for *more.*

Seventeen

"I can't wait till we leave this place, Pey. Just wait until we start a life together out there. No matter where we are or where we go, you've claimed me. My life makes sense when I'm with you."

Peyton rolled onto her back as she let memories of him keep her awake. She brought her fingers to her lips, missing the way that he felt against her. It had been a rookie mistake to kiss him, but inside her, something had snapped. She'd hated the way that he'd blamed himself for Jay's behaviour and her actions. There had been no logic, just the desperate need to take all the self-blame away from him.

"We just can't let it happen again, Peyton."

And it couldn't. It was bad enough that he was back; kissing him made it all the more complicated. He'd said that he could only offer her now and sometimes, nothing close to forever. The tension had been so thick when they'd returned to the hotel; she was almost drowning in it.

Peyton let her hand fall back onto the pillow and kept her eyes on the pendant light as she continued to replay today in her head. A day that made her question what tomorrow would bring. After what had seemed like forever, the tension had started to dissipate. Somehow, they'd found a comfortable moment when they'd discussed the wedding. With some adjustments to her original plan, the dance floor by the lake was feasible. All it needed was redesigning, and Callum offered to do just that. The moment she said, "Okay," to him, he picked up the design, said he had to leave, and walked out.

The moment the bell rang to signal his departure, Peyton was thankful. She couldn't take being so close to him, hating the fantasies of what could have been that bubbled up every time she looked at him. She was finally alone to breathe. But each time she thought about them kissing on the pier, she ended up more frustrated than before.

After being left alone with her thoughts, Peyton realised that she didn't want to hear from him after he left. She didn't want to hear about how he had found love and found happiness. She didn't want to hear about how another woman had ended up with the man Peyton had always seen as her happily ever after. But she knew deep down that she wanted to hear about this woman and thank her for making Callum happy. That's what her heart wanted.

Peyton turned on her side and stared at her phone on the bedside table. Taking a deep breath, she picked it up and rolled on her back again. With a firm grasp, she held the phone in front of her face and unlocked it. Then she found Callum's number, not even sure if it was the same as it was four years ago. She swore she felt and heard her heartbeat pound in her eardrums as she opened the screen to type a new text message.

She let out a breath of air as she hovered her thumbs over the touchscreen. She knew she shouldn't do it, but she was fighting an internal battle of want and need. The same battle between protecting her heart and freeing it. But the fight with herself didn't take long as her thumbs began to type for her.

Peyton: Are you awake?

She pressed send and immediately regretted it, wishing she could recall it back. She prayed that she had the wrong number. A second after pressing send, though, she got a reply.

Callum: Peyton?

She looked at his message. She knew she shouldn't reply, but she wanted to speak to him in any form she could get. To say she was confused hardly described what and how she felt.

> **Peyton**: It's me.
> **Callum**: How'd you know I still have this number?

Pure luck and hope.

> **Peyton**: I thought I'd tempt Fate.
> **Callum**: To answer your earlier question: Wide awake.

What am I doing?

Peyton placed her phone on the pillow next to her. Then, almost immediately, it lit up with every message he sent her, the vibrations alerting her. Realising her error in messaging him, Peyton reached over and powered the phone screen down. With a deep breath in, she closed her eyes before she exhaled. The uncomfortable thumps of her heart were relentless. Limits were needed. And they needed to be established quickly.

Three vibration alerts occurred before they stopped. She opened her eyes and rested her hands on her stomach, twiddling her thumbs. Her heart didn't calm, which annoyed her further. She was breaking—and at a more rapid rate than she believed possible. She chalked it up to loneliness, but she knew there was more. She wanted to be loved, enough to make her escape into some alternate reality of the current—and sad—life that she lived.

Tap. Tap. Tap.

Peyton quickly sat up. *Three.* She looked at the window to see a silhouette and held her breath for what came next.

Tap. Tap.

Pause.

Tap.

That was it. She swallowed hard, purely to give herself a

second. Then she reached over and turned on the bedside lamp. Not taking her eyes off the curtains, she removed the blanket and got out of bed. Slowly—to buy more time—she walked to the window. Once she reached it, she heard and felt her heart pick up. Excited and anxious. Her stomach clenched as a million different emotions filled her, making her head spin. She drew back the sheer curtains to see Callum's hands on the glass. With the light from the moon and the lamp, she was able to see his eyes. His lips curved up before his eyes looked up at the lock and then back at her.

If she let him in, that wall was gone. Any stance was over and any hate she held would slowly fizzle out until he left in due course.

Callum moved closer, his eyes never leaving her as he breathed against the window, creating condensation on it. Then he placed a finger on the glass and began to slide it, creating a message for her. Her eyebrows furrowed at the sight. When he removed his finger, Peyton stared at it. It was a symbol.

?

She stared at the question mark as it slowly faded away. Without even giving it another thought, Peyton reached up and unlatched the window. Callum was the one who lifted it open until it locked into place. Then he put his hand on the windowsill and smiled.

"What are you doing here?" she asked, hating the nervousness in her voice.

"Making sure that you're okay. You didn't answer my messages," he replied smoothly—unlike herself.

Peyton shrugged, not knowing what to say.

He tilted his head at her before asking, "Are you okay?"

She shrugged again.

"Can't sleep?"

Peyton shook her head and said, "No," at the same time.

"Me, either." He paused. "Can I come in?"

She leant forward, staring him down. "You know, some people use the front door."

He let out a low laugh. "When have I ever used the front

door?"

Peyton's shoulders loosened, not having realised just how tense she really was. "You have a point. Come in." She took a step back, giving him room to get inside. He made it look easy, as he had when he was seventeen, too.

When he stood in her bedroom, Callum turned around and closed the window. The second his eyes met hers, he took her hand and her heart quickened its pace. Her breathing wasn't quite cooperating, but it was manageable. *Just.*

"What are you doing?" she asked, a little breathless.

Damn.

"You can't sleep," he said before he pulled her close enough to wrap his arms around her waist. "And honestly, I can't either."

Peyton looked up at him, intrigued at the way he gazed at her. "I'm not going to get any sleep if you stay here."

"Right here?" he asked.

Peyton nodded.

Callum's hands made their way up her arms and then back down until he threaded his fingers with hers. She told herself all the reasons why she should take a step back and put distance between them, but before she could really debate, Callum led her towards the bed, the back of her legs hitting the mattress. Her breathing became shallow and an inconvenience as she looked to his eyes for answers to the question she hadn't asked.

He guided her down until she sat on top of the blanket. Then he crouched down and held her hands more firmly.

"Peyton, do you remember when I said that I couldn't give you forever?" he asked. The sadness in his voice broke her heart. An impossible thing was happening.

She gave him a sad smile. "I remember. I was there."

"I stand by that. And the reason why I can't sleep is because I can't stop thinking about you."

Oh, God.

He squeezed her hand. "I shouldn't, but I can't. And frankly, it's not something that's just happened since I came back. I haven't stopped thinking about you for the last four and a half years, Peyton."

Words that should have made her heart rejoice actually pierced her deeper than before. The fragments broke away, hoping to be found someday. It wasn't satisfying at all for her.

"What I'm saying is that I stand by what I said about saying goodbye to you after Oliver's wedding. I can't give you marriage or any of that. That's not my intention, and well, I'm not capable of it. I know that I sound harsh, but I don't want to mislead you. The only thing I can offer you is *now,* for as long as I can," he said.

And there it was—a now, not a forever. It was what she had asked of him and it pained her that it was all she'd really get.

"What does 'now' consist of?" she asked in a little voice.

Callum let go of her hands and stood up, wrapping his arms around her head and pressing her ear to his chest. She listened to his heartbeat. The uneven and erratic beats filled her with sadness and even more confusion.

"Enough to let me hold you like this," he stated.

And then those broken walls turned into ashes. She was officially a goner. A tear ran down her cheek, which was followed by another one. No forevers. It was agreed upon the moment Peyton wrapped her arms around his waist and held him tighter, afraid of their impending goodbye.

"I should hate you," she whispered as she closed her eyes tight, memorising the sequence of his heartbeat.

"You should and you will."

"I'm tired of hating you. What good would it do when it won't bring my parents back? I can't tell them how right they were when it came to you. I don't even think I hate you anymore, Callum. I'm just angry that I wasn't enough to make you stay."

He tensed underneath her. Then Peyton felt his warm hands rest on her cheeks before he pulled her back and bent his knees to face her. She was shocked to see the tears in his eyes.

"I hate that, for the last four years, I've made you feel like you weren't enough for me, Peyton. It wasn't that at all. You were more than enough. No answer I give you is worth you forgiving me. No damn answer." His thumb brushed the tears away.

The door to be truthful was finally open.

She looked him straight in the eye. "Did you cheat on me, Callum?"

When he didn't answer right away, her heart gave way. Falling, burning, and faltering. The breaths she inhaled added coldness to the heat, intensifying the pain rather than extinguishing it. She wasn't sure how to react if he said that he had. A slap in the face wouldn't be satisfying. She thought a knee in the crotch might be enough.

Callum closed his eyes and breathed out heavily. "Would it be easier when we say goodbye if you thought I did?"

Thought. Not that he had. But it didn't matter. Goodbye was still looming. The reason back then didn't matter anymore. It was here and right now that mattered.

"No," she replied, her voice had strained. The concept that he could have been with another girl killed her inside.

He gave her a tight smile. "Then no. I didn't cheat on you, Peyton. You were all I saw. I was lost in all that you were. There was no chance that I wanted someone else when I had you. I was faithful until the end."

Until the end.

Peyton believed him.

She moved away from Callum and sat back in the middle of her bed, letting her legs dangle over the edge of the bed. He hesitated a moment before he unzipped the hoodie he was wearing and let it fall to the floor. Then he took off his shoes, leaving them by the bed, before he climbed on the bed and Peyton patted her lap. She knew he understood what she meant the moment he positioned his feet near her pillows and lay his head in her lap. He looked up at her as she ran her fingers through his hair.

"Sometimes," she said as she continued to glide her fingers through his locks.

"Yes?" Callum stopped her left hand and held it in his.

She made a small smile. All so familiar.

"I wish you had cheated on me…that someone else had

gotten in the way of us. That it wasn't me who had changed your heart. That you had fallen in love with someone who wasn't me. I'd rather know you fell in love with someone else than know that I didn't make you happy. That I couldn't make you love me."

Truth.

She let her free hand fall to his jaw and softly trailed her fingers down. "Your leaving hurt me. Not because I lost the person I loved, but because I also lost my best friend. I had to figure out a life without you. And I missed you. A lot. Nobody got me the way you did. Not Jay and not even Graham."

Then she paused and brushed the wetness that had escaped from the side of his eye. "I've missed you, Callum. You were the part of me I loved the most about myself."

Callum let her hand go and sat up. Just as she was about to ask him what he was doing, he placed his hand on her shoulder and pushed her back on the pillows. He moved her so she was lying on her side before he settled next to her. Once he pulled her hair away from the side of her face, he moved in close, his mouth near her ear.

She was losing control. And she didn't care. She was giving it up…for sometimes moments. And she knew this was one of them. For her, it would be.

"I've missed you, Pey. I've missed you so damn much that I got your name tattooed on me. The cherry blossoms that wrap around my arm are symbolic of you. It was the only way I could feel close to you," he whispered in her ear.

She thought his heartbeat was her favourite sound he made. But it was actually the way he whispered and the way it made her heart ache and beat freely.

"Callum, we need a safe word," she said, looking at the Polaroid of them on the bedside table.

"Why?" he asked as he settled his chin on the top of her head.

"When this becomes too much. When we step over the concept of now. When one of us can't get over forever. Or when one of us can't take it anymore."

"Supercalifragilisticexpialidocious—that's our safe word," he said softly. "Close your eyes and let me hold you now, for as long as I can."

His voice sounded beautiful, and she let her eyelids fall. As she listened to his breathing until it finally settled, Peyton kept her eyes close. With one last sigh, he held her tight against his body before relaxing. After listening to each inhale and exhale Callum made, Peyton slowly opened her eyes. With a turn of her head, she was able to confirm that he was asleep.

This is when I know he loves me.

When he holds me in his sleep.

When he's exposed and vulnerable.

When he can't hide behind his fears and excuses.

When I know that there's still hope…

That he can love me again.

A tear fell before Peyton whispered to herself, "Super-cali-fragi-listic-expi-ali-docious."

Eighteen

After the bed dipped, a cool breeze fluttered over and settled on her arm and the side of her face. An arm wrapped over her, and she moved, her eyes slowly opening. A groan left her as she turned her head.

"It's me," Callum whispered, and she smiled, still half asleep.

She lay her head back down and closed her eyes. "You should go home, Callum. I don't want you to get sick," she said.

"Turn around for me," he instructed.

Peyton turned in his arms, her forehead against his chest as he held her tight against him.

"You're still burning up, Pey."

She snuggled into him. "I haven't been able to stay awake. Dad might take me to the hospital if I still can't stand tomorrow. Is Mrs West's cat still lying next to me? I'm too weak to make him move. Is Mr Lucky comfortable?"

Callum chuckled and kissed the top of her head. "There's no cat here, Peyton."

She raised her head, her eyes slowly opening. "Are you sure? He was by my feet just before."

"Mr Lucky isn't in your room. Close your eyes and get some sleep. We might have to take you to the hospital tomorrow, Peyton. You're burning up. I'll go get you a cold rag," he said, his hold on her loosening.

She gripped his shirt. "No. I'm freezing. Just hold me. Make sure you let Mr Lucky out the window when he wants to leave."

He laughed lightly. "Okay, I'll be sure to let him out. Goodnight, Peyton."

Peyton's head fell and she slowly let go of his shirt. "Goodnight, Mr Lucky."

Somewhere far away, she heard his beautiful laugh. Her head weighed too much to process another thought and her eyelids were too heavy to open. His hands rubbed circles on her back and her body no longer felt like her own.

Like a dream, she heard someone whisper, "I love you, Peyton."

"I love you, too, Mr Lucky. But I think that I'm in love with Callum. He'll let you out soon. Be a good kitty."

Blink.

Breathe in.

Blink.

Breathe out.

Blink twice.

And repeat.

All night, Peyton repeated the cycle of blinks and breaths. The way Callum held her through the night reminded her of when she was sick. That night, she'd been delirious, not really sure what was actual reality and what was the result of an extreme case of the flu. She had dreamed that Callum had said that he loved her, but she knew it was a dream. He never said anything when she woke.

Peyton spent the night staring at the Polaroid of them on her bedside table as Callum slept next to her. The need to say the safe word consumed her. She knew she was on the road to self-destruction. Taking a deep breath, Peyton turned in his arms until she was face to face with him. His mouth and brows were relaxed. When he was asleep, he seemed free and looked every inch the seventeen-year-old she'd loved. The thought caused heat to succumb her chest.

The reality was that the person she'd once loved no longer remained. Instead, he was a shell. He seemed lost, without a home. She wanted to touch him, have her fingers trail down the side of his face. See if he reacted the same way that he had when she used to do it under the cherry blossom tree outside her window. But she refrained from doing so.

Say it, Peyton. Say the word that will make him leave. End this now, her conscience screamed

Peyton squeezed her eyelids together. She knew that the right thing to do was wake him up and tell him to go home. She wasn't sure she could recover this time if he hurt her. She didn't have her parents.

"Why are you crying, Peyton?"

Peyton slowly lifted her lids, the tears she didn't realise she had dragged out sliding down the side of her face. The concern in Callum's eyes was hard to miss. She didn't wipe them away. Instead, two more tears fell before Peyton stared down at his chest.

"Peyton?" Callum asked softly.

Her eyes locked with his, and Callum's hand grazed against her stomach before he brought his fingers close to her face and brushed her hair back. She didn't say anything as he stroked her hair and then placed his palm on her hip, heating the skin underneath her pyjamas.

The corner of his lips deepened slightly, and his moves were a mix of familiar and unknown. He used to stroke back her hair plenty of times, but this time, the control on his face had her walls building. It wasn't the same. They weren't the same. She couldn't have the same.

Peyton shook her head. "I'm not sure," she replied and sat up.

She kept her eyes on the dresser opposite from where they lay and against the wall, unsure of what to do. Being lost in the past was risking her present and her future. 'For now' was too much of a risk. 'For now' wasn't what she deserved, and she shouldn't have asked for it.

The bed shifted, and Callum's hand was on her left shoulder. When she turned her head to look at him, remorse had filled his eyes, like he knew exactly what she was thinking. Another hand was placed on her right shoulder, his eyes never leaving hers. Then he sighed and pushed her back on the bed, his hands flat on the mattress by her head. Once he threw his leg over her body, he hovered over Peyton.

"You want to use the safe word, don't you?" His eyes darkened and her heart throbbed violently in her chest.

"Yes," she breathed out.

The features of his face hardened and his nose flared. "I told you that I didn't want anything from you, Peyton. You wanted this. You wanted now."

A whimpered escaped her lips. "I wanted forever," she confessed in a small voice. "I stupidly wanted forever from you."

Callum's arms tensed, and from the corner of her eye, she could see him fist the sheet under her. "I can't give you forever. Use it. Use the safe word, Peyton."

Do it, Peyton.

She blinked once, in time with the beat her heart made. Callum stared at her, waiting for her to say the word from one of her favourite movies. For a moment, she thought he'd cry. His mouth pressed together firmly and his eyes shone.

Peyton closed her eyes, mentally counting to three before staring at him. Then she took a deep breath and breathed out, "Super—"

Callum's lips crashing into hers stifled the rest of the safe word, almost taking it away from her. Peyton's hands reached up and held onto his waist as she kissed him back. She closed her eyes as Callum's mouth put more pressure on hers. Over and over, his lips worked with hers. It wasn't slow. It was fast and desperate. A kiss that screamed, "Let me keep you!" to Peyton.

His body tensed under her hands and she pulled him onto her. The pure weight of him caused her to moan. A sob was made somewhere between his mouth moulding over hers and his body falling on top of her. It wasn't a sob she made. Then something warm and wet hit her cheek and she opened her eyes.

The movement of her lips were slowed as she watched tears run from his closed eyes and down Callum's face, unaware that she was watching. Her heart throbbed and heated within her chest. She stopped returning his kisses as his lips continued to glide over hers.

"Callum, stop," she said.

And his lips did.

His arms tensed harder to the point where his veins protruded under his skin. Then he took a deep breath and rested his forehead against hers, his eyes still closed. When another tear hit her, she couldn't understand why a second sob escaped him.

"I don't want this for you, Peyton. You don't deserve this. This is why I made you promise to not let me kiss you."

The break in his voice had Peyton removing her hands from the side of his body, letting them fall onto the mattress. The cracks in her heart deepened at the desperation in Callum's voice.

"Then say it," she whispered.

Callum opened his eyes and moved his forehead from hers, staring down at her. "Say it?"

Peyton nodded. "Call it. Say the safe word."

He winced. "I can't. I can't say that word," he said, shaking his head.

Peyton reached up and wiped the wet tears from his cheeks. "You can say it, Callum. You know how to walk away. You've done this before."

"I'm not calling it, Peyton. Not on *this* bed. This bed holds everything for me. I'm not ending it here," Callum said.

She recognised the anger in his voice.

Callum looked her in the eye. "Not on this bed. *Never* on this bed." He didn't let her say a word as he got off the bed and walked to the door. But then he paused and hung his head low. "I'm sorry, Peyton. You don't understand how much that bed means to me," he said sadly before he opened the door and left her room and then the house.

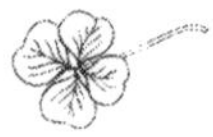

Peyton let her head fall back as she stared at the ceiling and listened to the sound of the water rushing out of the tap. She forced her eyes shut and tried to forget the image of him crying. Tried to forget the desperation. Tried to forget the apology and regret. But forgetting wasn't happening. It continuously burned holes through her chest.

Never on this bed.

She slowly opened her eyes and looked down at the bubbled water of the tub.

"Why my bed?" she thought out loud and turned off the tap. "Why didn't he use the safe word?"

Why didn't I use it?

Peyton's hands covered her face. "Because I didn't want to use it. I couldn't."

She quickly placed her hands on either side of the porcelain tub and submerged herself under the hot water in an attempt to drown herself. Death was an easier solution…if she weren't so afraid of dying. Instead, she started counting.

One.

You.

Two.

Still.

Three.

Love.

Four.

Him.

Peyton jerked out from under the water, gasping. Once her breathing settled, she wiped her face of the bubbles then shook her head. She was *still* in love with him. The concept was one she didn't welcome. She couldn't.

"Oh, God," she cried. "No. Anyone. Love anyone but him."

The sound of a new text message had her looking over the tub to her phone on the tiled floor. Reaching over, she picked it up, water settling on the screen as she unlocked her phone.

Callum: I need to see you. Meet me tonight.
Peyton: Why?
Callum: Because you want to see me, too.

Her breath caught and she swallowed hard. No denying it. She wanted to see him. Wanted an explanation for the tears. She wanted a lot of explanations from Callum Reid.

Peyton: Where?
Callum: You know where, Peyton.

Peyton hugged her thick jacket tighter as she walked over the hill and to the lake. The sun had already set and the temperature was dropping. After her morning bath, she'd pulled out the box from under her bed. It was a box of things he had left behind and little things they'd collected together. She'd gone through the contents for the first time in over four years. She'd come across a small, dried branch of pink cherry blossoms. It was the same branch he'd broken off for her the first time they'd sat under the tree outside her window. She'd kept it and cherished it until it had found its way into the box under her bed.

Her phone vibrated, so Peyton took it out of her pocket as she walked on the hotel grounds. She read the new message from Callum.

Callum: I'll be here waiting for you. Whenever you're ready.

She stopped just outside the path that took her into the woods and to their circle of trees. A place in this world that she both loved and hated. A place where she felt secure and insecure. A place where he never reciprocated her love.

Peyton: I should turn back.
Callum: You should. But I don't want you to.

Peyton: What do you want?
Callum: To be with you.
She stared at his message and swallowed hard.
Callum: And to not be with you.

Her heart plunged.

Callum: But I want to be with you. I've always wanted to be with you. But I couldn't and shouldn't. You're smart, Peyton. It would be stupid to be with me tonight.

Peyton looked back and stared in the direction of her street and then at the path. Then she glanced down at her phone and typed.

Peyton: I'm stupid.
Peyton: And I'm foolish.
Peyton: But foremost, I am stupid.

Once the message sent, she locked her phone and returned it to her pocket. The darkened forest that met her was one she stared at for a moment before she took a step towards it.

It didn't take long until Peyton found the circular rock, and she walked down the short incline, avoiding loose rocks and fresh mud, to see orange flashing. Slowly, she trekked through the dense foliage until she broke into the circle of trees. She stepped forward, dry leaves rustling under her foot, and Callum turned his head to her. He sat on a checker blanket, staring at the small makeshift fire that burned brightly enough to illuminate his face.

He gave her a tight smile as the vibrant red and orange of the flames reflected on his skin. She didn't say anything as she made her way over and sat on the blanket next to him. She crossed her legs as she appreciated the warmth from the fire. Peyton didn't look at him. Instead, she took in her surroundings. This moment resembled the night she'd lost her virginity to him.

The stars were brighter now than before, but there was no fog. Last time, they hadn't had a fire—they'd had lanterns.

The memories played heavy on her heart and Peyton shook her head to rid them. That had been the last time that he'd held her before he'd broken her heart.

"I'm sorry about this morning, Peyton," Callum quietly said.

She turned her head to see him staring intently at the fire like he had the night he'd kissed her. Another memory. Another moment.

Peyton clenched her jaw before she spoke. "You cried, Callum."

He flinched. "You don't know the truth, Peyton."

It was her turn to flinch. "Then give me the truth."

Callum slowly turned his head until his eyes met hers. "You don't want it," he replied.

Her heart burst in frustration. "I want it as much as I wanted you."

He closed his eyes for a second before he maneuvered his body so that he faced her properly. Then he looked down at his hands before meeting her eyes, the pain returning to his grey ones. Peyton leaned forward, never breaking eye contact, and gripped his shirt tight within her grasps. After a deep breath, she pulled his face close to hers, their lips almost touching.

"Why did you cry, Callum?" she asked.

She noticed his Adam's apple bob as he swallowed hard. "Because you don't deserve to have me in your life. I *will* hurt you."

The air in Peyton's lungs was drawn out and she was reminded just how temporary his stay is. Every inch of his face was filled with pain. Her heart wanted more, but it also wanted now. Callum couldn't offer past his stay, but he had promised now. And in some screwed-up way, she wanted what she could have in this exact minute. In this moment, she would let her heart win.

"Then I look forward to it," she stated, and she felt Callum flinch underneath her fingers.

My name is Peyton Spencer, and I am by far the stupidest woman on this Earth.

She nodded at her thought and ignored the way Callum's eyes were fixated on her lips. His breathing became heavy pants, and she held his shirt tighter.

"Tell me no, Peyton. Goddammit, tell me no," he begged desperately.

Her eyes met his before she whispered, "Yes," and brought his lips to hers.

Her head screamed at how irresponsible she was being, but she couldn't help herself. There was an undeniable draw to him. It had been there for as long as she could remember. Stupidity and heart were winning. Whatever she could have now, she'd rather take. No matter if a broken heart was what lay ahead of her.

Callum's tongue found hers and they discovered a rhythm of strokes begging of desperation and control. A moan escaped her, but she didn't care. The last time she was ever this close to anyone was when she was seventeen. *In this exact same spot.*

Peyton lay back on the blanket, bringing him down with her, and he settled between her thighs. They both sighed at the contact of their bodies. Every thought she managed was placed in a dark room in her mind and locked. She needed this. She needed the pain to go away. And Callum's mouth on hers was relief.

"Oh, God," she softly moaned the moment he moved against her. Then she arched her back, moving her lips away from his as she experienced the small burst of pleasure.

Callum's mouth went to her neck and slowly trailed up and down, ghosting his lips along her skin. The image of him crying wouldn't leave her and she hoped this intimate act between them would drowned it out. After Peyton found the hem of his shirt, he propped himself up and looked into her eyes. She noticed a glint to those confusing grey pools. The control was either gone or broken. One or the other. He was reluctant and she was offering. And she knew that he needed direction.

"Tell me you don't want this, Peyton. Tell me no," he said

between heavy pants.

Peyton, tell him no. You have some pride.

When she rested her body weight on her elbows, Callum moved back onto the blanket. She swallowed hard as she removed her thick coat, the desire and interest consuming Callum's eyes.

Make him realise his mistake of walking away.

Peyton stood up, her eyes still on his. And as her fingers reached the hem of her shirt, she said, "Four years ago, you ruined me in this spot. You broke my heart. You made love to me here. Callum..."

His eyes saddened at her reminder of their first and last time together. "Yes, Peyton."

She ignored the way his name sounded to her heart and bent forward, placing her hands on his cheeks. Then she looked him hard in the eye and whispered, "Fuck me."

He flinched and his nose flared. He blinked once and looked her over. This wasn't about love. It was about releasing the tension and feeling pleasure for the first time in a long time. He couldn't give her love.

Callum held onto her hips and brought her down to his lap. The moment she straddled him, his eyelids tightly scrunched together and he swore under his breath.

"Fuck me, Callum," she pleaded once more.

His eyes opened quickly just in time to see her pull the shirt off her body and throw it on the ground next to the blanket.

His fingers dug into her skin as he tried to compose himself, but his heavy panting was deceitful. He wanted this as much as she wanted it. Peyton hoped that this one moment of him fucking her would remove the innocent memory of their first time.

She reached behind and found the clasp of her red lacy bra. The sharp inhale from Callum was enough for her to unclip and remove it. His eyes never travelled south as she placed her bra with her shirt. The cool wind caused her to shiver, and his fingers dug into her more. When her hands moved to the button of her jeans, Callum's quickly covered hers.

"I'm not fucking you, Peyton," he said in a hoarse voice before he had her on her back. Then he quickly unzipped his hoodie and disposed of it and his shirt.

She tensed under him. Those weren't the words that she'd expected.

"Last time to tell me no," he said as he placed his hands on her jeans.

"You're not going to get it," she replied as she lifted her hips off the blanket.

His jaw clenched as he blinked at her.

Do it. Just fuck me, Callum. Taint our innocent times with this moment.

With a sharp inhale and a second to himself, he pulled down her jeans and underwear. The moment he had her naked, he stood up, unbuttoned his pants, and stepped out of them as well as his underwear. The light from the fire allowed her to take in the naked image of him. She admired the cherry blossoms wrapped around his arm and was just able to see the letters of her name on his wrist. Her heart ached. So instead, she kept focused on his face rather than his tattoos.

He reached down and pulled out his wallet, flipping it open and removing a condom. Her heart pounded loudly in her chest at the sight of the small package he held.

No. This has to be raw in order to taint our memories.

Peyton held out her hands. After a moment of his eyes floating over her naked body, Callum placed the condom in her palm and she threw it into the fire. He made a strangled sound, and she shook her head at him.

"I want you bare inside me," she instructed.

Callum looked at the fire, watching the protection burn. "Peyton—"

She grabbed his hands in hers and pulled him back on her body. "I'm on the shot."

Relief filled his eyes as he settled between her legs, and she felt him at her entrance. Then his hands were on the blanket as he held himself up. His eyelids were shut tightly, and Peyton refused to touch him. This wasn't about feelings or a connection.

It was about ruining her soul and memories.

When Callum opened his eyes, she winced the moment she saw them glaze over. It wasn't what he wanted between them—she saw it. His watery eyes brought violent throbs to her heart, the pain spreading through her.

No.

She wanted this to be love. Seeing the vulnerability in his eyes was a glimpse of the past. Her fingers wrapped around his wrists as her thumb smoothed over her tattooed name.

"Callum," she said.

The memory of him crying this morning flashed before. But it wasn't a memory. It was reality. Callum, naked and beautiful, had tears in his eyes.

I want the truth.

If I can't, I want as close to the truth as possible.

Peyton took a deep breath. "What's the most honest and truthful thing you have ever said in your life?"

He tensed, confusion sweeping over his face. "The most honest and truthful thing?"

"Yes," she said in a whisper.

He didn't answer straight away. Instead, his lips pressed on hers. Kissing her slowly and passionately. Not as rough as before. More like he was savouring and treasuring her mouth.

Then he drew back and looked her in the eye. This time, she saw fear.

He propped himself on an elbow and used his hand to push back her hair before placing it back on the blanket. The different emotions that filled his eyes had her heart slowing down painfully. *Waiting.* His lips parted and he blinked once. Then his hips slowly thrust forward as he entered her. Stretching her.

Ignoring the pain, she concentrated on the feel of him inside her. His heavy pants mirrored hers. He stopped mid-thrust as he held himself over her. The muscles in his neck strained as he swallowed hard, but he didn't push further, only stilling.

His eyes didn't leave hers as he whispered, "I love you, Peyton," and thrust hard and deep.

Her heart didn't regain its beats. Instead, it died inside her chest.

Dropping his head into the curve of her neck, he pulled out. His heavy pants hit her skin as tears filled her eyes. Not blinking, the stars above morphed into blurry shades of black and spots of white.

"I love you, Peyton," Callum he said breathlessly then thrust inside her, completely filling her. He stayed inside her before he said, "That's the most honest and truthful thing I have ever said."

Nineteen

"Say something," Callum said quietly, still inside her.

Breathe. Please. Breathe.

Peyton couldn't form words. *Nothing.* She kept her eyes on the night sky. With each moan of her name from his lips, she silently cried hard. She fell. Her self-control finally snapped.

Callum kept his word. Unfortunately, he didn't fuck her. Instead, it was slow, desperate, and passionate—something Peyton regretted. It was the final chain breaking.

I'm in love with someone who'll break me.

Four and a half years—that's how long it had been since she was last intimate. After Callum, she hadn't been interested in being that close to someone again. Being close scared her. But here she lay. Callum Reid inside her. She wished that he'd screwed her hard and painfully. But he hadn't.

Her heart was split on whether or not she loved what they did. It wasn't like last time. There were too many things unsaid, things that hadn't been expressed. Each time he looked her in the eyes as he entered her, there was a flash of an apology.

But then she came. And he came. Almost together, a fraction off from a perfect unison. It was like he needed to see more than just her eyes when he shouted her name one last time before he collapsed on top of her. It didn't help that she softly begged him not to stop as she dug her nails into his wrists. She wanted to touch him more. More than just his wrists and arms. But she couldn't. She wouldn't allow herself more. She needed the tattooed cherry blossoms under her fingertips as he filled her. Cherry blossoms gave her hope for the truth. He'd said it himself. They were a symbol of her for him.

Peyton continued to stroke the tattoo of her name on him. She couldn't look him in the eye. She wasn't sure how to feel. Wasn't sure who she was in this moment. So she let her eyelids fall, trying to rekindle the hate she had for him. It was still there. It lingered. Not quite touching her heart's surface.

"Please say something, Peyton."

His soft plea had her opening her eyes to stare into the grey ones that had undone her all over again.

"Why didn't you just—"

"I couldn't," he said, interrupting her.

The way his lips formed a frown had Peyton wanting to touch hers to his. She wanted to take away the pain, the guilt, and the secrets. But she knew it herself. She couldn't set him completely free. That was all him. She could only get him so far.

I love you, Peyton.

She tensed at the thought. He'd said it. *Twice.* Never in the space of their relationship had he ever said those words to her. She didn't trust the words he'd breathed against her ear as he'd found a slow rhythm that connected them in the most intimate of ways. She felt and heard her heart die inside her chest. The denial that she didn't love him was ultimately crushed. They were right. They all were. She was still in love with him.

"We should go," he said, shifting under her and attempting to pull out.

But Peyton gripped his wrist tighter. Her mind had finally succumbed to her heart's persuasion. Her brain had betrayed the rest of her.

I need him to stay. Right here. Enough to let me have this before he takes it away. I need these sometimes moments.

He turned his head and stared at the way her hands wrapped around his wrist before he met her glance.

Peyton blinked and she breathed out. "Okay," she replied, not really sure how these after-sex chats go.

"It's been a while for me, Peyton, but I swear I'm clean."

She nodded and relaxed her grip on his arms. Slowly, her thumb followed the branches of his tattoo. Once she circled the petals of a cherry blossom, he flinched, slightly thrusting inside her. A soft gasp escaped her lips at the surprise movement.

Don't turn this into anything more, Peyton. You know what happens. He leaves. You stay. Don't make this more. Make it a now.

"Peyton, I can't be inside you like this. It shouldn't have been this way. I don't want to end up fucking you when you don't deserve that," Callum said as he slowly pulled out and removed himself from on top of Peyton's body.

Peyton sat up then reached for her clothes. Without a word, they both dressed themselves. Callum's back was towards her, and she noticed the flames of the fire dance against his skin. Peyton reached for her boots, unsure of exactly when he'd taken them off her. The moment their lips had met, her traitor brain hadn't responded. Next she slipped them on and then her coat.

She crossed her legs and stared at the fire, not really sure what to say. The last time they'd made love, she'd lain in his arms until almost sunrise. Before they had packed up their things, he had dressed her and made her feel cherished. But this time, Peyton felt cheap and not of standard. She hung her head in shame and crossed her arms over her chest.

"How long has it been for you, Peyton?" he asked.

She turned to face him. His body was tense as he waited. "Don't worry. I'm clean, too, Callum."

"That's not what I'm asking," he said. "I could tell."

He could?

Peyton uncrossed her arms and let her hands fall to her lap. "How long has it been for you?" she asked, stalling.

"Months," he answered.

Her heart burned and then plunged. He had been with other women since her. She had known that, but it hurt to hear. Somewhere inside her, the old Peyton sobbed. The same Peyton who believed they would be forever.

"I need to hear you say it, Peyton. I need you to tell me that you've had others. I need you to say it. I need to hear it."

And there it was. The same voice. The same desperation. The same way he'd said that he loved her.

Peyton stood up and took a deep breath. She didn't look at him. Instead, she gazed out past the trees. Tonight wasn't what she'd expected. She definitely hadn't thought her resilience would break and she'd sleep with him.

"Would you rather I lie to you, Callum? I'm not the liar here." Peyton's focus shifted down to see him staring at the small fire. It was like his eyes flashed with every single fear that he had. His frown was one she didn't like to see.

"I haven't lied to you, Peyton."

She balled her hands. "No. You just don't tell me the truth."

Callum reached over, took the bottle of water that was next to the pit, and poured it over the fire. Peyton watched the fire extinguish and stepped off the blanket in time for Callum to pick it up off the ground.

He faced her. "The moment that I decided to come back to Daylesford, my intentions were to *never* sleep with you, Peyton. As I drove into town, I hoped you were with someone. The love of your life. Anyone. I didn't care who. I just wanted you to be unavailable to me. When I saw that ring, I was relieved. I was also jealous. But I was relieved because it meant I couldn't touch you. I don't lie to you, Peyton. I never have. I've kept things, but I haven't lied. I have *never* lied."

She pressed her lips together before she breathed out heavily. It was time to have the what-you-said-during-sex talk.

"When did you say those words?" she asked.

"I've said it three times in my life," he said and walked past her.

Peyton quickly turned around and saw him walking up towards the hotel. "Three?" she called out, and he stopped.

He turned around and gripped the blanket tighter in his hand. "The first time was when you were sick in bed. I told you that I loved you and you said that you loved Mrs West's cat. But you also said that you were sure you were in love with me.

The second time was when you were in hospital. I was sure you were okay when I said it to you, but you quickly passed out. And the last time I said them was in the car as I left this town. But there was a fourth time. The night I packed up my things, your dad saw us load the cars."

Her heart halted silently.

My dad.

Peyton took two steps forward and asked, "What did you say to him?"

He looked her straight in the eye. Without a blink, Callum said, "I'm in love with your daughter, Mr Spencer. I love her enough to do this to her."

Her eyelids fluttered quickly at him. Her father had known that Callum was leaving. He'd kept it from her. Callum had confessed his love to her father but never her. He'd been a coward then just as he was now.

"You obviously didn't love me enough, Callum. Love isn't hurting someone like you did. Love isn't what you've done or been doing for over four years." Peyton paused. "Tonight was a mistake. Holding hope you'd come back was a mistake. Being with you at seventeen was a mistake. Loving you, Callum, is a mistake!"

He didn't flinch. It was like he had expected it. He gave her a sad smile before he said, "Thank you."

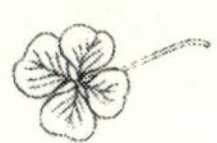

Madilynne: I hate you. I hate you so much!

Peyton: What for this time?

Madilynne: Because I have to return to that stupid town!

Peyton: So I'm guessing that you haven't left yet.

Madilynne: No. I've packed and unpacked several times. Since we're best friends, would you just give me the recommendation for my resume?

Peyton: You know I would.

> **Madilynne**: And that is why I love you. But word spread quickly. My folks know that I'm coming home. Can't run now. I'll see you in a few days. Be a good girl until then.

Peyton locked her phone and put it in her jacket pocket. She could last a few days until her best friend came back to Daylesford. By the time Mads returned, Peyton would be busy with prepping the hotel for reopening and for the Reynolds' wedding. She'd be too busy to deal with Callum.

Peyton's shoulders sagged and she let out a sigh. The soreness between her legs didn't help with forgetting him. Neither did the revelation that he had somehow loved her when they were seventeen. Not now. But then. It was Peyton who loved him now *and* then.

Shaking her head, she opened the front door and stepped outside, closing it behind her. She immediately hugged the jacket around her tighter. It was bitterly cold out and fog was in the air. She smiled, knowing just how beautiful the lake would look.

Peeking up, she stared at the Reid house. She'd been stupid to sleep with him, only because it meant more self-inflicted pain. After Callum had said, "Thank you," he hadn't said anything else. Instead, he'd walked her home. It had been different from their last night. When they were seventeen, it had taken them almost an hour for Peyton to sneak back into her room. They had sat under the cherry blossom tree until he'd decided it was best that she got back inside before her parents had discovered she'd snuck out.

I have to stay away.

The temptation to walk up to the house across the road swept through her. She wanted to speak to him. She also wanted to feel his lips on her again. Feel him close to her. But she couldn't. The safe word had to be said out loud. Last night had been the ending. Nothing more.

Peyton slipped her hands into her jacket pockets and quickly walked down the steps. She needed to get to the lake and fast.

There was no time to dwell on Callum Reid. She had already spent four and a half years doing so.

By the time she got to the bench, the lake was clear. She sat down and stared out at the lake, loving the way the fog didn't touch the water's surface. Instead, it rolled over, allowing the lake water to have its own space to breathe. One of the many reasons why she loved Daylesford. It was beautiful. There was no denying it.

Reaching into her pocket, Peyton pulled out her phone to check the time and the date. She wasn't imagining the date. It was the first Monday of the month and just after eight a.m.; Graham was never late. Peyton was never the first on the bench. It was always Graham who was there waiting for her. With a victorious smile, she settled onto the bench and waited.

After almost an hour had passed, Peyton unlocked her phone and brought up Graham's number. She looked over at the hotel, knowing that she was keeping Jenny, the hotel's operations manager, waiting. With a deep breath, she called Graham.

"Hi, Graham Scott here. Can't make it to the phone. Leave your details and I'll get back to you."

Peyton hung up and tried again.

And again.

And again.

The fourth time, she placed her phone on her lap and ran her hands over her face. Graham was never one to skip their tradition. Even when he was sick, he still made it.

Don't be so paranoid, Peyton. It's not what you think. You're not losing Graham.

But then again, he's never missed any of my calls.

She moved her hands from her face and stared out at the lake. The thought of losing Graham killed Peyton inside. She couldn't lose him. She loved him. She knew she did. That's why when he gave her the promise ring, she said yes. She looked at the faint tan line on her finger where the ring had once sat.

The screen of her phone lit up and caught her attention. Without a single thought, Peyton quickly answered her phone.

"Graham," she said, relieved that he had called her back. She had known that he hadn't forgotten.

"You called," he said, sounding bothered by her.

Peyton flinched. "It's the first Monday of the month."

She heard him sigh before the line went quiet. Her eyes followed the roll of the fog on the lake as she waited for him.

"Honestly, Peyton, I don't want to look at you let alone talk to you on the phone. I'm hung over."

No.

Peyton let out a strangled sound. It was a sound she tried to suppress, but it escaped her. Her eyes stung as she held the phone tighter.

"It's Monday, Graham," she said, her voice betraying her. It made her appear weak.

She heard him take a sharp breath in. "You told Jay that I'd understand, but I don't. We're best friends. You could have just told me. I didn't have to hear it from Jay. Right now, I'm disappointed in you. Let me be mad at you, Peyton. Just this one time, let me be mad. I'm sorry." Before he let her respond, Graham hung up.

Peyton slowly removed the phone from against ear and stood up from the bench. She looked at the screen, hoping he'd call her back and say that it was a joke. But he didn't.

Graham Scott had officially broken tradition.

Twenty

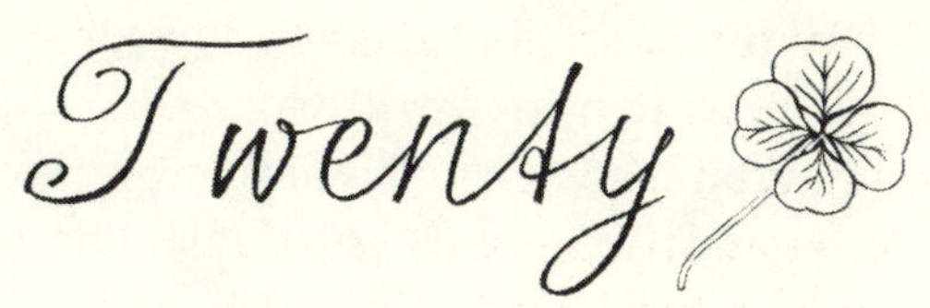

A cup was placed in front of Peyton. She stared at it until she looked up to see Jenny frowning at her. Besides her aunt and uncle, Jenny was like a second mother, making sure Peyton never missed meals, always went to school, and always kept focus. While she had completed her bachelor, Jenny Fields had managed the hotel with Aunt Brenda and Uncle John.

"You seem like you need it," Jenny said, sitting on the seat in front of Peyton's desk.

Peyton gave her operations manager a tight smile—one that Jenny squinted and shook her head at. Then Jenny pushed back her auburn hair over her shoulders and sighed. Jenny was the same age as Peyton's mother. Forty-six. But unlike Jenny, Cindy Spencer had only made it to forty-two.

"Thanks," Peyton said as she moved the folder to the pile and reached over for the cup of coffee. Picking it up, she stared at the light-brown liquid that was inside.

It was Wednesday and she still hadn't spoken to Graham. He never called. Never texted. But she'd let him be mad at her.

"What's on your mind, Peyton?" Jenny asked. Her light-blue eyes filled with concern.

"I'm running a hotel. Between new bookings and a new business plan, I'm... I don't know. Some days, I just think this place would have been better in your hands and not mine," Peyton confessed.

Jenny's facial features softened. "This is yours now, Peyton. I know it's a lot sooner than you or your parents would have liked, but it's yours. I'm always here to help you," Jenny assured.

Peyton saddened. Jenny was just like her—staying in Daylesford because of responsibilities and loyalty. And she regretted the fact that she'd held Jenny back. Peyton put her coffee down and pulled the drawer open, taking out a large envelope.

"This is why you have to do this for me," Peyton said, handing the envelope to Jenny.

"What is it?"

"Orientation papers for the Park Hyatt in the city. I called in a few favours from June; with her uncle being Park Hyatt's HR manager and my recommendations, she was able to get you the managerial position they had open," Peyton explained.

The disbelief washed over Jenny's face as she opened the envelope and took out the papers. Peyton sat and waited. She would be losing a valuable employee, but Jenny's dreams were more important than the hotel or the town. Only some were able to leave, and Jenny should be one of them. The hotel was losing a great asset, but Peyton didn't mind.

Jenny stood up and placed the envelope papers on the desk. "I love this hotel, Peyton. It's no Park Hyatt, but it's something special. I wish you'd see that. You're doing well. Your parents would be proud of what you've achieved for this place. *I'm* proud of you. Tell June I said thanks and I can't wait for her new album, but I'm not leaving you or this hotel."

A knock on the office door had Jenny stepping aside. Peyton stood up to see a man in a pair of cargo pants and dark-blue shirt holding a clipboard.

"I'm looking for Miss Spencer?" he said and smiled at both women.

Peyton walked around the desk towards him. "That's me. How can I help you?"

He tipped his head at her. "I have the wooden frames and

planks for the dance floor. I have the rest of the boys with me to start digging into the dirt and putting them up."

"Right," Peyton said with a nod. "How about you get them to start unpacking everything you need and I'll show you where we're building it all."

"Sure thing, Miss Spencer," he said, tucking the clipboard under his arm.

"It's Peyton," she corrected.

"And I'm Nigel. I'll get the utes unloaded," he said and walked towards the front door.

Peyton felt relieved. She finally had things under control. Over the past few days, she'd worked on a new business plan that meant incorporating more of the community into the hotel. But that part of the plan would take some time.

"See? You handled that perfectly," Jenny said from behind her.

Peyton turned around and smiled. "I guess so."

Jenny stepped forward and looped her arm through Peyton's. "Let's go see if we can't find you a tradie husband."

Peyton let out a laugh and shook her head. "I'm good."

"Because Callum's back in town?"

Peyton tensed next to Jenny. "He'll be gone soon," she said.

"And you don't want him to go?"

"I didn't want him to leave the first time. But that doesn't matter. Callum is nothing to me. Shall we go out to the cabins? I'd love to show you my plans for some of them."

"First, the tradies," Jenny said, excitement in her voice clear.

"You're old enough to be their mother!"

Jenny laughed. "And I'm married, too. But we can always look. There's no harm in looking."

Looking is the first part to wanting and touching. Looking is the start of the harm.

"Do you want to go to the party tonight?"

Peyton peered up from her Russian revolutions textbook and raised her brow at Graham. He pursed his lips and returned to his methods homework. He didn't ask for an explanation. Ever since Callum had left, the people in town had started to treat her differently and Peyton hated it. She didn't want their pity. Besides Graham, Jay Preston had begun to speak to her. He had always been nice to her, but with Callum gone, Jay had given her more of his time. At first, she'd been flattered, but then she'd come to appreciate him.

"Would you like to go, Graham?" she asked, placing the book down on the patio table. It was what they did every day since their moment on the bench – homework at either of their houses.

"I don't want to force you. We can skip the party. We can either hang out at the farm or here?"

His dimple greeted her, and Peyton refrained from rolling her eyes at the grin he directed her way.

"We can go to the party."

"What, my farm isn't nice enough for you?" he sassed.

"I would much rather be at your farm than the back of the boathouse. But I have a feeling you need to be at the party. I'm thinking Krista?" Peyton raised a brow as she stood up from the chair.

Graham's cheeks turned bright red. "Whatever," he muttered, embarrassed.

Peyton let out a laugh. "I knew it!"

"You know nothing," he bit back.

Peyton shook her head and pointed at herself. "I know everything."

Graham rolled his eyes and returned to his homework.

"I'll get us drinks before you go home and change," Peyton said before she walked into the house.

Upon entering the kitchen, she noticed her dad sitting at the dining table. He was wearing a frown as he stared at her. Her father hadn't been the same since Callum left Daylesford. He seemed guarded, like he was keeping a secret from her. But Peyton knew otherwise. She knew her father was waiting for the breaking point. The moment that she exploded and became reckless.

"I didn't know you were home, Dad," Peyton said as she made her way to the fridge.

Her father didn't reply as she opened the door and took out two cans of Fanta. Once she held them firmly in her hands, Peyton closed the fridge and stared at him.

He pressed his lips tightly before he said, "You and Graham are getting close."

She froze.

He stood up from the chair and glared at her with a concerned look. "He's a nice boy, Peyton. But what if Callum comes back? You going to hurt that boy for Callum?"

Peyton shook her head. She was her daddy's little girl. But she was tired of being babied. She didn't need anyone's pity or concern. The way her father's eyes flashed in pain wasn't something Peyton liked to see.

"He's not coming back, Dad. No one comes back after they leave this place," Peyton said, staring at the cold cans in her hand.

"That's not true, Peyton. Your mother and I always come back." He gave her a sad smile. "You never know. One day, he might come back."

"You and Mum come back because the hotel is here."

"We come back because you are here, Peyton. You come first. If you'd like, you can come with us to the city? We're leaving tonight."

She wasn't sure how to tell her father that she was scared to leave town, afraid that she might see him, so she shook her head. "Thanks, Dad. But I promised Graham that I'd go to the boathouse party with him."

He gave her a nod. "Maybe the next business trip, you'll come."

She shrugged before she said, "Maybe," and exited the kitchen.

The first lie her father had ever told her was when he'd said that he and her mother would always come back. That weekend, her parents had died in a hit and run. The night of the party was the last time she ever saw her parents alive again. If she had gone with them, she most likely would have died, too. Some days, Peyton wished she had. To stop the pain. To never experience the loss of the two people who had brought her into the world. And to never see Callum Reid again.

In theory, dying sounded easy. But the thought of never seeing him was shattering. She could say it a million times and never mean it. Callum meant a lot more to Peyton than she wanted to admit. She wanted every laugh, every touch, every belief of them to be tarnished in pain and deceit. But they stayed pure.

Peyton stopped her steps as she reached her street. She looked to her right and stared at the double-story house across from hers. Biting down on her lip, Peyton weighed her options. The truth was that she missed him. Missed the way he held her in his sleep. Missed the little smiles that went unguarded. Missed the moments when she could tell herself that she was his. The moments she believed could be enough for them. But they weren't. They never would be.

Her feet made the decision for her as she crossed the road and made her way up the path. She stepped on his mat and studied the door. She concentrated on finding a normal rhythm of her heart. She was anxious and hopeful. She was also regretful and broken. The only reason she was at his door was to see him. To prove that he was worth losing Graham and Jay for.

Along with the sun setting, a cold gust of wind blew, causing Peyton to shiver. She'd spent most of the day watching the construction of the structure for the Reynolds' wedding. Besides that, she'd hid in her office, not wanting to return home. Her thoughts had been on Callum. They shouldn't have been, but they were. It had been days since she'd last seen him. She should have been worrying over her friendship with Graham, but she had to give him space.

Forming a fist, Peyton raised it up at the door and gently rested her knuckles against the wood. She took a deep breath and let her head fall forward.

What am I doing? I'm just making it worse for myself.

With a sigh, she pulled back from the door and stood straight. She hadn't imagined them apart until it had happened. This time, she couldn't imagine them together. She wanted more. She would always want more from him. She wanted to be given what she was being denied—a future with the one person she loved, no matter how much he tore and destroyed her soul.

Maybe, in another life, I could have had him.

She took a backwards step. And then another. Her eyes were

on the door before she spun around and made her way back towards her house. When she looked at the steps, she thought of the morning when he'd left. She'd sat on these exact steps. Moments later, she'd had her heart torn out. Placing her bag on the step, Peyton turned around and sat down next to it. Her eyes roamed every inch of the brick house as her heart ached at the years she'd needed him.

My biggest lie: wishing I hadn't fallen in love with Callum Reid.

Twenty-One

Aunt Brenda: We went fishing by the pier. Your uncle is hopeless. We love you, Peyton. Are you eating? How's the hotel?

Peyton: Aunt Brenda, you should worry about him falling in rather than the fish. I love you both, too. You're getting good at texting. Hotel's good. We have everything under control. Jenny turned down Hyatt. The building for Marissa's dance floor starts today. Yesterday's weather was too risky to pour the cement for the posts.

Aunt Brenda: Jenny loves the hotel, too. She won't leave unless you do. Your uncle wants to go down to the shops. We both love you. LOL.

Peyton: I think you're using LOL wrong.

Aunt Brenda: We are sending you lots of love.

Peyton: You might want to find out what LOL means, Aunt Brenda. I'll speak to you soon x.

"God, this town got uglier!"

Peyton lifted her eyes off her screen to see her door burst open. She knew that voice. She wasn't surprised when her best friend, Madilynne Woodside, walked through the door. As usual, Madilynne wore her blonde hair in her natural curls, her long, dark eyelashes framed her blue eyes perfectly, and her lips were coated in a matte-red lipstick. Peyton placed her phone on her desk and stood up.

"What happened to calling me from Ryder's?" Peyton asked as she walked towards the door.

Madilynne rolled her eyes. "Drove right past. Kinda forgot to look out for it. Dammit, I forgot how pretty you are. I'm glad that I don't have to compete with you in the city."

Peyton shook her head. "I'm sure you do just fine in the guy department, Mads."

Madilynne shrugged. "It's a tough department. The city isn't very kind, Peyton. Neither are some of the girls. But enough about me. How's everything in 'Peyton Spencer is a hotel owner' world going?"

I should tell her about Callum...and Jay...and Graham.

As Peyton looked at her best friend, a sense of relief washed over her. She finally had someone in town to spend time with. Someone she could be around. Someone to distract her. It had been two years since Madilynne had last been in town, too busy with university and city life. They had continued their friendship through calls and messages.

"Mads, it's Friday. You should have been here a lot earlier," Peyton said, deciding that she'd keep Callum's return to Daylesford from Madilynne for a little longer.

Madilynne wrapped her arms around Peyton and said, "It's good to see you, boss. I'm also happy to see that you haven't been struck by lightning."

After a laugh and a quick hug, Peyton stepped back and adjusted her silk blouse. "Would you rather we get work orientation over and done with or catch up and go through work stuff tomorrow?"

Madilynne made a gagging sound. "The work bullshit now and then we can go drink and talk."

"*I would* much rather be doing this internship under your rules than Jenny's," Madilynne complained as Peyton locked the hotel's front door.

By the time Peyton had explained what Madilynne would be doing and filled out the paperwork, it was late in the afternoon. She'd agreed when Madilynne had slammed the stack of papers on the desk and stated that wine was necessary.

"How are you supposed to learn anything from me, Mads? I know nothing," Peyton said, throwing the keys into the bottom of her bag.

"We would have *so* much fun."

"You're not here for fun. You're here for a recommendation," Peyton stated.

"Ugh, you are such a boss. Come on. Let's go drinking and unwind at the pub," Madilynne said excitedly.

Peyton winced. She hadn't been at the pub since Callum and Jay had had their confrontation. She also hadn't spoken to Jay since they'd both called each other traitors. Before Peyton could even suggest wine at her house, Madilynne had made her way towards the turn into town. With a sigh, Peyton followed, knowing it was time to face Jay. With each step she took, she could see the pub's large sign more clearly. Her breathing became unsteady as she tried to control her nerves.

All Peyton could hear was Madilynne's voice, but she wasn't listening. Instead, she tuned out her best friend and kept her eyes on the old brick building on Main Street. When they got closer to the doors of the pub, she saw Graham. Peyton halted at the sight of him. It had been almost five days since she'd spoken to him.

"If you don't tell her, I will! She doesn't deserve this. You shouldn't have come back!" Graham yelled.

Peyton and Madilynne had stumbled across the heated argument that Graham had been involved in.

"I know that, Graham. I'm trying to fix things." Callum's voice drew out the air from her lungs. She couldn't see him from behind Graham, but she heard him.

"Peyton, what's going on?" Madilynne asked next to her.

"You deserve my fist in your face. How dare you do this to

her. I've spent over four years trying to help her and you come back and ruin her all over again."

"Whoa. What's the issue here?" Madilynne asked.

Graham turned around, and Peyton's eyes met Callum's.

"Oh my God," Madilynne breathed out and looked at Peyton.

Peyton ignored her and stared at Callum. She didn't understand the hurt and pain in his eyes. And he wouldn't let her. So she slid her gaze to Graham, and an unspoken apology consumed his eyes.

Graham swore out loud and ran his hands through his hair before he walked to her. "I'm sorry, Peyton. I shouldn't have done that to you on Monday. It's the first Monday I've missed. I was angry and I shouldn't have been. But *this*, Peyton? This, you don't deserve. You don't deserve what he's doing to you. You're one of the best people I know and it's not fair!"

"Graham," Peyton said before he wrapped his arms around her. She breathed in the lavender fragrance that lingered on his clothing and hugged him. She had missed him. The concept of losing him was one she couldn't fathom.

"You have to walk away now, Peyton. He's only going to hurt you. Please walk away," Graham begged.

Peyton blinked slowly before she said, "It's too late, Graham. I'm sorry."

In that moment, she chose. She chose Callum Reid breaking her heart over salvation with Graham Scott.

Graham untangled his arms from around her body and took a step back. "I want to say that I'm disappointed in you but I'm not. I get it. I get why he's doing this. I would do it, too. Just know that I'm always here, Peyton."

He didn't let her reply. Instead, Graham walked past her and down Main Street.

"I'll go after him. I'll speak to you later, Peyton," Madilynne said before she left Peyton and Callum alone.

Alone with Callum was not what she wanted. Because all she wanted to do was kiss him, feel him, feel pleasure because of him, and forget the impending pain.

She looked up at the terrified expression on his face. No words were shared, only glances. She should listen to Graham. She should also listen to the voice in her head that was telling her to run and never look back. But instead, her heart instructed her to stay.

"You're going to hurt me, aren't you?" she asked in a small voice, needing his confirmation.

Callum's jaw clenched before he said, "Yes."

Peyton nodded, allowing her entire body to feel the ache in her chest. "What did you say to Graham?"

He didn't blink as he said, "The truth."

Peyton pressed her lips together as she tried to fight back the tears. The nearing end terrified her. They were close to reaching it.

"And what is the truth?" she asked as she took a step forward and grabbed his jumper in her hands.

He remained silent.

"Please tell me," she pleaded, making sure his eyes never lost focus on hers.

Callum shook his head.

"Please," she begged one more time.

"Peyton," he warned. His hands were over hers, trying to pull away from her.

His refusal was one her heart appreciated. The moment she knew the truth meant the end of them. And as hard as she fought against him, she wanted Callum to stay, which meant the truth couldn't come to light just yet.

"Callum." She gripped his shirt tighter.

His nostrils flared as he held her harder. "I'm calling it, Peyton."

Her heart stopped. The staples that held it together were slowly and painfully being removed one at a time.

"Please don't," she begged softly.

"Super—"

She pulled on his shirt to find his lips. Crashing and burning—her heart did both. He tried to pull back, but she kissed him harder, begging him to keep his mouth on hers. This was what she had missed. The attraction, the want, and the need he resisted between them. His lips moved against hers, prolonging the inevitable. Prolonging the safe word being said out loud. Prolonging their goodbye. Prolonging the death of her heart.

Painfully perfect.

It was the only way she could describe it. She was at fault for this, at fault for a lot of things. But right now, this was right. It was always right when she was with him. They fit. They made sense. At least she believed so.

His hands held her shoulders, steadying the pace, and her knees went weak. The breathless whisper of her name had her holding on to his shirt. Every kiss of hers was answered with his own desperate and willing ones.

She would rather spend the rest of time with his mouth on hers, but as all things do, his lips slowed down and their kiss ended. He lingered his lips over hers before he pulled her back at an arm's length.

They searched each other's eyes. She waited, hoped, and even prayed that he'd keep the safe word to himself. She had already made a choice. Unknowingly, she had chosen Callum over the two men who had been by her side as the seasons changed.

"Peyton, I'm giving you an out, the turn off the highway. Listen to Graham and take it. Walk away," he said sadly.

She stared at her hands and slowly let go of his shirt. Then she looked up at him and shook her head. "I can't. I've tried, Callum. My heart wants to forgive you. I don't think I'll be truly free until it does," she confessed.

"That's what you want?" Callum asked.

Peyton nodded. "Give me closure. Give me right now. Make me believe you. That's it. That's all I want."

Lie. I want more.

But I can't have more. Truth.

Relief filled his eyes as he gave her a slight smile and a nod. "I wish I could offer you more, Peyton."

"But you can't. So, why try? Let's just make the wedding

something amazing. Then *mutually* part ways this time."

"Okay," Callum said and dropped his hands from her. "Want me to walk you home?"

She gave him a bittersweet smile. He used to ask her that same question after every shift she finished at the hotel.

Peyton nodded, not trusting her voice. Then she turned around and made her way back to the lake. He didn't grab her hand like he used to. Instead, he walked in sync with her. When she turned her head and looked at him, his lips were pressed hard together as he concentrated on what was ahead of him. The old him was in there somewhere. The moment he caught her staring, she decided that she would try to find him again.

Get ready, heart. We won't survive this time.

Twenty-Two

"Peyton," he whispered in her ear.

With her eyes still closed, she smiled. "Yes," she breathed.

He placed a kiss on her neck, and she leant back on his chest, letting his arms circle around her waist.

"Look up at the cherry blossoms."

Opening her eyes, she peeked up to see the light shining through. Beautiful and glorious. It reflected off the pink flowers, making them almost clear.

Her smile grew larger as she softly said, "Beautiful."

"I know," Callum said.

Peyton turned her head to see him staring at her.

"But they're nothing compared to you. Nothing will ever be as beautiful as you."

She twisted her body so that she was on her side then cuddled up next to him. The ridiculous smile on her face didn't go away and she kissed his jaw. It never felt real when he complimented her. It was new. But she was in love with the way he saw her and spoke of her. Since being released from hospital, she had spent her days in bed recovering. Today was an exception. The moment Callum had shown up at her window, she'd handed him a blanket and had him help her out of her room. Then he laid out the blanket and they sat under their tree.

"This is my favourite spot in the world," he said, holding her

tighter.

Peyton glanced up at the flowers one more time before she said, "I told you it was just a kiss."

"It wasn't. I knew it even before you asked. I've known it would be more with you the moment I held your hand when we were thirteen. It took four years, but I'm finally yours. I love this tree. Each time I think of it, I think of what it felt like kissing you for the first time."

He didn't let her reply to him. He made her speechless. It also didn't help that he pressed his lips on hers, kissing her the way he had claimed her heart.

Falling in love with Callum was as simple as falling in love with breathing:

One of the most unknowing, willing, natural and completely necessary tasks one does.

Peyton stopped at her door and stared at the stained-glass panels. She wasn't sure if she should invite Callum in or not. She wanted time with him to discover if the old him was still inside. Just wrapped in him somewhere. One last time before fate caught up with them.

"I'll let you go, Peyton. I have to finish up work on the designs," Callum said behind her.

She felt both disappointed and relieved. Pulling out her house keys, she turned around and then smiled at him. In this moment, he didn't seem so guarded. Instead, he looked comfortable. It filled her with hope. There was a chance that he would open up to her. In time.

"Do you mind stopping by the hotel tomorrow? We can go over it before the tradies come back on Monday."

He nodded. "Sounds good to me. I'll see you tomorrow. Goodnight, Peyton."

"Goodnight, Callum," she said, turning back to her front door. Then she placed the key into the lock as she heard his footsteps trail down the stairs. With a small sigh, she twisted the key and opened the door.

She wanted to turn around and watch him walk across the road. She wanted to know if he looked over his shoulder just before he walked into his house. But she didn't. She wanted her heart to miss him more, to make all the pain somehow worth it in the end.

Peyton stepped into the quiet house and dropped her bag on the wooden floor, not caring to put it away. The only work she had to concentrate on was the plan for the cabins. Renovating them would be costly, but replacing the windows with floor-to-ceiling size ones would be a great selling point for guests. It would be like the lake and forest were an extension of the cabins.

She closed the door behind her and went into the kitchen. Since her aunt and uncle had moved to enjoy their retirement on the peninsula, the house had become dark and quiet. Peyton used to welcome the loneliness, but now, she hated it. When she had been with Callum on Sunday night, she hadn't been quite alone. She had been wrapped in him as they'd opened themselves to sharing the loneliness they were in. She'd felt connected and wanted.

It probably hadn't been the best idea to kiss him in the middle of the town's main road. Anyone could have seen. No doubt the town gossipers had. She didn't care about their opinions, though. She loved this town and the people, but this was between Callum and her.

She couldn't ignore the way that he had kissed her and held her. The way he'd begged her. The way he'd sighed her name. It was utterly unforgettable. She wanted more. But he wouldn't let her. The truth was stopping him. And the truth was something Peyton wanted and didn't want. The truth, she was sure, would break her to the point where breathing wasn't enough.

The vibrating of her phone in her pocket had Peyton pulling it out. When she swiped the screen and checked her messages, she had found a new one from Madilynne in her inbox.

> **Madilynne**: I'm sorry that I left you with him. We'll talk about him being back tomorrow. You should have told me, Peyton. I'm not mad. I

understand. Graham isn't mad, either. He wants to talk to you. Come over, but he says you can't ask him about Callum. He says that it's Callum's choice to tell you and that Graham can't take that away from you and him. I'll see you soon.
Peyton: Okay. I'm on my way.

She needed to see Graham. She needed some assurance from him. That the choice she was making was one that would be worth something in the end. It didn't have to mean forever. It just had to mean something.

Peyton took out the keys from her pocket and walked out of the house. Graham wanted to see her. Even though he'd broken the tradition and trust they had, she couldn't turn her back on him.

After closing the door behind her, Peyton ran down the stairs and to the driveway. Then she unlocked her Volkswagen Golf. The moment the lights flashed and the car made a sound, she opened the driver's side door and got in.

Peyton reached for the seatbelt and clicked it in place, desperate to speak to her best friends. She put a hand on the steering wheel as she inserted the key into the ignition. The second it clicked, she froze. She didn't turn the key all the way. Instead, the click brought flashes of the pictures she had seen in the newspapers the day after her parents had died.

Images of the mangled car brought tears running down her face, and then images of flowers placed by the side of the road brought the sobs. It was the first time she'd sat in the driver's seat since the accident. Her aunt drove her if she needed to be anywhere that wasn't within walking distance. Her heart twisted as she remembered the picture of her mother and father's happy faces on the front of the paper. They had been taken from her. That was the day her father hadn't fulfilled his promise.

Tears streamed down her face as she tried to fight off the pain. She reached into her pocket and took out her phone. Then unlocked it and pulled up Graham's number. Her eyes were firmly set on the steering wheel before she pressed the green button to call him.

It rang twice before he answered. "Hello."

Peyton didn't answer, but rather, she sobbed.

"Peyton, are you okay? What's wrong? What did he do to you?" Graham's voice was heartbreaking. She hated that she was this weak, this scared of the past, that it affected her present.

"I can't get out, Graham," she cried.

"Out of where, Peyton? Tell me! Where are you?" he asked in a desperate yell.

"I want to see you, but I can't. I keep seeing their faces. I keep seeing the wrecked car. I can't get to you." Peyton placed her forehead on the wheel and cried.

It was too much. She didn't think. She just needed to be at the farm. She needed her friends.

"No, don't think about them like that, Peyton. I'm here. Think of your parents with you and laughing. Don't think of the accident. Please. Please don't," he begged, sounding like he himself was about to cry.

"I can't get out of the car, Graham. I can't get out. Help me, please. I need you."

"Madilynne, call Callum right now!" he yelled. "I'm here, Peyton. I'm here. I can't get to you."

"Why?" Peyton asked in a small voice.

"I've been drinking. I didn't think you'd want to see me. I'm sorry. I shouldn't have told Madilynne that I wanted to see you. I'm getting Callum, okay? You're not going to be alone. You're never alone. I'll be here until he gets there." He was trying to calm her, but Peyton could still hear the fear in his voice.

"He's not picking up!" Peyton heard Madilynne cry out desperately.

"Try again!" Graham roared. "Don't slip, Peyton. I don't want to see you go into that state again. You're strong. You've been strong. Don't shut down on me."

Darkness started to encroach, attempting to suffocate the light around her. So she closed her eyes and concentrated on his voice. Her heart pounded violently against her chest and her breathing was gasps as she tried to inhale enough oxygen to calm her body.

She felt her phone slip from her fingers and she whispered, "I'm sorry. I'm so sorry."

She was afraid of the darkness that was swallowing her. But she wanted the pain to stop, so she welcomed it. She'd let it win. She was too tired to fight.

"It's okay, Graham. I have her now." His voice sounded so close, but she knew he wasn't. Physically, he was, but emotionally, he was too far gone. "No, don't worry. Sober up. I'll stay with her. I won't leave her alone tonight. Make your time with Mads count. I'll let her call you. Okay, bye."

Peyton squeezed her eyes, seeking the light. She'd spent years fighting the darkness. She didn't want it to win. But the loneliness enticed the darkness. It fed it temptation.

"Pey, I'm here. Let me take care of you."

Pey.

She slowly opened her eyes and stared at the Volkswagen logo. His nickname for her drew her out of the state that she'd been falling into. She couldn't look at him, though. Her heart had bled too much pain. It had been denied too much from him. Her heart decided that it no longer needed a filter.

"I'm in love with you," she confessed. "Don't you see that?"

Callum placed a hand on her thigh. Peyton looked down to see the cherry blossoms poking out from the long sleeve top he wore. Then she dropped her hand from the steering wheel and placed it on top of his. Her fingers slowly stroked his until suddenly Callum flipped his hand over and threaded his fingers with hers.

"Look at me, Peyton."

She turned her head and saw those grey eyes full of pain and relief.

"Let me take you inside. I'll take care of you."

Peyton's eyelids fluttered once and she nodded. Callum stood up and reached over, unbuckling her seatbelt. Then he crouched down and pulled out the key from the ignition. He gave her a reassuring smile before she looped her arms around his neck and he pulled her out of the car. As she held him tightly in her arms, he used his body to close the car door and then carried her up the steps to the front door.

Her car sounded as Callum locked it and she rested her head against his collarbone.

"I think I left the door unlocked," she said quietly.

He bent down and, from under her, reached for the doorknob. Then twisted it once and the door opened. Not saying anything, he walked into the house and kicked the door close behind him. Looking up, Peyton stared at the way his eyes roamed over the dark and quiet house. The confused expression on his face was like he was thinking of where he should put her.

"Bedroom," she said, answering a question he hadn't voiced.

He looked down at her and nodded. The way his eyes flashed gave her a glimpse of the person he was hiding from her. She had confessed that she was still in love with him, but he hadn't said a word. She had known he wouldn't. But her heart had needed the relief that came from expressing those words. It had liberated her.

Callum walked them to her bedroom door and pushed it opened with his shoulder. The moment they stood inside, he made his way to the bed and laid her on it. From head to toe, his eyes slowly swept over her. Then he inhaled and exhaled before his eyes met hers.

"I have to confess something and I want to say it right. Tell me yes," he said as he pulled the shirt over his head.

Peyton sat up the moment his hands were on his jeans. "Yes," she breathed out and sat on the edge of the mattress.

"Thank you," he said as he undid the button of his pants.

He gave her a smile that warmed her aching heart. She wanted whatever he could give her.

Peyton's fingers reached her silk blouse, but Callum's hands were on hers and stopped her. He didn't say a word as he unbuttoned the top she was wearing and pulled it off her body. Her breathing was embarrassing. No sequence, just pants of anticipation.

"Stand up for me," he instructed, and Peyton did.

She felt empowered the moment he got on his knees and dug his fingers into her hips. The sight was one she'd mark as one of her favourites. His hands left her and trailed the side of her body until he reached the knee-high boots she had on. He slowly unzipped one boot before pulling it off her leg and then the other. Then he stood back up and wrapped his arms around her waist as his fingers found the zip of her skirt.

Callum held his breath as he pulled the zipper down. The control in his eyes snapped, and she could see the desire in them. She would beg him if he tried to stop this. She needed him like she needed the next breath of air to enter and relieve her burning lungs.

He pulled down her skirt and said, "Lie back, Pey."

Her knees went weak at just the sound of that three-letter name. She took a step back and sat on the bed. Callum's pulling down of his jeans and underwear caused her to freeze. He noticed her staring, but she didn't care. He was glorious and beautiful. And for however long this lasted, he was hers and she was his.

He stepped forward and kissed her deeply. The feel of his lips on hers caused her to ache all over, needing him. Then his hands made their way to the clasp of her bra, and in one swift move, he had it off her. Peyton moved back on the bed before he softly pushed her on the mattress. His tongue passed her lips and found hers as they stroked, kissed, and sucked. Fighting against each other before conceding defeat. Over and over until his hands reached the side of her underwear. Then he broke from her lips as she lifted her hips for him to take off the last piece of clothing she was wearing.

The moment he threw it on the floor, he settled between her legs. Then he propped himself on his elbows as he stared at her with a look she hadn't seen in years.

Next, he kissed her lips once before the tip of him was at her entrance. Holding her breath, she expected him to thrust straight into her. But he didn't, so she waited. Peyton wet her bottom lip as she kept her eyes focused on him, wondering.

Callum took a sharp breath in and studied where their bodies almost connected. He lifted his stare back at her. The sweet glint in his eye had made her heart beat harder in her chest.

"I'm confessing to you this way because, the moment I'm in you, I'm the most fragile. I'm the truest form of me when I'm in you, Peyton. I'm at my weakest when I'm this connected to you, emotionally and physically. This is the right way to show you how true and honest I am."

She felt him tense, so she reached up and held his arms, making sure that he knew she was right here with him. Then she nodded her approval before he slowly entered her. It was achingly slow, but she loved it nonetheless.

"In this moment, right here and right now," he said, pushing himself farther into her.

She bit back the need to close her eyes. She kept them open, memorising him and the look of utter pleasure that consumed his face.

He was halfway in when he thrust hard into her, making her gasp. "I'm in love with you, Peyton Olivia Spencer."

"Say it again," she whispered.

Her heart hadn't found a way to operate its basic function. He'd said it. Words she'd never expected, words that had been meant for this moment and words that were about now and not the past.

She expected him to pull out and enter her again like last time. But Callum rested his forehead on hers for a moment before he drew back to see her.

Still inside her, he whispered, "I'm in love with you, Pey. I've always been in love with you. Then and now. Forever and always. I love you."

Instead of protecting her heart, she brought his left wrist to her face and let the tattoo of her name touch her lips before she placed it on her chest and above her heart. Then she closed her eyes and allowed the pulse from his wrist to touch her chest. His heart beat for her, as did hers for him.

Peyton opened her eyes and said without reserve, "I love you, too, Callum."

Twenty-Three

She softly stroked the back of his head as he slept. Inhale and exhale, his breathing was constant and steady. Each breath he let out touched her chest. Callum had fallen asleep resting his ear to her heart.

Four times. That's how many times they'd made love. Each thrust, each digging of her nails into his flesh, each groan and moan had made it difficult for her to breathe. Peyton wasn't sure how her heart had functioned after he'd said that he was *in* love with her. Not then, but now.

"I've spent the last four years in hell. Life hasn't made sense since you."

They were the words he'd whispered before he'd fallen asleep. Peyton had closed her eyes and let them brand every cell in her body. She believed him. Callum's being inside her as he confessed his love was something that she hadn't been able to imagine. It had been powerful, moving.

And it had also been heartbreaking. They'd made their ending even more difficult. She'd known that the moment that he'd let those words be heard. But she had seen the freedom in his eyes when the truth had been revealed.

Peyton continued to run her fingers through his hair as she stared at the ceiling. She'd been up for most of the night, terrified that he'd leave her or that it had all been a dream.

Callum Reid is my nightmare, my dream come true.

He's my sometimes and my forever.

He's the man who will undoubtedly destroy the person I am.

He will either liberate or kill my heart…

And I would let him do it.

I would let him crush my soul to redeem his.

In some way, he had already achieved her forgiveness. He had put the doubts to rest. Throughout the years, she'd believed that it had been nothing but a lie to him, that his feelings for her had never been genuine. These doubts had clung to her heart and told her not to ever forget. But when he'd said that he was in love with her, those doubts had detached themselves and faded away.

This is a now moment.

She knew that it wasn't a forever moment. The ending was close; she felt it in every beat of his heart and her own. Until she knew what a sometimes moment was, she would file last night as one of them. Sometimes didn't mean all the time. Sometimes meant once, maybe twice. *They* were once, maybe twice. The thought had her heart beating fast in aches.

"Your heartbeat picked up. What are you thinking about, Peyton?"

The caressing of her fingers stopped at the sound of his voice. He didn't move to meet her glance. Instead, he let his fingers trace the skin of her stomach. She held her breath and thought of what to say.

The ending? That you're in love with me? That I'm in love with you? Our ending?

Peyton breathed out and let her fingers resume their strokes, not saying a word. Unable to trust the words that would come from her mouth, she kept quiet.

"I meant what I said last night," he said before he propped himself up and looked down at her.

Peyton nodded her head at him and sat up, resting her back on the headboard. Then she let out a sigh and combed her hair with her fingers.

"We just made things a lot more difficult, Callum," she pointed out.

"The sex part? Or the 'I love you' part?" he asked, sitting up and facing her.

"Both."

Callum took her hands and pulled her into his lap, straddling him. She felt him under her, but the look in his eyes wasn't just about making love again. There was something more and she hoped to find it someday. But for now she leant forward and placed a kiss on the cherry blossom that was on his shoulder.

Her lips left Callum's tattooed skin when he said, "Just because we can't have forever doesn't mean I'm going to love you any less, Peyton."

She straightened her body as she looked into his grey eyes. This morning, they were light, reflecting the honesty that was evident in his voice.

No forever. We have love, but no forever.

"Unlove me, Callum," she instructed.

He tensed and his face grew sad. His hands were on her waist, holding her to him almost as if he were afraid of her leaving.

"Could you unlove me, Peyton?"

She wrapped her hand around his left wrist and turned it over, looking at her tattooed name. Using her right hand to steady his wrist, she let her left index finger trace each letter.

"No," she said and met his eyes. "I've spent over four years trying to. Unloving you is impossible and so is loving you. Could you unlove me?" she asked once more.

He gazed down at his tattoos, and a sad smile touched his lips. "No. Every part of me has loved you since the start. I could never unlove you, Peyton."

Even though she knew what the end held for them, she let herself fall in love with his words. This was what seventeen-year-old Peyton had wanted and what twenty-one-year-old Peyton had avoided. But in this moment, there was no difference. The Peyton in this moment loved him and his words. From now on, she'd only listen to 'in the moment Peyton.' She would be the one to benefit from his love for now.

Bringing his wrist to her mouth, she kissed her name and

then let her lips touch every tattooed cherry blossom up his arm. When she reached his shoulder, she left a lingering kiss on the largest one near his collarbone. Letting go of his wrist, she placed her hands on his cheeks and kept eyes locked on his. Then she breathed in deeply before she lifted her hips and positioned herself over him.

"Love me as hard as you can for the rest of the moments we have together," she breathed before slowly sank down on him.

His fingers dug into her waist as he panted. Her breathing mirrored his, and she let out a soft moan. The feeling of being complete washed over her. Dropping her head to his shoulder, she stilled and memorised the feeling of him filling her.

"If forever existed, I would have wanted it with you," he whispered in her ear.

Peyton's eyes fluttered closed at his words. The same words that had caused her heart to shrivel and throb. Lifting her hips, she slowly sank back down. With Callum's hands on her hips, guiding her, she repeated her movements, finding a rhythm of undeniable pleasure.

Forever doesn't exist.

The concept of it all is just a process, a thought we create to give us confidence in our choices, a promise before the end.

Forever is like a blooming cherry blossom, beautiful even after the wind has blown it away from home to settle on the tainted ground below.

Peyton kissed his neck several times before she trailed her lips up to his jaw and then his ear. The way Callum thrust hard into caused her to moan as he took control.

"If I could have forever with anyone, I'd want it with you, Callum."

Callum and I are cherry blossoms.
We flourish.
We taint.
We lie about what we really want.
We want a forever that has died long before us.
Callum and I,
We're dying.

Twenty-Four

Dear Peyton,

I don't know where you are in life at the moment, but I hope you're happy. I hope that, whatever happens, you don't hate Callum Reid. If you do, I'm sorry. That's entirely my fault. In this moment, right now, it was a choice I made because I wanted him to make me happy. I wanted him to make me better. Being with him, I feel, and I haven't felt in a long time. But you know that all too well.

You're probably reading this because he's gone and you're wondering why you did this. You love him, Peyton. That's why. Because you would rather be loved by him for now than not at all. Whatever his reasons are for leaving this time round, accept them. You got a lot more than last time.

I know that I should have forced him away a lot sooner, but he's the one I can't let go. I know he will break my heart, I knew that going into it all. But I've been lonely for so long that I just wanted to be loved by him, like I always have. I hope that he's told you what 'Sometimes Moments' are, because I have a feeling it was what we were and all we could have.

Maybe, in the short space of time he allowed us to have together, we had our forever. That's what I'll tell myself. It's been a lonely life, Peyton, but it's been a good one, without or without Callum. I hope that you've mended things with Jay and Graham. Being with Callum again made me realise just how much my love for them all differs. I love Graham more purely because he gave me the strength I needed. And Jay... I will love him for his friendship. But Callum I love the most. I have always loved Callum the most. I love him more than I love breathing. I love him more than the pain I have to endure to be with him and to save him. I love him more than I love myself, and I love him enough to sacrifice a forever with him for now.

I know you're hurt, Peyton. I can feel it right now. But your heart loves him enough to give up a future with him. You see, the heart is a funny thing. So vital yet so easily broken. It doesn't take much to destroy an organ. But he will destroy more than that; he will destroy your soul and your belief. Give it time, Peyton. You will learn all over again. You will be okay.

I know that, in the end, this is all worth it. I hope that you told him that he found redemption the moment he walked back into your life. Give him his freedom, Peyton. Let him walk away.

Your heart will beat again. It will find a will to live and love.

I believe in you.
Peyton.

Pressing save and labelling the document "When he's gone," Peyton closed her laptop. Then she looked down at the rug to see him asleep near the fireplace, his designs sprawled across the floor.

After they'd made love, he'd kissed her and lain next to her until he'd gotten off the bed and put his clothes on. The sight of him dressing had been an eye opener. Words were nothing in comparison to actions. And Callum's actions had proved that this was temporary for them. He'd given her one last kiss before he'd said that he had to go home and shower.

She hadn't expected him at her bathroom door as she'd lain in the bath this morning. He had placed the designs on the sink counter, walked over to her, and sat next to the tub. He'd held her hand as they'd enjoyed the peaceful moment. By the time the hot water had turned lukewarm, Callum had let go of her hand and stood up. She'd tilted her head at him, and he'd kissed her forehead before telling her that he'd let her bathe. Once he'd walked out, she'd sat in the water until it had gone cold before she'd gotten out and changed.

Now, sitting on the couch, she watched him sleep. He hadn't been himself since returning to her house, his smile never quite becoming full and his eyes filled in concern. When she'd asked him what was wrong, he'd blamed it on a mild headache and exhaustion with working on the designs so late.

Peyton removed the laptop from her lap and placed it on the blanket she had been using to cover her legs before approaching the fireplace. After picking up a log from the basket, she threw it in the pit and watched the flames inhale the wood.

Turning around, she got on her knees and started to pick up the pens around Callum. She was just able to see the design of the lakeside dance floor, but he was sleeping over most of the design. Slowly, she pulled on the piece of paper that was under his arm. When she got it out from under him, Callum opened his eyes and sat up. She couldn't help but laugh at the startled look on his face.

"How long have I been asleep?" he asked, rubbing his eyes.

Placing the paper on the coffee table, Peyton said, "Not long. Few hours, I think. It's almost two."

Callum threw his head back and sighed. "Should have woken me. We missed lunch."

"You looked like you needed sleep. I got work done and prepped everything for when my first guests arrive on Monday.

I've been busy." She smiled and picked up the creased design. "Is this for the lakeside dance floor for the wedding?"

She took in the design. It was beautiful. From what she could see, the dance floor would be an octagon. On the edges, small lights were to be placed in a cut in the wood, and in the middle would be a glass plate.

"You like it?" he asked.

Peyton couldn't help the smile that developed on her face. "I love it."

"That's a relief. It's not quite done yet. I need to modify some of the measurements and add an inner row of lights. I want posts outside of the dance floor where we can have lights above them while they dance. On the water, I was thinking floating lanterns. That way, it adds to the scenery. I think Marissa would like that."

She could just imagine the bride and groom dancing after the sun had set. The way the lanterns would reflect on the water would be a perfect backing for photos. She couldn't help the jealousy she felt. Marissa and Oliver's wedding would be absolutely stunning.

"It is going to be beautiful, Callum. Thank you for this," she said gratefully.

The concept was just what The Spencer-Dayle needed. It would be as beautiful as it had been when her parents had run the place. Callum Reid was her saviour.

Peyton frowned the moment she saw the sullen expression on his face. "What's wrong?" she asked.

Callum scratched his head and his shoulders sagged. "I'm leaving Daylesford tonight."

No.

Peyton held the design tighter, almost ripping it. She had expected him to leave sometime, but the breathtaking ache in her chest proved that she wasn't ready for him to go. Their ending had caught up with them. He would be gone in a matter of hours.

She placed the paper in her lap and said, "Okay."

She wasn't sure what else to say, but her eyes had started to water. Blinking quickly, she gave him a smile. When she went to stand up, Callum grabbed her wrist to stop her and pulled her into his arms. He held her tight against his chest, and that's when the tears she tried to prevent started to roll down her cheeks. She would now know a life without him.

Peyton wrapped her arms around his waist. It would be for the last time, and she'd memorise it and reflect on it later in life.

"It's only for the rest of the weekend," he said.

Peyton pulled back and stared at him. "What?"

Callum's hands cupped her face before his thumbs wiped away her tears. "Tonight's Oliver's bachelor party."

Relief poured through her. The end had once again been prolonged. She needed him for bit longer. Her heart wasn't ready to let him go just yet.

"I thought..." she managed out before she shook her head.

"We have until the wedding," he reminded her. Then he pushed back her hair and kissed her lips once.

"What time are you leaving?"

"I have to stop by my apartment before I see Oliver. I would need to leave town at about four."

Her eyebrows furrowed. "That's in two hours."

"Yeah. I'm sorry. I've spent the week trying to tell you, but I thought I'd give you space. And then, well..." He stopped, referring to their confessions and the sex between them.

"I have you for two hours."

He nodded. "You do. I'm at your mercy, Peyton Spencer. What do you want to do for two hours?"

The grin on his face had her rolling her eyes. Peyton stood up and looked down at him. "I'd like you to hold me for two hours."

It surprised her to see his grin grow larger.

"I can do that. I *want* to do that."

Callum stood up and threaded his fingers with hers. She peeked at and then smiled at their connection. Her heart approved of their hand holding with heavy beats against her ribcage.

"Bedroom or couch?" he asked with a raised brow.

"Couch," she said, leading him to it.

He picked up her laptop and placed it on the coffee table. Her eyes stared at it sitting on the glass top. Her letter to herself was saved there. For a moment, she had believed that she was hours away from rereading it. Pushing the thought of the letter away, she took in his chin dimple that she loved. Callum tugged her onto the couch, and she placed her head on the cushion, lying next to him. Then he shifted and placed his chin on the top of her head, before he wrapped his arm around her body.

She felt his chest rise and fall against her back as she stared at her laptop. Less than two weeks. That's what they had left. It would only be weeks until she read the letter she wrote. Weeks left of enduring the slow death of her heart.

"I'll be back on Monday," Callum said softly.

She held her breath. Déjà vu. In that one second, she was back in his arms in the forest. He had said the same words moments after she'd lost her virginity to him.

Knowing these were potentially the last moments they had together, Peyton closed her eyes. "Okay."

Twenty-Five

Peyton stared at the calendar on her laptop. *Tomorrow.* He promised he'd be back tomorrow. But the doubt was still settled in her heart. She wouldn't hold her breath. He had kissed her goodbye before he'd gotten in his car and driven away. This time, Peyton had watched. His kiss hadn't felt final against her lips. But then again, if it had, she'd have ignored it.

Her phone buzzed and she reached for it immediately. The moment that she saw his name, a foolish smile broke upon her face.

> **Callum**: Less than twenty-four hours, Peyton.
> **Peyton**: Unless something happens.
> **Callum**: Like?

Like you could be in an accident like my parents. Like you could find the love of your life at lunch.

> **Peyton**: You might meet your future wife. If you do, stay with her. Spend all night with her. Make her laugh. Make an impression. Fall hopelessly in love with her. And most importantly, forget me. She will make it possible.

She turned off her phone and placed it on her desk. It was the truth and it had needed to be said. It would make their goodbye easier if he were to meet *her* in the city. Peyton would be happy. She craved it to happen.

There was no future with him. She had the hotel and Daylesford. He had the city and his job as an architect. There would be no compromise. She could never leave this town. She could never walk away from the hotel. It was what had kept her alive all these years. She lived for the hotel.

"When am I ever going to see you happy again?"

Peyton looked up to see Madilynne leaning on the doorframe of her office. She looked over her best friend and was instantly jealous. Madilynne was the beautiful one. She had the amazing, petite figure and the personality. But most of all, Madilynne was free. And Peyton was grounded, not meant to fly.

She shrugged at Madilynne and reached for the folder that Jenny had left her. "Some people don't deserve happiness, Mads."

Madilynne pushed off the doorframe and sat in the seat in front of her. "That is bullshit and you know it, Peyton. If anyone deserves to be happy, it's *you*."

Peyton put the folder down and looked at her best friend. "Because my boyfriend left me days after I gave him my virginity and then, months later, my parents died in a car accident? Is that why I deserve to be happy above others? Because I'm slightly unfortunate?"

"What happened to you, Peyton?" Madilynne stared at her as if attempting to find the old Peyton somewhere on the surface.

"You know I'm right, Mads."

"This hollow shell of what you were saved your life, Peyton. I don't like not seeing that smile you had and that love in your eyes, but you would have died, too. You should see that as the light to start over. We would have buried you. And that's the worst pain any of us could have gone through."

Peyton winced and noticed the sad gleam in her friend's eyes. She decided it was time they changed the subject. "How is Graham?"

Madilynne sighed. "He's okay. He's worried about you. He's always worried about you. I respect the way he loves you."

Peyton heard the sadness in her voice, and that's when she remembered what Callum said to Graham on the phone.

"Make your time with Mads count."

"Madilynne, what did Callum mean by making Graham's time with you count on Friday?" Peyton asked.

Madilynne looked away for a second before she met Peyton's eyes. Her eyes pleaded for Peyton to silence the topic of Graham.

The sad look had Peyton feeling guilty and realising that for a long time she had been pushing Graham to the wrong person. For years, she believed their high school friend, Krista, was the one Graham had been in love with. "It was never about Krista, was it?"

Madilynne shook her head. "The moment Graham saw you on that bench, it was game over for us. He wanted to protect you. We let you believe it was Krista. And when I found out about the promise ring, I hated you. But I knew it could be the chance for you to smile again. I told him to stay here in Daylesford. You needed him."

I'm a misfortune to people's lives.

Peyton hung her head and let out a sigh. She had been selfish all these years. She truly did deserve to be lonely.

"I'm so sorry that I took him from you, Madilynne. I didn't know. I was pushing him to pursue Krista. Had I known it was you… I'm sorry. You had every right to hate me and still hate me."

Madilynne let out a laugh. "You're my best friend. I was envious. We decided not to start anything because you needed us. We couldn't upset you. We lost you for a long time. Graham somehow brought you back. That's why I made him stay."

Peyton gave her a tight smile. Madilynne and Graham had sacrificed a relationship together for her. This time, there would be no more sacrificing.

She looked Madilynne in the eye and breathed out, "Please

tell me you both made your time together on the farm count?"

Madilynne's cheeks reddened. She never blushed. "You mean did we have sex?"

Peyton nodded.

"We made our time together count. We felt guilty because we couldn't get to you since we had drunk a little. And well, we kissed and you know how sex works."

She should have been sick at the thought of her two best friends hooking up, but Peyton was relieved. She didn't think she could live with the guilt for the rest of her life. That she was the one to prevent them from being together.

"Do you love him?" Peyton asked.

"Yes. But I love you more. That's why it could only be a one-time thing."

Peyton ignored what Madilynne had said. She refused to believe that it was. "Do something for me."

"You know I would do anything for you, Peyton."

She smiled, knowing that Madilynne had sacrificed more than she should for her. "You get him the hell out of Daylesford and off that farm. Take him to the city with you."

Madilynne let out a sigh. "He won't leave without you. He'll never leave if you don't."

Peyton gave Madilynne a smile before she said, "We'll figure it out. I owe you both it."

"No you don't, Peyton. We chose this for us."

Before Peyton could argue, a knock on the door had her lifting her eyes. Her breath caught the moment she looked at Jay. He didn't have a smooth, relaxed expression on his face. Instead, he was a brute version of what she had known of him.

"Mads, your daddy's looking for you. He's down at the pub," Jay said.

Madilynne leant forward, and Peyton met her eyes. "Unlike Jay or Graham, I approve of Callum. You never have to explain yourself to any of us," Madilynne softly said. Then she got up from the chair and walked out the door.

Peyton's eyes locked with Jay's. She expected him to turn and follow Madilynne out of the hotel. But Jay took a step into her office. And then another, continuing until he was standing in front of her.

"I'm sorry to do this to you, Peyton. But you need a little perspective," Jay said. Hate laced in his voice.

Peyton's eyebrows furrowed. "What do you—"

Jay interrupted her by pulling out a folded bundle of papers and dropping it on her desk. Confused, Peyton picked up the papers and opened it. Her heart sank the moment she looked at what was written.

Termination of Contract for Breach.

She inhaled and exhaled, but no air reached her lungs. As her eyes scanned the paper, she felt every painful throb of her heart.

Then her eyes landed on a sentence she never thought she'd ever read.

Please take notice of the intended termination of the business relationship between The Spencer-Dayle and Daylesford Pub.

"You're terminating our business relationship?" Peyton asked, utterly shocked.

Failure to carry out contractual obligations.

She couldn't look away from the letter. The Spencer-Dayle heavily used their relationship with the pub to generate more visitors. Without the pub, it would financially and reputably cost the hotel. The pub tours of the area included Jay's and the tour included lunch at The Spencer-Dayle. If her hotel had any chance of surviving she would have to focus on what made money—weddings.

"Yes. It's the *only* way."

Peyton stood up and stared at the man she had once called a friend. "Only way?"

"This isn't you, Peyton. It's a small goddamn town. We know what you've done with him. We've all seen it. You're better than that. You let him touch you? He broke your fucking heart! It's the town or Callum. You can't have both!" Jay roared. So much anger filled his voice.

"No," she bit back. "This is more personal for you. This is about you and Callum."

"You're acting like a love-struck teenager. Don't you see how your actions reflect on all of us? If this hotel fails because of you and your foolish heart, we all go down with it. Terminating the contract means that what happens only affects your hotel. It's the town or Callum, Peyton. Or better yet, it's your parents' hotel or him," Jay said. His body was strung up tight, and she saw the vein in his neck sticking out.

Peyton flinched, dropped the letter onto her desk, and blinked. "This is all about you, Jay. No one sees this the way you do. You're being ridiculous."

"I'm being ridiculous?" Jay hissed. "I'm not the one *fucking* someone who'll toss me aside. He ain't ever staying for you."

Peyton swallowed hard, hoping it would numb the heated pain in her chest. Jay was her friend. At least she'd thought he was.

"He'll never love you. I was here for you when he wasn't. You should have loved *me*, Peyton."

She picked up the termination letter, held it tight, and looked at Jay. The anger and hate in his eyes were ugly on him. Right now, he wasn't the person she had once adored.

"I can't love a man who will selfishly hurt me, Jay. I could never love you," she said without hesitation.

Jay winced. "You're a hypocrite! You love Callum and he has hurt you."

Peyton shook her head. "But Callum would never damage my livelihood. This hotel is my life. He would never do anything to jeopardise its survival. You, Jay... You are a selfish man."

"Then you're gonna wanna hope he sticks by you when this place dies," Jay said with so much disgust that it made her sick. Then he stormed out of her office and the hotel, the slammed door echoing throughout the entire building.

Peyton sank down onto the chair and stared at the letter in her hand. Her head spun at the sight of it. The Spencer-Dayle embodied local partnerships and produce. If it lost all these businesses, it lost its image.

She hoped Jay's decision wouldn't rub off on the rest of the town businesses.

Twenty-Six

Sitting at her desk, Peyton looked at the termination letter from the pub. The letter never suggested arbitration, just straight termination. It had been just over half an hour since Jay dropped the notice in front of her, now she held and stared at it. So much hate ran through her veins. If she wanted to play unfair, she could have dragged Daisy into it, but she hadn't.

The town or Callum...

That's what Jay wanted. In his eyes, she had betrayed him and the town. He was punishing her more than the hotel. The hotel happened to be in the crossfire. Without the pub, she wouldn't be able to keep the hotel running after the wedding. The Spencer-Dayle pub had been the hotel's biggest business partnership other than the Scott lavender farm.

There would be no negotiation, and right now, the hotel would be out of business by the end of the month if other businesses followed Jay's actions. Nothing she had saved up for could pull The Spencer-Dayle out of that. Finding businesses outside of town would be difficult. Most of the towns that surrounded Daylesford had their own community business relationships.

Peyton sighed and covered her face with her hands. "What the hell do I do?" she asked herself, hoping to come up with an answer.

"You stand tall and show him that *he* needs the hotel, not the other way round."

Peyton looked up to see Jenny standing at the door with her arms crossed over her chest.

"You know how important the pub is," Peyton said, holding the termination paper up to her.

"Yes, but you have still have one of the most important businesses that still believes in you. And sometimes, Peyton, that's all it takes. Just one," Jenny said.

"Jenny, this is where, as your friend, I tell you to take the Hyatt position. I can't keep this place alive for much longer. I have enough to pay everyone severance pay…unless I find a new owner and negotiate them keeping the same staff," Peyton said, placing the letter on the desk and shaking her head.

Jenny leaned in close. "We're going to be okay. You're overthinking this. None of us will be here without you running this place, Peyton. Our loyalty is to you. If only Jay knew the importance of loyalty... Then he would never have done this to you. Talk of what he's done is starting to travel around town. The next move is yours. Whatever you do, we support you. As long as you're here, Peyton, we will be here."

Jenny's support had Peyton's tears forming. "I let you all down. I'm so sorry."

"You didn't, Peyton. Listen to me," Jenny said as she took her hands. "We didn't think we'd have jobs after your parents died. With the state you were in, we were sure that was it of this place. But you fought hard—not because of Jay, but because you had people who love you and support you."

Peyton smiled. She would figure out a way through this. She didn't need the pub. She would just find a new partnership, even if that meant outside of town.

"And I know Callum would support you. He may not have physically been here, but I know he would have been by your side. The way he looked at you when you were teenagers… A love like that doesn't go away in time. You've never been alone, Peyton. We've been here. We will always be here. No matter your choice, we will support you. You come first to us—then the hotel. Realise that order. I may not be your mother, but I see you as my daughter and I will always treat you like one. I've never tried to replace your mother. She was a wonderful woman. But I have tried to be the maternal figure you needed all these years."

Peyton removed her hands from Jenny's and quickly wiped away the tears that were running down her cheeks. "Thank you, Jenny. I promise I will do everything in my power to make this hotel succeed. Not only for my parents, but for all of us. For everyone who believes in The Spencer-Dayle."

Jenny stood up and brushed the tear that had escaped away. "I'll always be proud of you, Peyton."

"Thanks, Jenny. For being here when you could have easily left," Peyton said and picked up the pub's letter.

"I wanted to watch you grow and make this place beautiful. I owed it to your parents to be the one to do it when they couldn't," Jenny said before she walked out of the office and the bell rang to signal she'd left the hotel.

The moment Peyton was alone, she reached for the closest pen and read through the termination contract between The Spencer-Dayle and Daylesford Pub. There was no need to contact the hotel's lawyer. She didn't want to go into arbitration or court over it. Jay was not only terminating the relationship between their businesses, but also their friendship.

Peyton looked through the pages to see that the hotel hadn't fulfilled its obligations in providing a reputable image for both organisations. She shook her head and placed the tip of the ballpoint on the paper. Then she took a deep breath and signed *Peyton Spencer* on the dotted line and added the date.

Peyton stood at the door of the pub. Her heart was beating so fast and hard that she was scared it would force itself out of her chest. But she needed to do this. She needed to prove just what she was capable of as a business owner. This wasn't a game.

This was her hotel's future that Jay had meddled with. If he was upset with her being with Callum, then he needed to take it out on her, not the hotel. But he had known it would hurt and that was why he had done it.

You can do this, Peyton.

She placed her hand on the door and pushed it open. The loud pub quietened the moment she took three steps inside. Countless pairs of eyes were on her, but she ignored them. Instead, she locked eyes with Jay.

He looked surprised to see her. Whispers could be heard around her, but Peyton tuned them out as she walked towards the counter.

"Mads isn't here. She just left with her folks," he said, wiping down the wood counter.

Before Peyton could say anything, Jay's father walked from the door to behind the counter, holding a clipboard.

"Jay, where are the invoices from today's del– Oh, hello, Peyton." He smiled.

Peyton looked at him, wondering why he was being so sweet to her. He sounded genuine, considering that now the hotel and pub were no longer associated with each other.

To be nice, Peyton gave him a tight smile and said, "Hello, Mr Preston."

"What the hell do you want?" Jay growled, annoyed.

Mr Preston dropped the clipboard on the counter with a bang. "I didn't raise you to speak to women like that, Jayden. You apologise to Miss Peyton."

Jay let out a short laugh. "I ain't apologising to her. I will never apologise to an ungrateful bitch."

And there was the truth. Peyton wouldn't challenge him. Reaching into her back pocket, she pulled out the letter. She saw the startled look on Mr Preston's face as his jaw dropped. Turning her attention towards Jay, she saw him eyeing the paper.

Ignoring the painful blows from his words, Peyton placed the termination notice on the counter and said, "It's signed and dated. I've emailed a copy to my lawyer."

Mr Preston picked up the letter and quickly read it. The moment he reached the last page, he winced. "Peyton, I had no idea he was doing this. Please retract this."

"Dad, no! We don't need her!" Jay roared.

Peyton saw the anger in Mr Preston's eyes as he looked at his son.

"Are you crazy, Jay? We need her and that hotel. Why do you think we've lasted this long? That hotel brings in revenue for us. That hotel brings in revenue for the entire town!"

No matter how much Jay had hurt her, she didn't want them to fight. "Mr Preston," she said, and he turned to face her, an apology filling his eyes. "It's signed. It's legally binding. I retract it and we have a lot of issues on our hands. It's easier and more affordable than arbitration and negotiation. Thank you for what this pub has done for the hotel."

He shook his head. "I had no idea my son was going to do this, Peyton. The pub wasn't in the best state when your parents approached me to sign a deal. When they came to town, they wanted to rebuild the hotel and include the town's businesses. Your parents are what made this town strive."

She ignored the remorseful look on Mr Preston's face and looked over at his son. "You got what you wanted, Jay. I got perspective from your letter. You showed me what an awful person you can really be. You're supposed to be my friend and you haven't. You have too much pride. Like our businesses relationship, our friendship is over."

He flinched like she had stabbed him in the chest. "You turned your back on this town. We've done nothing but be there for you."

Peyton looked down for a moment, saddened by what he said. "I'm choosing *me,* not you or the town. I will always be here when you or the town need me. I'm not a horrible person. I will never turn anyone away." She turned to Jay's father and smiled. "Thank you for trusting my parents."

Mr Preston frowned. "I am so sorry, Peyton."

She wanted to reassure him, but she couldn't. She wasn't sure if things would be okay. But she believed in her hotel. She would make sure The Spencer-Dayle flourished. It would go through some darker times to make it to the light.

"Jay," she said, getting his attention.

"What?"

She didn't like the flare in his nostrils. She missed his grin, but she knew they wouldn't be friends again.

"You're welcome at The Spencer-Dayle any time you'd like."

His eyes were wide in shock. "Why?"

Peyton gave him a smile and held the strap of her shoulder bag tight in her hand. "Because I'm not a spiteful person."

Refusing to give Jay or his father time to reply, Peyton turned on her heel and walked out of the pub. When she hit the sidewalk, she looked out at the afternoon sky. She took a moment and appreciated that she was living a good life, no matter the pain she had endured.

By the time she got to her street, it was getting close to sunset. In the end, even though it would cost her financially, she felt free. It was time to finally start new and find people who supported her. It was about her heart's choice. Callum and the hotel were a combined choice. He was what was rescuing it with his design. It would lure in more weddings.

She wanted a long bath to forget what a day she had. Jay's betrayal stung, but she would get over it. He was not the friend she'd once known.

After turning for the steps that led to her front door, Peyton stopped at the sight of Callum sitting on a step with a bundle of pink cherry blossoms in his hand.

"What are you doing here?" she asked.

He stood up, a smile on his face. "I needed to see you, Peyton. Your message had me driving back."

"But Oliver's—"

"You're what's important to me right now. You have no idea how much your message hurt me. It made me realise how little time we have and I didn't want to waste it. Oliver knows."

Peyton stepped in front of him and looked into those grey eyes she loved. No matter how much the ending would hurt her, she needed and missed him.

"I meant that message," she said.

He nodded. "I know you do, Pey. But I would never find her. Not when she's been here my entire life. If I could have forever with a wife, I'd want her to be you. No one could ever get me to fall hopelessly in love like you have."

Words that mask our timely death.

"How long have you been waiting here?" she asked as she took the cherry blossoms from him.

"An hour. I thought I'd surprise you."

"Are these from the tree?" she asked.

He nodded with a smile.

Peyton frowned at the beautiful flowers. Today had so many twists and turns and Callum's surprised appearance had been one of them. But she couldn't forget the fact that she had come between Madilynne and Graham and that Jay had terminated his business relationship with the hotel.

"Callum," she said, looking up to meet his eyes.

"Yes, Peyton?"

She swallowed hard before she asked, "Do you believe in the hotel and me?"

His eyebrows met and his eyes filled with concern. "I've believed in you since we were kids. I've always believed that you would do great things for the hotel. I stand by this belief."

Her eyes started to water. Jenny was right. He did believe in her—unlike Jay. She quickly wrapped her arms around him, her head resting on his hard chest, and she let out a sob.

"Thank you for coming back," she cried as he circled his arms around her.

"I was always going to come back for you, Peyton. I just needed time. I just needed you to be patient with me," he said, rubbing her back.

She held the cherry blossoms tighter in her hands as they rested against his back. This, she knew, was a sometimes moment. She knew that she would look back and smile on this memory. But she knew that imminent heartbreak was fast approaching them.

"Being in your arms, after everything… This goes against everything I believe in when it comes to you," she said. "I'm meant to hate you, but instead, I'm foolishly and hopelessly in love with you."

Callum held her tighter, like it was the last time he'd hold her. "I know, Peyton. Just know I'm sorry for what comes next. Only because I'm aware of how hard you've fought against me. You've defied your morals and beliefs…and your pride. I don't deserve to have you in my arms, but I'm thankful to have you love me in the slightest. I'm so sorry for what happens next, Peyton. I am so sorry."

He was talking about their end. The thought broke her heart, but she had always known what she was doing when it came to him. She had to prepare for life after him all over again.

I wouldn't trade our sometimes for forever with anyone else.

"Pey, wake up," he whispered in her ear.

She groaned and snuggled into something hard. A chuckle and movement occurred under her.

"Come on, Peyton. Time to get up. We'll miss it," he tried once more.

"Miss what?" she asked still half asleep, her eyes remained closed.

"What we used to do. Sneak out and watch the morning pass us by from the pier."

Peyton slowly opened her eyes to see that the something hard she was sleeping on was Callum's naked chest. She smiled at the sight she thoroughly enjoyed. Hugging the blanket around her naked body, she removed herself from his chest and glared down at him.

"Really?" she asked biting back a smile.

Callum sat properly and kissed her lips. "Yes. Now stay still. Do not move," he instructed.

Peyton arched an eyebrow at him. Callum smiled, reached over the bed, and rummage through the bag he'd brought over after dinner. Then he turned to face her, and Peyton noticed what he was held.

She let out a laugh. "You still have that?"

"Don't knock the Polaroid," he teased. "Now, stay right

there. You look breathtakingly beautiful with the sun seeping through the window."

When she was just about to burst out laughing, a flash stunned her and a Polaroid picture slid out of the camera. Then Callum held it up to her, and she looked at it, astonished. She blinked twice. The Polaroid had captured a genuine smile that made her look beautiful. Even though her hair was all messy from sleep, she appeared happy and free.

"That's how I see you, Pey. You are undeniably beautiful when you smile."

Her heart swelled at his compliment and she knew she was blushing.

After setting the picture down, she took the camera from Callum and held it up. Closing one eye and looking through the tiny glass box, she counted to three before she took a picture of him. Before he could take it away from her, she studied it.

A lump formed in her throat as she asked, "Can I keep this?"

Her eyes met Callum's, and he tilted his head at her. She returned her focus to the picture she had taken of him. It was there—that smile and look in his eyes. She had the old Callum back, even if it were only in a picture. He was still there, the one who had claimed her heart and was free. She'd treasure this one picture since it was all she'd have of him by the end of the month.

"Only if I can keep the one of you," he countered.

Peyton looked up and smiled. "You have a deal," she said.

Callum took the camera from her and brought her close to him. After a moment, he positioned the camera in the direction of their faces and took a picture of them. When she turned to face him, his lips found hers, and the sound of the shutter went off.

"I was not ready for that!" Peyton complained once she pulled back.

Callum had a pleased grin on his face as he held up the picture of them kissing. "You look pretty ready here."

Peyton stood up from the bed, dragging the blanket from him and leaving him exposed. "I can say the same thing about you," she said, eyeing his lap.

"Doesn't help that I know you're completely naked under that blanket," he said, not bothering to cover himself. Then Callum turned and snapped a shot of the cherry blossoms on the bedside table.

"Why are you taking so many pictures?" she asked as she walked to the bedroom door.

"To reflect on," he replied. Then he held the camera up, smiled, and took another one of her.

"Do not come into the bathroom with that. I'm warning you, Callum. I would say come join me, but I really need us to get going so we can get to the pier. Otherwise, I'm going to be late for the Swan's checking in," Peyton said firmly to demonstrate her seriousness.

If her were to even kiss her longer than with a quick chaste one, they'd wind up in bed. Last night, he'd taken away the pain. Lost in the pleasure, she'd forgotten Jay's hurtful actions and the future of the hotel. All she'd cared about was keeping her with him for as long as time and Callum would permit her.

"Meet you back here in thirty?" Callum asked, reaching for his discarded underwear and pants.

Peyton's eyes lingered below his waist. If she didn't have to work, she'd jump him right then and there. Instead, she nodded and said, "Thirty."

His arm brought her closer to him, and Peyton rested her head on Callum's shoulder. Peeking up at him through her lashes, she saw him staring out at the lake. The sadness that swept his face had replaced the carefree one he'd had while they had been in bed. Something was always hanging over him. That same something had him guarded.

With a deep breath, she turned her gaze back out at the water. She would always love Daylesford. All her favourite memories had happened in various parts of town, especially the ones that were made within the walls of The Spencer-Dayle. Peyton looked over at the hotel. It was beautiful. She would do everything in her power to keep it standing.

"Graham messaged me this morning, Peyton. He said that

Jay's pub terminated their relationship with the hotel. He's worried that Jay could affect the rest of the town."

The blame could be heard in his voice, but all she did was nod against him.

"I still have Graham's farm," she said.

Callum was silent for a moment before he sighed. "You lost the pub's business relationship because of me, didn't you?"

Peyton sat up, lifted her legs from over the edge of the pier, and turned her body to face him. "It's not your fault, Callum," she tried to assure him.

His eyes gave her the attention she wanted. Reaching over, she took his hand in hers and pulled him to face her.

"It is *not* your fault," she repeated.

His posture slouched. "No, it is. You would have never seen that notice of termination if I had just stayed away. God, Pey, I never wanted this to happen to you or the hotel."

She smiled when he said Pey. Callum was becoming more comfortable around her. Squeezing his hand once, she grinned before she threaded her fingers with his, loving the feel of his touch. Peyton brought their joined hands to her lips and kissed the spot where their hands connected.

"The hotel will be okay," she said.

"And what about you?"

"I'll be fine."

"And us?"

She stilled at his question. Then she turned his wrist over and stared at where he had marked his skin with her name. Sometime after he'd left, he'd cared enough to tattoo her name on him. It gave her hope, but when she met his eyes, she saw the goodbye in them.

"I'm not sure, Callum," she answered truthfully.

"You can't be unsure," he said softly.

She gave him a tight smile. She didn't know if they'd be okay when they got to goodbye. Deep down, she had been delusional and believed it would never catch them.

"Sure I can. Just like how grey isn't sure what colour it should be. If it should be black or white. So, it decides to be unsure. It decides to be grey. *I* am grey. *We* are grey."

She believed they weren't sure how to get to goodbye. The moment they did, the future would blend with the past and the present. They had less than two weeks left.

Callum's mouth pressed into a fine line. "That's a beautiful way to mask our ending, Peyton Spencer."

Letting go of his hand, she turned and let her legs dangle over the edge of the pier. She looked out at the lake, enjoying the purity in the image. "It gives me enough denial to make it to the ending, Callum Reid. I tell myself that we'll be okay and part ways with a mutual understanding, but honestly, I'm not sure. There are no bright lights waiting for us at the end."

Softly swinging her legs above the water, she kept her eyes on her lap. The sound of a camera shutter had her turning her head and Callum held the Polaroid in his hand.

"There are always bright lights waiting for you, Peyton. I know it."

She looked at the photo as it started to develop. Seconds later, she saw that it was an image of the hotel. Callum handed it to her and she clutched it, knowing that, no matter what happened, she would always have The Spencer-Dayle and all the memories that had been created in it and around it.

"This is the brightest light that's waiting for you. You don't need any of them. You're a survivor and you will be something great."

Her heart throbbed at his belief. Peyton turned and saw the way that he looked at her. *Love.* It was love that filled his eyes. A love so beautiful and unattainable. A love she couldn't keep.

"Want to go lie in the boats until I have to start work with Jenny?" she suggested once she stood up.

Callum chuckled and picked up the camera and the pictures they had taken on their way to the pier. "Like old times?"

She nodded her head. "Like old times."

It didn't take them long to walk off the pier and around the lake to the boathouse. Once they stepped onto the wooden boardwalk that wrapped around the building, they made their way to the posts. Then Callum got into the wooden boat first and held his hand out to her before he helped her in

They didn't untie it from the post. Instead, they lay down and stared at the blue, cloudless sky above. It's what they'd always done. They'd watch clouds and time pass them before she'd have to go home for dinner or get back to the hotel.

It was a bittersweet moment, lost in the past and the present. Both so similar, but this time, she was aware of the end. Last time she had been oblivious to it. Ignoring their impending end, Peyton took a deep breath and closed her eyes.

You were right, Mum and Dad. Forgive and forget. It's time I let the past go, and soon – Callum too.

When the boat rocked slightly, she opened her eyes to see that Callum had moved closer to her. Feeling his gaze on her, Peyton tilted her head and was met with his saddened eyes. The smile she had developing stalled and instead her lips made a fine line.

Callum inhaled deeply before he blinked. Slowly, his hands reached up and brushed her cheek then it returned to the wood of the boat. The moment his touch left her, she had already missed the way it affected her heart.

His lips parted before he asked, "Do you know what a sometimes moment is, Peyton?"

We did it. We're coming up to the ending.

Peyton swallowed the lump in her throat. She'd heard him whisper it as she'd fallen asleep the first time he slept in her bed. She was scared to hear him define what she was basing their time on. She was scared to hear him admit that it wasn't forever. But the truth was that she had always known.

"It's us," she replied in a soft voice, knowing that he could hear the sadness lacing it.

Callum gave her a tight smile. "In a way, we are sometimes moments. What we have right now embodies it. Sometimes moments are the moments you'll look back on later in life and smile. They were points in time that were occasional and brief. They are a reflection of a memory. They are moments that are looked upon fondly. They are what we live and breathe and know as now but look back on someday. They are not forever,

Peyton. They are reflections. They are the times you think of when you're married and have children. You'll think of me and smile because we had something in that tiny period of time we had together. That, when you have your forever, you will look back at the moments we shared. Even if it's rarely, they were ours. They were our sometimes moments."

Sometimes doesn't mean forever.

"And is this a sometimes moment, Callum?" she asked.

Callum nodded. "Every moment we've experienced since I returned to Daylesford has been a sometimes moment, Peyton. Memories that I hope you'll look back on one day."

She thought of the times they'd shared the past few weeks. Every kiss, every touch, every breath of air and 'I love you.' They were more than she could have believed she'd share with anyone. She hadn't imagined being close to anyone after him. Peyton had believed that she'd live a lonely life, wondering what life's pleasures were about. But he'd come back and restored her faith in a better, happier life—even with the pain.

Callum's thumb brushed her tear away and he kissed her lips. "Thank you for our sometimes moments, Peyton. I will hold on to them for far longer than my last breath." Then he pulled her into his arms.

She lay her head on his chest and looked up at the sky. The moments they had shared, although brief, were treasured. They were moments where she believed that he was hers and that she was loved.

She breathed him in and memorised the beats of his heart. She took in her surroundings and the man who held her. Then she closed her eyes and let every sound and movement Callum made sear themselves into her heart.

Life is a cluster of sometimes moments, more beautiful when more are grouped together. Our sometimes moments will be my forever moments. There is no one else after Callum Reid, the boy who kissed me under a cherry blossom tree and the man who gave me a forever in a sometimes.

Twenty-Eight

"You finally made it," Callum said once Peyton had walked up the small hill.

She stood next to him and said, "I had to wait for my parents to leave, and Jenny's covering for me."

Callum wrapped his arms around her and kissed the top of her head. "I'm glad you're here. I wanted you to be here when it happens."

Peyton squinted up at him. "When what happens?" she asked, slightly suspicious.

He rolled his eyes before untangling himself from her. Then he picked up his SLR camera and adjusted the lens. "Look out at the lake, Pey."

When she looked in the direction that he'd suggested, the view took her breath away. It was beautiful. The setting sun filled the sky with purples and reds, and the water sparkled before her eyes. She had never seen the lake look more beautiful than in this moment.

The sounds of the camera shutter had her turning her head. She watched the awed expression on Callum's face transform as he looked at the photo on the screen. He saw the beauty. He saw the innocence of nature. And Peyton saw that in him. Her heart throbbed at the sight of him taking in the view. The way he appreciated life had her envious of his perspective on the world, and a slow smile developed on his face.

When he turned and his eyes met hers, the sparkle in them made her breathless. And it was in that moment that she knew what she had always known deep down.

I'm in love with Callum Reid.

"Pey, wake up."

A nudge had Peyton groaning.

She hugged the blanket around her and said, "Callum, I don't have your kind of stamina. I'm not an expert at lasting long when it comes to sex. Give me a couple of hours."

He shook her this time, so she rolled on her back and opened her eyes.

"As much as I love the idea of sex right now, that's not why I woke you up."

Peyton sat up and rubbed her eyes. Before she could even ask him what was going on, Callum handed her the phone.

"It's Jenny," he said.

She looked at the clock on her bedside table to see that it was just after two a.m. She knew Jenny would never call her this late, especially with this week's guests having already checked out. It had been four days since Callum had told her that their time was limited and four days since she had started operating the hotel to guests. The feedback that she'd received from her customers had been great, and it had given her the confidence boost that she'd needed. Now she could concentrate on Marissa's wedding and the building of the lakeside dance floor.

Peyton scratched her head before she put the phone to her ear.

"Peyton!" Jenny cried out hysterically.

Peyton stilled. "Jenny, are you okay?" she asked desperately.

A million scenarios on Jenny's safety ran through Peyton's head. She couldn't lose Jenny. She couldn't lose anyone else.

"Jenny, please talk to me."

There was a loud bang in the background, and Peyton looked at Callum. He was just as confused as she was.

"What's going on?" Callum asked.

Peyton shook her head to tell him that she didn't know.

"Peyton..."

"I'm right here, Jenny. Tell me that you're okay. Do I need to come get you?" Peyton asked as she threw back her blanket and stood up from the bed. Then she walked to the hook near the door and grabbed her dressing gown, slipping it on over her silk nightdress.

Jenny let out a sob. "It's the hotel, Peyton."

Peyton froze. "The hotel?"

Callum was by her side instantly, holding her. His supporting touch couldn't stop Peyton's throbbing heart. Fear overtook every inch of her body. Flooding she could fix. A fallen tree on a cabin would dent her finances, but it wasn't impossible. A broken window would be easy to replace.

"It's on fire, Peyton. The hotel's on fire."

The phone slipped out of her hand and fell onto the floor. Numb. That's what she felt. Her heart had stopped functioning and she was sure her lungs had, too. She was breathing, but her lungs weren't inhaling the oxygen.

Callum let go of her and bent down to pick up her phone. Before he could even stand, she bolted out of her room and the house.

Shoes weren't important. More clothes to protect her from the winter night weren't a concern. She ran. Faster and harder. Stepping on sharp rocks as she desperately sprinted to the lake. She felt pain. In her chest, her lungs, the side of her body, and her feet. But she didn't care. She heard her name being yelled out from behind her, but she kept her legs moving up the hill and to the lake. She didn't stop to see if there was smoke or flames—she just kept running.

The moment she reached the path to the hotel, she slowed down, taking careful steps towards the hotel. Tears ran down her face as she painfully willed her body forward. Flames and smoke. That's all she saw. Dark, black smoke filled the sky, providing the backdrop for the fire that engulfed the building.

She had never felt so helpless. In front of her, she watched everything she had ever loved and treasured die before her very eyes. Each memory of her parents, Jenny, the staff, and Callum. The flames were destroying the future she had carved for herself. It was symbolic. The hotel's burning down was a reflection of her future—she didn't have one.

When a part of the hotel collapsed, she fell to her knees, sobbing. And when she heard voices around her, all she could do was stare at The Spencer-Dayle sign as it burned before it fell to the ground.

She was voiceless. All that came out were sobs and strangled sounds she had never made. Her hopes and dreams were dying. The last four years of keeping the hotel alive were now a waste. A loud explosion blew out some windows and she heard people gasp the moment parts of the building started to collapse. The fire was relentless in its destruction of her hotel. Arms were around her, but she didn't have to turn to know it was Callum.

"Don't just stand there. Save it! Do something!" Jenny screamed.

Peyton cranked her neck to see her manager pointing at the burning building. Timmy, the firefighter Peyton had gone to school with, looked conflicted as he held the hose. When his eyes met Peyton's, there was an apology in them.

"I'm so sorry, Peyton," Callum whispered as he put his hand on the side of her head and brought her to his chest.

"It's gone," she managed out.

The tears continued to fall—the only form of water near the hotel. Peyton focused on the firefighters to see them standing there watching the fire consume The Spencer-Dayle.

"Why aren't you trying to save it? It's your job!" Jenny cried.

Timmy flinched and his eyes averted hers. Peyton followed his stare to see him looking at Jay as if he were asking if it was okay to put out the fire.

"They're just standing there, staring at Jay," Peyton cried unbelievably.

After what seemed like for the first time, she blinked, hoping it was just a dream. But it wasn't. The fire still burned and the smoke entered her nostrils.

She watched Jay shake his head at Timmy. She knew Callum had seen it too when his arms loosened around her. Timmy's older brother, Thomas, had been Jay's best friend in high school. And growing up, Timmy had idolised his brother and Jay, doing anything to received their approval.

"Stay here," Callum instructed.

Before she could stop him, Callum stood up and marched over to Jay. Callum didn't say anything as he punched Jay in the jaw. Jay stumbled back, holding the side of his face.

"Right now, Timmy. Put out that fire!" Callum yelled.

When Timmy didn't move, Callum shook his head, walked to the firefighter, and pulled the hose out of his hand. Then he pointed the water to the building, but it did nothing to extinguish the flames. The hotel was far too gone to be saved.

Peyton walked over to Callum. His eyes met hers and she could see the refusal in them. He didn't want to give up on trying to save it. And for that, she fell in love with him all over again. She blinked away the tears as she stepped next to him. Giving the hotel one last look, she mentally said goodbye to it and her parents. She wrapped her hands around the hose and pulled it away from him.

"No, Peyton! I can save it. I can save it!" he cried.

She shook her head. "It's gone, Callum."

Tears filled his eyes. "You don't deserve this."

She dropped the hose and wrapped her arms around his waist. "It's not about if I deserve it or not. It's happening."

Callum wrapped his arms around her and apologised numerous times. That's when Peyton closed her eyes, knowing that everything she would love would leave her. The last thing that remained was the man in her arms. Soon, she'd say goodbye to him, too. She held him tighter because in this moment he was the only tangible thing she could hold onto.

"I love you," she said into his chest, knowing it could be one of the last times she'd say it out loud.

"I love you, too, Peyton." He kissed her head before he said, "Come on. Let's get you to safe distance." Then he unwrapped his arms from around her and took her hand.

This was their moment of defiance against the town. They could take away her hotel but they couldn't take away what they had. In the near future, it would be Peyton and Callum who'd destroy what they had. Not the town.

A ute pulled up near them, and Graham and Madilynne got out of the car. If Peyton weren't so broken, she'd smile at the sight of them together. The moment Graham raced towards them, Callum let her hand go in time for Graham to wrap his arms around her. She couldn't cry in his embrace. It was like she was dry inside.

"Why the fuck are they just standing there?" Graham growled in her ear.

Peyton tensed. Graham was never one to cuss. Suddenly, he pushed past her. Peyton pivoted to see him storm off towards the firefighters.

Timmy was saying something, but she was too far.

Graham picked up the hose and slammed it into Timmy's chest. "Do your job! You listen to Jay again and I will make sure you lot see a commission!"

The firefighters all nodded and went to their engine, pulling out the equipment. But she knew it was too late. With a heavy sigh, she walked towards them and looked at the men who would rather see her hotel die than save it. She would be the bigger person, no matter how much they had scarred her. It wasn't because they deserved to be pardoned but because her aunt and uncle had taught her forgiveness. And Callum taught her that sometimes, it's better to just let go.

"It's long past saving. Please make sure it doesn't travel too far back and burn the rest of the town. People's lives and homes are at stake," she said.

It was like common sense had clicked in their eyes, and they all nodded and mumbled their apologies to her.

Graham wrapped his arm around her back and led her towards Callum and Madilynne. "We'll rebuild it, Peyton. We'll make it better," he promised.

"I know, Graham," she replied quietly as they passed by Jay and some of the firefighters.

When Peyton locked eyes with Jay, he was emotionless. Graham stopped and let Peyton go.

"I can't believe you told them not to save the hotel. Fine.

Be angry at her for being with Callum. Taking away the hotel's partnerships was one thing but letting it burn to the ground? You're a son of a bitch, Jay."

She wanted to yell and scream at Jay. She wanted to hurt him, but she just wasn't that person. In all honesty, she was far too tired inside. And what good would hurting Jay do? She had all but lost The Spencer-Dayle. She had spent so many years trying to keep it afloat, but it had all been for nothing.

Peyton stepped away from Graham and stood in front of Jay. As she stared at him, she saw no remorse in his eyes. There was no salvaging a friendship with him.

"I would never wish this on you or the pub, Jay. I would never wish it on any of the town's businesses. Whatever you wanted to achieve out of this, I hope you got it. Hate me all you like, but I have always been in love with Callum. I'm sorry you can't find a way past that and be my friend."

She could never trust Jay again. She'd believed in him. Believed he was a good person. Tonight revealed that he wasn't. He was a selfish man full of pride. Realising that they'd never be friends again, she walked into Callum's waiting arms and let his heartbeat distract her from her own stalling ones.

"Peyton."

Jenny's voice had her pulling away from Callum. She noticed Jenny covered in ash, and in her hand, she was holding something.

"It's the only thing I could save. I couldn't get farther. The flames and the smoke were too overwhelming. I'm sorry I couldn't save some of your parents' things."

Peyton saw that it was the picture Callum had taken of the lake. And that's when she burst into tears and hugged Jenny tight. "I would rather the hotel and everything in it burn to ash than lose you, Jenny. You shouldn't have risked your life for the picture."

Out of anything that could have been saved, Peyton was glad that Callum's picture was it. The moment he had taken it, she'd known she was madly in love with him. It was a picture she'd always want, no matter how much pain he had caused her with his leaving.

Callum took the framed picture and said, "Thank you for saving this, Jenny. I appreciate it more than you could possibly know. I'm going to take Peyton home now. You go home to your husband. We'll survey what's left in the morning."

Peyton let go of Jenny and wiped at her cheeks.

"There was no one inside during the fire. I'll call those with bookings tomorrow morning and explain the situation. I'll handle everything, Peyton. I'll deal with the Reynolds' wedding, too," Jenny said, trying to reassure her.

"That's okay, Jenny. I'll speak to Oliver in the morning. Come on, Pey. I'll get you home." Callum's hands entwined with hers, his thumb caressing hers. "Graham, you mind dropping us off at Peyton's?"

"Yeah, I'll take you both. Madilynne, do you want me to drop you off at home?" Graham asked, leading them to the ute.

Callum opened the car door for Peyton, and she got in the backseat. Then he clicked her seatbelt in place before he got into the backseat with the picture sitting in his lap.

Madilynne got in the front seat and said, "No. I'll stay at yours for the rest of the night. I don't want to hear what my dad says about tonight."

Peyton watched Graham nod and adjust the rearview mirror so that his reflection met her eyes.

"You 'right there, Peyton?"

She nodded. "Yes."

Lie.

The only thing she could feel was Callum's hand in hers.

"Okay," he replied, no doubt seeing through her lie, and started up the car.

Peyton didn't look back as the car reversed away from the burning hotel and towards her house.

I am helpless.

I am hopeless.

I am a failure.

I have nothing,

I am fading.

I am dying.

Twenty-Nine

Peyton shivered at the cold air that touched her skin. She hugged the blanket tighter and reached out for Callum's warm body. When she felt the cool mattress, Peyton sat up and rubbed her eyes, searching the room for him. She noticed the door open and his muffled voice trailing in from the lounge. Pulling the blanket aside, she swung her legs over the bed and stood up. Then she made her way out of her room and walked down the hall, but she stopped when she heard him speak.

"What do I do now, Oliver? How do I do this to her?"

The worried tone in Callum's voice had Peyton pressing her hand on the wall to keep herself on her feet.

"I don't want to say goodbye. I don't want to leave her. It was hard the first time, but now… How do I do it now?"

Breathing failed her as her heart burned within her chest. He was discussing their ending. Hearing that he didn't want to say goodbye broke her heart. She found the concept as difficult as he did.

"I love her, Oliver. I can't do it to her. I can't tell her the truth—not after tonight. I can't do it," Callum cried.

Peyton closed her eyes and let the tears roll down her face, hitting the nightdress she was wearing. She counted each slow beat of her heart. Time was catching up to them. Time would separate them. Time would end them.

But the truth was that Peyton didn't want to hear the truth. Not when it meant that the ending had reached them. She didn't want it. For, as long as she could prolong the truth, she'd still have him. So she'd stopped asking for the truth. She hadn't asked why.

"I shouldn't have come back. I should have just let her be here and hate me. Right now, I hate me. I want her to hate me. It would be easier. Her life would be easier. She's lost everything because of me. I should have stayed in the city. I should have never suggested Daylesford for your wedding. I should have just let her live her life."

Peyton pushed off the wall and walked into the lounge. The moment her eyes landed on him, she saw Callum holding the phone in one hand and the other covered his face.

"Stop saying I should hate you, because I don't. Not in the slightest," she said.

Callum moved his hand from his face and looked up at her. The defeated expression on his face made her heart ache. Dropping to her knees in front of him, her hands rest on his thigh. Then he leant forward, allowing his forehead to touch hers.

"I need you to hate me, Peyton," he begged.

She shook her head, their foreheads not breaking contact. "I can't give you that."

He squeezed his eyelids tight and said, "I know, Oliver. This is why I have to leave. I—"

Reaching up, Peyton took the phone out of his hand and held it to her ear. "Oliver, Callum will call you back in the morning. We need to talk about the fire and your wedding," she said.

"Wait, Peyton." Oliver stopped her from hanging up. "Why can't you hate him?"

Callum sat straight and pulled away from her, as if he knew what Oliver had asked. He seemed afraid of what she would say next as a forgiving plea swept his face.

Peyton stared in his lost and conflicted eyes before she answered, "Because I want to feel loved by Callum Reid, even if it's only for a little while. I want his love more than I want to live another day. I want to be with him for as long as I can, because for the last four and half years, I've been deprived of his love and his touch. I can't hate him because he's the love of my life."

Oliver sighed. "He's never stopped loving you, even when he moved to the city. You were the girl whose picture was by his bedside table. Whatever happens, just know he loves you and has always put you first."

Peyton hung up the phone and placed it on the couch. Then she peered up through her lashes to see Callum staring down at her. He looked tormented, like he was in his own version of hell. When Peyton stood up, she held out her hand to him. Callum rubbed his palms over his face then let out a groan.

She stepped forward, rested her hands on the back of his head, and brought him to her stomach. She hoped that this one embrace could show him that she'd be okay. That she would rather see him free than stay here in Daylesford. His arms were around the back of her legs, holding her tight.

"I shouldn't have left you, Peyton," Callum said and gazed up at her. "I'm so sorry. If I could go back, I would. I'd change it all. I wouldn't have left you here on your own."

Peyton moved her hands from the back of his head to his cheeks. "Don't do that to yourself, Callum."

"God, why can't you hate me?" he exclaimed, frustrated.

"Because I've spent years trying to. I'm tired of holding you accountable, when the reality is that I didn't fight for you to stay. I didn't do enough to convince you that what we had was worth you staying," she said, brushing his skin with her thumbs.

"You were worth staying for. You will always be worth staying for. I was just a coward. I couldn't let you be held back by me. I had your happiness in mind when I left," he explained, untangling his arms and standing up.

Callum cradled her face in his hands before he brought his mouth as close to hers without touching. Placing her hands on his waist as she held him to her.

"Leaving you, Peyton... I was like the after events of a revolution. I was liberated, but I was lost. I had no direction in my life. But when I came back, my sad and lonely life made sense. Life is better with you in it, Peyton. It always has been," he revealed before his lips lightly touched hers.

"Thank you for letting me have sometimes instead of never," she said softly.

His lips brushed hers again, this time harder, more desperate. Open kisses that slowly tore away the loneliness of her heart and replaced it with need and desire. Her fingers dug into the side of him as his tongue found hers, moving and sucking, and she found it impossible to breathe.

Callum's lips moved back and he pressed his forehead to hers, panting. "Peyton, you're trying to mask the pain of losing the hotel with sex."

She shook her head. "I'm not in as much pain as you think I am, Callum."

"Pey—"

"No," she interrupted. "I know what it's like to lose it all. It hurt to see it burn down, but it is nothing compared to the feeling of losing my parents. And it comes nowhere close to losing you. That broke the person I was."

"I don't think it's hit you yet. And I'm okay with you blaming me, Peyton."

Her heart squeezed. She couldn't and wouldn't blame Callum for the fire. He had been in her bed when it'd happened. If she were going to blame anyone, it would be Jay. He had stood back. He'd influenced the firefighters. He'd let it burn to ash.

"I don't want sex from you, Callum."

His breathing hitched. And she pushed her body into his.

"I want you to make *love* to me. I need you to make me feel better. I need this sometimes moment with you."

"Couch?" he asked before his lips crashed into hers, making her both her stomach and heart dip.

She answered each of his kisses with her own desperate ones, the need in her growing. She needed the pleasure he drew out of her. She needed the explosions and the momentary period of forgetfulness. She needed him and his heartbeat on her skin.

His lips moved from hers and trailed slowly from her jaw to her neck. She let out a soft moan, unable to suppress it.

"Bed," she let out. Her heart beat hard against her chest as she cupped his face, making sure his eyes were on hers when she said, "Make love to me in my bed. No teasing or games. Just make love to me."

"I love you so much," he said with a hint of hesitation.

Then his hands were at her waist as he picked her up, her legs wrapping around him. His hands went to the back of her thighs, holding her securely. She panted at the intensity in his eyes.

"God gave me you and I gave you up. He gave me a small window to make this time count. I'm going to make sure that I don't waste my time with you. Until we can't take it anymore, I'll keep making love to you," he promised.

She warmed all over as her heart throbbed at his words. She blinked once before her mouth founds his, needing to feel him on her and in her. Needing every little bit of him.

Lie. God gave me you to love you twice as hard as last time, if not more.

Thirty

"Are you sure you're okay?" Callum asked just before they walked down the small hill to the lake.

Peyton stopped, her hand shaking. Callum was right. Last night, it hadn't sunk in. The hotel had caught fire. She didn't know if anything remained. The firefighters on the scene had done nothing until Callum and Graham had stepped in. It was then that Peyton had understood how much power Jay held in their town—the same power that could have minimised the extent of the damage.

"You look tired," she pointed out. The exhausted look on his face confirmed it.

Callum shook his head and took her hand in his. "I'm okay. Just got a little dizzy," he said as they walked around the lake towards the hotel.

She refused to look at the sky for the hotel building. Instead, she watched each step they took. Carefully examining the way their steps had been in sync. Then suddenly, Callum pulled on her hand and stopped her. She felt him tense, gripping her hand harder. Peyton closed her eyes and took a deep breath before she slowly opened them. Then her breath caught in her throat as she took in what little of her hotel was left. The large Victorian building had completely burned to the ground. The fire made it possible for her to see right through where the hotel had once stood. It seemed that the fire hadn't spread; the dance floor and posts outside the hotel had remained unharmed.

Just seeing the dance floor had her sighing in relief. Nothing else was damaged. The firefighters had contained it. It looked nothing like the large hotel that once had stood where burned wood, furniture, and ash lay. The smoke was still in the air, enough to make the situation feel so real.

"Peyton," Jenny said.

Turning her head, she saw the hotel's operations manager walk towards her, a phone in one hand and an iPad in the other. It was just after eight a.m. and Jenny was already working.

"How'd you sleep?" Jenny asked the moment she stood next to Peyton.

"Fine, considering," she answered.

"The reporters will be here soon. I have Darryl coming in. He'll make sure they don't harass you. I'll handle the media."

Peyton turned and smiled at her co-worker. "I'm glad you married a constable."

Jenny rolled her eyes. "He's glad he married me is more like it. Don't worry. I have the insurance paperwork going. I have a list of guests I'll call soon, too. I'm so sorry this happened, Peyton. The County Authority will be here soon to investigate the cause of the fire."

Although she wanted to know the cause, Peyton didn't answer. Instead, she looked at where her hotel had once been located. It looked like the remains of a bushfire that had rolled into town. There was nothing else to do but rebuild. It would take months, but she'd see it through. She had grown up within the walls of the hotel and she wanted to rebuild it and make it her own. No town to hold her back. The community had turned their back on her. Last night had made it obvious.

After letting go of Callum's hand, she walked up to the sign that had previously been bolted above the hotel's entrance. The 'Dayle' had burned, and all that remain was 'Spenc.' Crouching in front of the sign, she wiped away the ash and debris from her surname. One of her fondest memories was when they had hung the sign her mother had spent months creating above the hotel's main entry. Her mother and father had stood back a few metres from the door and smiled at the sign that signalled their hotel.

Peyton wiped the tear that ran down her cheek. Rebuilding the hotel was more than just for her. She wanted to do it for her parents. She wanted to take a step back and watch a brand-new sign being bolted up on the new hotel.

Upon turning around, she was met with a tired and concerned Callum Reid. She gave him a small smile. "Do you think you could talk to Oliver and Marissa? If I talk to some of the businesses I've previously worked with in Creswick, we can have the guests stay there. The dance floors are almost complete, and I could get Nigel to build anything else we need for the wedding. I know it's not what they would have liked, but if they want to go elsewhere, I'm more than happy to refund them the entire wedding out of my own pocket."

Callum dug out his phone from his pocket and said, "They don't care about the money, Peyton. Believe it or not, Marissa is very much in love with Oliver. She just wants to marry him. I'll call now." He turned and walked down the path away from her and Jenny.

She watched him talk on the phone, aware that, somewhere down the line, she'd blink once and he'd be gone. That was all it would take.

"I saw the fear in his eyes last night, Peyton. He was scared for you," Jenny said.

Peyton spun and looked at her before she gave Jenny a tight smile. If anything, she was scared for him. He had punched Jay last night, and that was something she couldn't forget. Callum had never been a violent person. But she understood why. With a sigh, she looked up at the clearing sky to see specks of blue through the lingering smoke. It amazed her how pure and beautiful the world was once it had taken something away from you. It played innocent. Acting oblivious to the mess it had made.

"I need to be somewhere," Peyton said, shifting her attention to Callum.

"Are you okay?" Concern laced Jenny's voice.

She didn't take her eyes off Callum as she said, "I just need to be alone for a minute. Do you mind keeping him busy? I won't be long."

From the corner of her eye, she could see Jenny nod.

"Thanks, Jenny. I have my phone," Peyton said before she walked towards the back of the hotel, taking the longer way to town.

The guilt added further pressure to her chest. Peyton hadn't stepped foot here in a long time. She passed the office and kept walking. When she reached the graves under the large oak tree, she sat on the grass.

As soon as she noticed the cherry blossoms on each of their headstones, she smiled. She didn't have to guess. Callum had visited her parents' graves while he had been in town. It touched her heart. He wasn't the cold, guarded person that he was trying to be. Deep down, he was the Callum she loved. Fears and insecurities hindered his freedom.

"I'm sorry that I haven't visited in a while. It doesn't get any easier as the days go by. You probably know that Callum's back. I fought him off for a while until I realised there was no point fighting or denying my heart. You were right, Mum. Forgive and forget. And you were right, Dad. He came back. I wish you were both here to give me that 'I told you so' brag." She laughed at herself as she wiped her face with the back of her hand.

"You also probably know that last night the hotel burned down." She paused, her heart now twisted. "I'm so sorry, Mum and Dad. I didn't mean for this. I didn't mean for the one thing you both worked so hard for to burn to the ground. I didn't mean to be a terrible owner. I was going through all this blind. Somehow, I made the choice between the hotel and Callum even before it burned down. And I chose Callum. I'm not sorry for that. I'm just sorry that I let you both down. You're probably up there disappointed in me for not saving the hotel. I tried. But every time I think I'm on the right track, something goes wrong or I just make a mess. I'm a burden and a liability to the hotel and to this town."

She ran her hands through her hair and shut her eyelids tightly. "I miss you both. I wish you were here so I could make mistakes and you could teach me how to do it right. I didn't get a goodbye. I don't get one more 'We love you, Peyton.' I don't get anything else in life with you. And that's what makes me hate the hotel and this town. They're all constant reminders. But now… Now, the hotel's gone. And soon enough, Callum will be gone, too. I've never hated life more than right now. But I'm going to try. I'm going to build our hotel my way, and whether or not I have this town's support means nothing. I'm doing this for me and for you both. I'm a Spencer, and I'll be damned if I let a fire take away what we've done for this town. I will make this a bright light in a town with so much disbelief. It'll be like a beacon in the fog," she promised—not only to her parents, but also to herself.

Minutes turned into two hours as she sat at their graves. She didn't say anything more. She had neglected to visit because it had been too hard. She had hid in her loneliness, afraid of the world. Peyton reminisced on the good times and what loving parents she'd had. She had been blessed to have them, and even though she hadn't been able to keep them, she had the memories. She still had the house. That house with the cherry blossom tree in the backyard would always be her home.

Suddenly, she heard the footsteps but didn't bother turning as someone sat next to her. She didn't have to know who it was that had followed her to the cemetery. Peyton took his hands and threaded her fingers with his.

This is also home.

"I thought you'd be here," Callum said.

Peyton shifted her gaze to him and smiled. "Thank you for

visiting them," she said, acknowledging the cherry blossoms.

He let go of her hand and uttered, "It's been four years. Long overdue," before he wrapped his arm around her, holding Peyton tight.

She let her head rest on his shoulder. "You're here now. That's all that matters."

They sat quietly with her long-gone loved ones. She had never felt more loved by him than she did in that moment. A moment she thought she'd never have—Callum by her side at her parents' grave. She memorised the way he breathed, how long he inhaled, and the space of each heartbeat hers made when in his arms. It was about collecting the memories she'd reflect on. The sometimes moments she would appreciate and love later in life.

"I have something for you," Callum said, breaking their silence.

Peyton straightened her back and turned to face him. He reached into his jacket pocket and pulled out a piece of folded paper. Then he stared at it for a long second before he handed it to her.

Her eyes looked back and forth between Callum and paper, unsure of what it contained. When she unfolded it, her eyes watered at the sight.

"I made it last night while you slept, so it isn't to scale or anything. I know it's rough, but it's just an idea. We'll work on it," he said.

Peyton took in the black-ink drawing of a Victorian-inspired building. She looked at the sketched path that led to the entry, and on either side were small drawings of a flower she recognised.

She looked up and asked, "Lavender?"

He nodded with a smile. "Graham's always supported you, and I think it would be beautiful against the cream stones of the building."

Then, as Peyton stared back at the sketch, her heart stopped at the sight of the door and what was above it. "The Spencer?" she breathed out, her eyes filling with tears.

"It's time you started new, Peyton. This rebuild is about you, not the town. This town doesn't deserve to have their name even close to yours or the hotel," he explained.

The Spencer.

She let those two words replay through her mind. In that moment, life made sense and hope returned to her. She dropped the paper in her lap and grabbed his face.

"I love you," she said with as much honesty and purity as she could voice out loud. Tears rolled down her face, but she didn't care. "I love you," she said once more before she kissed him fully on the mouth.

She had all but forgiven him. He had given her a path in life to take and she would. He had given her a form of freedom to be her own. He had given her the chance to be who she was instead of what the town believed her to be.

"I forgive you," she said against his lips.

Callum stilled instantly and pulled back. "What?" he said breathlessly. His eyes were wide in disbelief.

"Callum Reid, you have your redemption," she confirmed.

His eyes glazed over in unshed tears and his hands wrapped around her wrists. "Thank you," he breathed. "Thank you, thank you, thank you."

For the first time in a long time, she gave him the most honest and truthful smile she could make. Her mouth inched closer to his, ready to be lost in the pleasures of his lips, but her phone vibrated in her pocket, interrupting them. That's when she let out a groan, pulled it out, and looked at the screen. She quickly swiped across to answer the call.

"June, this is a surprise!" Peyton's voice hitched higher and she moved back from Callum.

"Peyton, I saw the news. Your hotel," June said unbelievably.

"Jenny was going to call you later. I'm sorry to have to cancel your spring booking," Peyton said, devastated not to have June at her hotel working on another album.

"Oh, I'll still be coming in spring. I'll just stay at your place. You, Peyton Spencer, are a great person to run songs with. Do you need me to come help out?"

Peyton heard someone play a song she had never heard and she knew June was in the recording studio. That's when the idea hit her.

"Callum, does Marissa like June Sinclair?" she asked.

His mouth dropped. "Marissa loves June. Is that who you're talking to?"

Peyton nodded her head. "June, I have a wedding next Saturday. Do you mind performing? We'll discuss an appearance fee and everything."

June laughed lightly. "We're friends, Peyton. I'll only do it for free. The band and I will be up Saturday morning. See you then!"

"See you then, June." Peyton hung up with a large grin on her face.

When she looked down at Callum's rough design, her heart twitched at the sight of The Spencer he had drawn her.

I will make his plan a reality.

Thirty-One

Eight days passed. Eight days of clean-up and planning. Eight days, she spent with him, loving him harder. But those days passed far too quickly. Setting up Marissa and Oliver's wedding took up most of their time. When he wasn't with her, Callum was redesigning his rough draft of The Spencer onto blueprints. People in town stopped by the burned remains and offered their condolences, but Peyton kept her head down and thanked them. The town had lost a source of income—that, she was aware of—but she couldn't dwell too much thought on anything other than the hotel.

Investigators who had searched the remains had put the accident down as an electrical fire that had come from the kitchen. But Peyton knew the source. The dishwasher—the same one Jay was meant to have fixed weeks ago. Peyton hadn't told them, though. She'd just agreed that the burning of her hotel had been an accident. Jay's mistake had cost her, but she wouldn't let him go to jail for faulty electrician work. No matter how much wrong he had done to her.

"That's going to be you one day," Jenny whispered.

Peyton looked as Oliver and Marissa danced on the lakeside dance floor. The lanterns on the lake as the sun started to set were breathtakingly beautiful. She couldn't deny wanting this someday. Wanting the man she'd married to dance with her, their first dance of forever.

Peyton just smiled. In reality, this would just be a dream for her. There was no one else after Callum. Her heart had been stained by his name, and she would rather it that way.

"He can't keep his eyes off you, even with that bridesmaid in his arms."

She moved her eyes away from the bride and groom and stared at Callum, who was dancing with Victoria, Marissa's maid of honour. His eyes were on Peyton. They were filled with an apology she understood. If life and time were working with them, this could have been a possibility for them one day. But they weren't. Life and time were working against them. Tonight was their last. The ending had finally caught up to them.

"He leaves tomorrow," Peyton finally said before she looked down at the clipboard.

Thankfully, the hotel in Creswick had been more than happy to help out with the wedding, providing Peyton's staff with everything they needed to make the wedding happen. Oliver and Marissa married near the path that led to Callum and Peyton's spot under the large trees. Callum had been right—Marissa had been heartbroken that the hotel had burned to the ground but she didn't want to change venues. She had just wanted to marry Oliver.

The moment June started setting up with the band, Marissa cried and kissed her new husband like crazy. The song June played was new and heartbreakingly beautiful. The soft sound of the guitar and June's voice made the song Peyton's favourite.

Timing got us wrong.
Life put us on show.
Separating all that we knew.
The dark times stole you.
I hid from all I knew.
Waiting for you to find me.

Peyton looked over at Callum the moment she heard June sing and smiled at him. In some ways, she had been waiting for him for all these years. She didn't take her eyes off him as his lips curved when he caught her staring. Callum blinked once, and without a word, he walked away from Victoria and approached her.

"What are you doing?" Peyton asked as she looked over Callum's shoulder to see Victoria less than impressed.

"About to dance with the woman I love," he said, holding out his hand.

She looked down and shook her head. "I'm working, Callum."

He took the clipboard from her and gave it to Jenny. "I'm sure Jenny doesn't mind taking over for a bit."

Peyton turned away from his grin and faced Jenny. The moment she saw Jenny nodding, she rolled her eyes. "Fine. One dance. Then I have to get back to work."

"Okay," he said and took her hand.

The way her heart picked up from his touch was one that she would miss come tomorrow. But for tonight, he'd be hers and she'd be his.

Callum pulled her away from the dance floor and up the hill.

"Where are we going? I thought we were dancing?"

He didn't stop or look her way as he said, "There's only one place I want to be with you."

Her heart ached—both in pain and pleasure. She knew where he was taking her. Hand-in-hand, they walked through the path, into the forest, past the circular rock and down the small incline until they reached their spot.

Once they were in the middle of the circle, he brought her close to his body and placed his hand on the small of her back. The music from the wedding was almost like a whisper in the wind as he swayed with her. Nothing else mattered in this moment.

Another sometimes moment.

She smiled at the thought. She would rather sometimes than never. Because Callum's holding her under the purple and red sky was beautiful. The end was hours away, but she didn't care. She couldn't let herself care or she'd taint the rest of the time they had together.

She glanced up to see the frown on his face. "What's wrong?" she asked.

Callum sighed. "Tomorrow," he stated.

Peyton took a deep breath and nodded. "Still hours away," she pointed out.

"It's still happening, Peyton."

"I know. Let's enjoy our last night together." She smiled, hoping to assure him.

His forehead touched hers as they swayed. "A night full of sometimes moments?"

"A night full of them," she confirmed and then kissed his chin.

They stopped moving as they took in this moment. If life had been fair, four and a half years would have never come between them.

Peyton closed her eyes and let her ear rest on his chest. His heartbeat was one of her favourite sounds, so she listened to each thump it made as his chest rise and fall with each breath he took.

"I have something for you," Callum said.

She lifted her head and stood straight, staring at the frown on his face. It wasn't the look she wanted to see on their last night together. But she took a small step from him and gave him the room he needed anyway.

"Okay," she said as nervous trembles made their way through her body.

Callum reached into his jacket pocket and pulled out an envelope. When she looked, she saw her name written on it and her heart dipped. Goodbye was coming earlier than she had anticipated. Then a sob formed and lodged in her throat, making breathing and speaking impossible. Her heart decided it would be the perfect time to slow down and throb painfully.

When he handed her the envelope, Peyton blinked at it.

"What is it?" she finally asked. She didn't look up at him. Instead, she followed each letter of her name.

"Our epilogue," he said.

What little air that was in her lungs was drawn out by those two words. Her hands shook as her eyes blurred. They were now meeting their end. She had their epilogue in her hands, and her heart smashed into a thousand pieces.

Ours.

She gazed up to see the pain in his eyes before she said, "Read it to me."

Callum shook his head vigorously. "I can't do that."

The agony in his voice had her shaking her head at him. "Then I don't want it," she said softly and held it out to him.

I don't want our conclusion. I don't want us to end.

Callum wrapped his arms around her and sobbed. "God, all I want is more time with you."

Her hands were squashed between their bodies as her head rested on his chest. "Then stay," she said. It was the first time she had asked him to. It wasn't a thought. It was a vocal plea.

His arms tightened around her once more and his chin rest on the top of her head. "I can't. I want to more than anything, but I can't."

As they stood still for longer than they should have, she memorised the feel of him breathing, the feel of his body on hers, and the way she fit in his arms. Peyton knew she'd memorise them in her room for the last time tonight, but right now, she memorised them in their spot. The one spot in the whole world that held their love, the one spot where life made sense to them both, and the one spot where she felt whole and true. The one place in the whole world full of their sometimes moments.

"Promise me something," she said and looked up at his jaw.

Callum took a sharp breath before his eyes focused on her and said, "For you, Peyton, anything."

"It's two promises."

He nodded. "Okay. What's the first one?"

It was her turn to inhale deeply. These promises had constantly lingered her thoughts over for the last few days. It was a thought she had known that she'd have to voice.

"Promise me you'll find someone to love you more than I could. You know how much I love you, and if someone can love you more than I do…then keep her. Have forever moments with her. Promise me that," she begged.

"I-I." He sighed. "I promise to keep her forever. What's your second promise?"

Peyton took a step away from him and looked at his note one last time before she met his cautious stare. "I will read this when you leave if you promise you'll give me a goodbye."

He tensed and his fists balled tight beside his body. He didn't say anything as he looked at her. The agony that filled his eyes almost had her retracting her requests. She wanted his pain gone, but she had thought of her closure first. She needed closure in order to live a life without him.

"I promise," he said before he hung his head.

Peyton inched forward, placed the letter in his pocket, then cupped his face. "I mean it, Callum. I don't want to wake up and find that you left me at some point during the night. I deserve a goodbye. You and I both know that."

He looked up at her and nodded. "I know you do, Peyton. You always deserved one. I was a coward last time. This time, I'll do it right. I promise."

She kissed him slowly enough to remind herself of the pain in her chest. If she let his mouth quicken or deepen their kiss, she'd never get back to the wedding and goodbye would be far more impossible.

Then she pulled back. "Thank you. We better get back or Jenny will kill me."

She didn't let him say anything as she took his hand and led him out of the forest.

Goodbye, Callum. Goodbye, forever, and goodbye, my heart.

Thirty-Two

"Pick a country," Callum said.

Peyton gazed down at her lap to find him staring at her. Gently, her fingers continued to stroke his hair as she thought about her answer.

"Austria."

"Why Austria?"

She picked off the cherry blossom that landed in his hair and said, "Because of Mozart, Belvedere Palace, Wiener schnitzels, and sachertorte."

He chuckled. "Liar. I know the real reason why you want to go to Austria."

Her eyebrows furrowed. "Oh yeah? What is the real reason why I want to go to Austria?"

Callum raised his eyebrow and confidently stated, "Inspector Rex."

"Don't you dare make fun of Komissar Rex!"

Callum sat up and placed both palms on her cheeks. "I will not make fun of your beloved detective dog." His lips lightly touched hers before he said, "We need to go to Austria one day."

She tilted her head at him. "We?"

Callum nodded once. "I need to try Wiener schnitzels."

We'll never make it to Austria together.

Peyton frowned at the thought and the memory. It would only be a dream. The idea of going to Austria without him left her empty inside. Those were their dreams, and she didn't want to share them with anyone but him. But it was a broken dream they'd never live. Tonight would be their last.

"That's him, isn't it?" June asked next to her.

"That's him," Peyton agreed.

"So I should thank him for my album?"

Letting out a laugh, Peyton turned to face June. It was incredible that a famous, Billboard-charting artist consider her a friend. June was smart, talented, and absolutely stunning with her green eyes, black hair, and sun-kissed skin tone. June was flawless and every inch the celebrity. But Peyton saw the real June, the June who struggled with writer's block and enjoyed sitting by the lake with her guitar.

"That album was all you, June." Peyton smiled.

June rolled her eyes. "I wouldn't have been brave enough to show my producers without you. I was thinking about having a small release party here, promote the hotel's rebuild."

Peyton's mouth dropped. "Really?"

"Of course, Peyton. This hotel was my inspiration and I want to be part of its new beginning. How is next week? It'll be enough time to market it and I'll have the team set up a giveaway for some fans to come down for an intimate concert."

Just as Peyton was about to reply, June's guitarist was dragging her to the stage.

"We'll talk in the morning, Peyton," June told her.

Peyton smiled at June before she let her eyes sweep the wedding. Everything looked perfect. People seemed to be enjoying themselves as they laughed and danced. Somehow, she pulled it off.

Towards the end of the cliff, she noticed Callum talking to Jenny. Callum nodded a few times and gestured with his hands before he hugged Jenny. When they finished their embraced, Jenny wiped her cheeks and then they both started walking in Peyton's direction.

"You okay?" Peyton asked once they stopped in front of

her.

Jenny nodded and said, "Everything's perfect. Listen, Peyton, I have things here covered. You've been up since five. You go home and rest. I'll make sure everything is taken care of. It hasn't been an easy week for you."

Peyton's eyebrows met as she looked at Jenny and then Callum. "I can't leave the wedding. Oliver and Ma—"

"Peyton, Oliver and Marissa won't care. I just have to stay a little longer and then I'll come by your place," Callum said.

"Fine," she said. Truth be told, she was tired. Hanging fairy lights and setting up lanterns had really done a number on her. It wasn't how she'd wanted her last night with Callum to go.

Callum stepped forward, placing his palms on her jaw as he lips softly grazed her forehead. "I won't be long," he promised.

She gave him a tight smile. "Goodnight, Jenny," Peyton said before she walked over to the small, portable building that acted as her office and grabbed her things.

Peyton stared at the ceiling as she waited for the bathtub tap to drip. Once the drop landed in the hot tub of water, she breathed out.

"Twenty-seven."

Then another drip.

"Twenty-eight."

And another.

"Twenty-nine."

And another.

"Thir—"

"Peyton?"

Callum's voice stopped her count. She turned her head to the side and stared at the bathroom door.

"In here," she called out. Then she submerged herself a little more into the hot water and let her head rest on the porcelain tub.

Seconds passed before Callum walked into the bathroom.

Then he walked over to her before he crouched so they were eye level. Her lips curved into an honest smile, grateful to see that he hadn't left. As she'd walked home, that's what she had feared the most—his leaving without a goodbye. After a call to Aunt Brenda about the success of the wedding, she had tried to silence her over-calculating mind with a hot bath. But the silence of the bathroom had just served to further increase her mind's activities.

However, seeing him squashed the doubts. Having him in front of her made her heart leap and ache. Her heart was bipolar when it came to him.

"How's the rest of the wedding?" she asked as she placed both hands on the tub and turned her body to face him better.

"Beautiful. You and Jenny did an amazing job," Callum said.

"You helped, too."

He leant forward and gave her a chaste kiss. "Don't sell yourself short, Peyton."

Her mouth tugged upwards at his compliment. Each drip she heard behind her made her realise just how quickly seconds were passing them. Soon, morning would come and they'd say goodbye.

"Take your clothes off and hold me," she instructed in a soft voice.

Callum didn't say anything as he removed his suit jacket and dropped it on the floor. She took in every movement he made until he was only left in his dress pants. Then his hands were on his belt as he unfastened it and unbuttoned his pants. Her heart beat fast against her chest as he pulled down the zipper and let the slacks fall to his feet. Stepping out of them, he stood naked in front of her.

Crouching back down to face her, Callum stroked her wet hair back and kept his grey eyes on her. She saw it in the way he looked at her—he wanted tonight to be memorable as they closed their book. They'd had a lifetime of love in a short period of sometimes. It was more than she thought she'd have with him and more than most people would have in life.

"I will never forget you, Peyton Olivia Spencer," he whispered. His words travelled through her veins and settled into her burning heart.

Afraid she would plead for him again, she pushed up from the tub, away from his touch, and sat straight. She gave him the room to sit and hold her. Carefully, he placed one foot in the water and then the other before he lowered himself behind her. He stretched out his legs on either side of Peyton's body and rested his hands on her hips, pulling her in to lean into his chest.

Peyton drew up her legs as Callum's chin settled in the curve of her neck and his hands were on her shins. She felt all of him against her back as she stared at the bubbles that surrounded their bodies.

"Callum," she said, trying to ignore the sad tone to her voice.

"Yes, Peyton."

"This is going to end horribly for us, isn't it?" she asked, already knowing the answer.

His lips grazed her neck, sending shivers down her spine, and then he pressed another one just below her ear. His breath touched her skin before he said, "Yes."

Peyton's lips made a fine line, and she nodded. "Then bring it on."

His soft chuckle influenced the smile on her face. The moment Peyton moved, his hands left her, giving her the space to turn her body to his. When she positioned both palms on his chest, his breathing was heavy rather than consistent intakes of air. Then she tilted her head slightly and stared into his eyes.

"What are you thinking about?" he asked, covering her hands with his before bringing her left hand to his lips and kissing her palm.

"Austria," she replied.

"Oh," he let out, staring at their connected hands. "I'm sorry we never got there." The remorse was thick in his voice.

"It was just one of those things, Callum. Things we said because we were young and dumb. We thought we were invincible. But the truth of it all was that we were naïve and high on love and the belief of forever. We were teenagers who thought we could outplay the universe."

Callum looked down at their hands before he said, "The universe outplayed us in the end."

The sad look in his eyes could break her heart all over again. She didn't want this to be sad. She wanted a few good memories. Ones that would keep her company at night. Ones that would guide her through the shadows and into the light. Peyton pulled her hand from his and placed it on his shoulder. Then Callum's eyes met hers before her hand mirrored her previous actions.

"Hold me, please," she said.

Callum nodded. "All night I will."

That made her smile. She wrapped her arms around the back of his head and sat in his lap. That's when she felt him touch her *there,* but she didn't want them to make love in the tub. She wanted him in her sheets for the last time. Then she pulled his ear to her chest, allowing him to hear her heart beat for him.

She didn't care that this embrace was eating away the seconds, the minutes they had left. This was a sometimes moments. Hers. His. Theirs. No one would ever take this exact moment away. She knew what sometimes moments were. They were a beautiful way of hiding the fact that sometimes doesn't mean forever. That sometimes leads to 'The End.' *Their* end.

Sometimes moments would keep her living in denial for the rest of her life, and she was okay with it. Because sometimes was what she would have and hold on to. This time, she was sure she couldn't have a life after Callum. He had marked her further. There would be no man after him. It was Callum or no man at all for her heart. It was a choice her brain had agreed upon.

"Callum," she said as she closed her eyes.

"Yes, Peyton."

She held him closer to her chest. "I don't think I could love anyone as hard, as strong, as pure, as intense, or as heartbreakingly as I love you. You should know that I've only ever wanted to love you."

Callum's arms wrapped around her back and held her tight. "I've only ever wanted to love just you. I only loved just you. I will only love just you—all of you, Peyton. When I leave, you'll be the one my heart loves more than anything that has breathed or existed."

Peyton didn't even try to hold back her tears as her heart began to crumble. "You'll find her," she whispered, letting go of the hope that it could have been her.

Callum shook his head against her breasts. "I found her when I was a teenager. I found her again almost a month ago. I'm holding her...but I have to let her go."

He has to let me go... I have to let him go. I have to let him be free.

Peyton untangled her arms and placed both her hands on the side of his head, pulling him up to face her.

She took a deep breath.

And then exhaled.

She let her heart beat twice before she said, "If you ever need me, I will be right here. Maybe, one day, you'll find your way to me again. I will be here, right where you left me. We don't have to talk. We could just exchange glances and then you leave, knowing that it's enough for us. I'll hope for those stolen glances."

I'll hope for forever someday. I'll hope for forever in our next lives. I'll ask God for his love in our next lives, too. I'll ask him for Callum to love me until the very end of existence.

Thirty-Three

The sun lit her bedroom brightly and beautifully, like it were mocking them. Like the sun knew of the end the exact same way it gave the moon the space to glow above the skies. But unlike the sun, they would never have another rise. It was their sunset for good. Her world would soon be consumed by black, no light from the moon to guide the waves to shore and no sun to warm her body. Just black. They had moments left of their time together.

They had both been awake long before the sun had risen but both had stayed quiet, their hands touching and their fingers circling – whatever they could do to make the other know that they weren't alone just yet.

Each breath Callum made she considered her favourite until he made another. Each heartbeat that thumped against her ear was memorised. With each circle he made, the pattern was engrained into her skin. Each squeeze of her arm was cherished. It was all about memorising, waiting to feel, hear, touch, and breathe the last of them.

Last night was the last time they'd make love. If they were to do so now, it'd make goodbye much harder. Every inch of pleasure, every moan, groan, pant, and whisper of love was sent directly to her heart. They had loved harder than they had before. They had cried more. They had reached euphoria for the last time in each other's arms. It had been a perfect ending. It had been the perfect last time.

"I'm sorry, Peyton," he whispered before his chin dipped and he kissed the top of her head.

Her eyes burned as salty tears tried to escape. She wanted to dig her nails into his torso to stop them from running down her face, but to no success. They fell and pooled on his chest.

"It's okay," she whispered back, the pain engulfing her chest.

This is my closure.

"I thought I was strong enough to not let this happen between us. I told you I wasn't cruel, but I'm a liar. I told you that I wouldn't let you fall in love with me, and I lied to you. I am a liar. I'm sorry, Peyton."

The sheer agony in his voice had Peyton squeezing her eyes shut. "Don't be sorry, Callum. I promised that I wouldn't let you kiss me and I let you. I broke a promise… We're both liars," she said and opened her eyes, still feeling the stings.

"Honestly, I'm glad you broke your promise. I'm glad for Mr Lucky. I'm relieved to know you still love me. I'll be thanking the universe for your forgiveness."

Peyton sat up and looked down at him. "You earned my forgiveness. You stood by me and chose to support me. You gave me my life back."

Callum sat straight, wrapped his arms around her, and leant back on the headboard. "Right now, knowing that we're about to say goodbye… You have given me a reason to hate the universe. To hate everything that gets to breathe. But I can't be angry with the world because I've had the chance to love you all over again."

His words settled deep within her heart—the same place that held his love and never wanted to let him go. Desire, want, and need flowed through her veins until they reached her chest. Placing her hand on his stomach, Peyton pushed herself away from his arms and swung her leg over him. She then set her free palm on his lower torso and hovered over him, straddling him.

Callum sighed out and rested both his hands on her waist,

stopping her from lowering down on him. "Peyton, we said last night would be it."

She shook her head. "I'm always going to want more than just last night, Callum. I need this with you. I need this one last time. I need to see you in the sunlight, in the pureness of the day. I need you to say goodbye to me this way."

When his hold on her loosened, she knew that he was submitting to her wants. She ran her hand from his stomach to his chest before finally settling on his shoulders. His eyes were locked on hers as she eased down on him slowly enough to memorise the sharp inhale of breath he made and the way his fingers dug into her. There was something empowering about being on top, controlling their pleasure.

The moment he was completely inside her, Callum groaned before breathing out, "God, Peyton."

She didn't move, loving the way he filled her and completed her. She knew it would never be this satisfying or right with another man. Running her fingers up his neck, she cupped his face, ensuring his eyes stayed on hers.

"When you come, can you tell me you love me? Is that possible?" she asked in a nervous voice.

Callum panted and nodded his head. "For you, Peyton, I'd freeze hell over."

A small smile touched her lips. "So, yes?"

He leant forward and placed his lips on her neck. "God, yes," he breathed, looking up at her.

That was all it took for her to lift her lips and sink slowly back down on him—not to tease, but to savour the feel. This wasn't about teasing. It was about making memorable love between them. To say goodbye to their old memories and have this one moment to reflect on where their love was mutually shared and mutually craved.

Again, she raised her hips and slowly immersed herself around him, but this time, his hips bucked and Peyton moaned. She let her head fall into the curve of his neck.

"Again, please," she begged, wanting him to take control, loving the way he thrust inside her.

He rolled them over so Peyton was on her back. Then she leaned up and kissed the cherry blossoms that tattooed his arm before she wrapped her legs around his waist and her hands around his strong arms.

Her heart stopped the moment he pulled out, and it regained its beats the moment he entered her with a hard, powerful rock of his hips.

"Callum," she moaned as she arched her back and met his thrust.

Harder.

Slower.

Harder.

Faster.

Her heart beat the same way he made love to her. She felt the tension build, waiting to be explode. And by the way Callum threw back his head and groaned, she knew he was close, too. The way their lovemaking brought him pleasure made her heart swell. No one could make her get so lost in pleasure the way he did. Unique, heartbreakingly beautiful, and hers—just for now.

"Kiss me," she half-instructed and half-breathed.

Callum's lips found hers and then his tongue mimicked the movements he made inside of her. She softly cried out as the pleasure built, and her breathing became pants.

"Fuck, Peyton," Callum murmured into her mouth.

"Harder," she begged as she moved her hips to meet him.

Her heart continued to thump harder as he sped up his thrusts. Their cries were no longer soft as her nails dug into his tattooed cherry blossoms. This emotional connection between them, knowing it was their last time, was about to throw her over the edge, reach a pleasure she had never known.

"It's always been you. Never anyone else," he whispered as he moved even faster.

When Callum propped himself, she could see a line of sweat settle on his forehead. Then his hands were on her waist as he held her tightly. His deep thrust had Peyton fisting the sheets as pleasure overtook her body and her orgasm hit her hard.

He thrust inside her twice before he groaned, looked her in

the eye, and said, "I love you, Peyton," as he came inside her.

Then he collapsed on top of her breasts, and Peyton's hands were stroking the back of his head.

"Goodbye, Callum," she whispered.

Callum panted heavily before he managed to say, "Goodbye, my love."

And once again, I'm here.

Sitting on the same step.

But this time, I know goodbye is imminent.

The double-story brick house she stared at was one she had known all her life, but over four years ago, it'd become a stranger to her. If she could have bulldozed it away, she would have. But unlike the summer he'd broken her heart, they were saying goodbye in winter. A winter's day where the sun was shining bright, with a cool wind in the air. It was a perfect day to break her heart.

The moment after they'd made love, she'd showered, allowing him the time and space to pack the remainder of his things before he was to leave town. She'd cried in the shower, sitting on the floor as the water fell over her. She'd cried as she walked into her bedroom and saw her unmade bed. She'd cried until the tears had dried up and she'd had enough in her to sit on the step.

When the door opened, the first thing she saw was a suitcase. And then Callum. He closed it behind him and looked over to her. The pain that consumed his face tore her heart wide open. It was like he was conflicted.

His Volvo sounded as his car unlocked. Then he gave her a tight smile before walked to the boot of his car, his back turned to her. Callum didn't move. After almost a minute of standing there, he lifted the boot, put his suitcase inside, and closed it. Then he turned around and met her eyes.

Callum crossed the road. Each step he took brought goodbye and their end closer. They were moments away from the obliteration of them. She wished he'd take slower strides, but he was at the bottom step within in seconds.

"So, this is it," Peyton said as she got to her feet.

He nodded. "This is it, Peyton."

She walked down the steps until she was just in front of him. A sigh left his lips before Callum cupped her face and then stroked her cheeks with the pad of his thumbs.

"I don't want you to go," she croaked out. Then she placed her hand on his left arm, turning his arm around to see his tattoo.

"If I could stay, I would," he said in a tight voice.

Peyton looked down at his wrist. His name was tattooed on her heart. But ink didn't have to be visible on her skin for her to be reminded. Callum Reid, her heart's only.

"I'm going to miss you, Callum Reid," she sobbed.

His arms were around her instantly as he held her close. She wrapped her arms around him, keeping him for just a little longer. Then she cried into his chest, staining the light-grey shirt he was wearing. Her heart burned with her lungs because she wanted the concept of forever. And she wanted him for longer than they had.

"I wish you could have given me the chance to love you for those four years we were apart. I wish you would let me love you for another four years and longer. I wish you'd stay." She weeped harder. "This is the worst breakup I've ever had, and the last one destroyed me."

"Promise me something," he said.

Peyton glanced up to see him staring at her. "For you, Callum Reid, I would freeze hell over."

He smiled. "No matter what you hear or what is done, you live a good and happy life, Peyton Spencer."

An involuntary whimper escaped. It was honest and beautiful. But she hated that he wanted her to have a happy life without him. She wasn't sure it would be possible.

"There isn't one after you're gone. I love you," she cried.

He brushed her tears away and pressed his lips to her forehead. The moment he pulled away, he whispered, "There will be. I am your sometimes, Peyton. Go find your forever."

"No, I don't—"

He shook his head, stopping her. "I've held your heart for far too long. Your forever moments are waiting for you. I will always love you and our sometimes."

The tears that escaped him made it so much harder for her to let him go. She shook her head.

"Callum," she struggled out. "I love you," she said, knowing it was the last time. Their sometimes was their end. No matter how much it broke her heart, a future was no longer valid.

He took a step back onto the path and reached into his jeans pocket. Then he pulled out an envelope she recognised.

"Our epilogue," she breathed out.

He wrapped her hands around the letter. "You promised me that you'd read this when I left. Please don't break this. Do this one thing for me, Pey. Read our epilogue."

She nodded and held it tight in her hand.

"No one loves you like I do," he promised.

Peyton wasn't sure why, but she smiled. "No one hurts me like you do."

Callum's lips made a fine line before he said, "Touché."

There was silence until they both let out a light laugh.

"I'm going to miss you, Peyton."

She closed the distance and tangled her arms around his neck. "You're my favourite sometimes moments. Not the things we did, but you. All of you."

His mouth found hers as they kissed one last time. It wasn't desperate or controlling. It was purely to let their lips know that it was the end and to always remember each other. Each movement of his on hers had her heart aching. Goodbye was bittersweet. She got it in the end, but she didn't want it. She wanted him.

Once he pulled his mouth away, he rested his forehead on hers. He didn't close his eyes, and it was almost as if he were almost afraid to. His arms were around her, their bodies meeting.

"Goodbye, Peyton Spencer, my greatest love."

Peyton blinked hard to remove the tears. She wanted one final look of him, one final look of the man who would always have her heart.

"Goodbye, Callum Reid. I will love you long after our goodbye and you leave town."

A loving smile developed on his lips. She gave him one in return before they both fell silent, knowing they were prolonging their separation.

"Get the fuck off my property, Callum," she finally teased, reminding him of the first time he was back at her house.

Callum let out a soft chuckle and took a deep breath. "I love you. Never forget that," he said before he kissed her forehead.

He let his lips linger on her skin for a second longer before he pulled back, putting distance between them. Then he looked at the letter she held before he turned and walked towards his car. Peyton's knees buckled, so she sat on the step, watching him leave.

Callum didn't look over his shoulder as he got into the car. Tears ran down her face as the brake lights disappeared and the Volvo reversed out of the driveway. Holding her breath, she watched the dark-blue car drive away from their houses and towards the town's exit. It was quick. Their goodbye ended as quickly as they had started. Peyton stayed on the step long after he left, letting the tears to vertically roll across her cheeks.

Her heart throbbed painfully in her chest as she willed the car to return. But it didn't. After the wind picked up and grey clouds covered the sun, she wiped the tears away and felt the nothingness in her body. Then she looked at the envelope. Her name was written exactly like Callum's tattoo, and that's when she realised his tattoo was actually in his handwriting. The knowledge caused her to sob as she ripped the envelope open.

Pulling out the letter, she unfolded it, and read it.

If you ever forget, it's all on the back of the picture.

- Callum.

Peyton looked up from the letter and stared at the house across the road.

"What picture is he—"

Quickly getting on her feet, she ran into the house and then into her bedroom. She looked around her room to find the framed picture of the lake leaning against the wall below the windowsill. After picking up the frame, she sat on her bed and placed Callum's letter on top of the blanket.

She turned the frame over, slid the pins back, took off the backing, and set it next to Callum's letter. Her breath dissolved in her lungs and her heart froze the moment she saw it.

October 2nd 2009 – I love you, Peyton Olivia Spencer.

June 29th 2014 – I will never stop loving you, Peyton Olivia Spencer.

Thirty-Four

Two days later, life was the exact same as before, just different in some ways. The emptiness in her grew larger, and so did the aches. She missed him. Missed the sight of his smile, the tattoo cherry blossoms that ran up his arm, and the way he loved her.

Life had moved on after Callum had left town. At night, she'd lie in bed and think of him, stare out at the cherry blossom tree, and hope that he thought of her, because she thought of him with every minute that ticked by.

Peyton sighed as she looked around her. The small, square box that was her office barely fit her and Jenny. She shook her head and concentrated on the paperwork in front of her. Yesterday, she'd heard from the insurance provider—her claim had gone through without a hitch. Now, she was waiting for the building permits to be approved by the council. Unsure of how the town council worked, she didn't hold her breath. For now, the staff was on paid leave until she figured out the next move.

Checking the time on her phone, Peyton saw that it was just after six p.m. She figured she would stay in the portable building for as long as she could, too afraid to go home alone. But then her phone buzzed in her hand at the new message from Madilynne.

Madilynne: You want to come to Graham's for dinner?
Peyton: Not really. I have a lot of paperwork.
Madilynne: Piss-poor excuse, Peyton Spencer.
Peyton: I think I'd rather give you two alone time.
Madilynne: Better excuse. Are you in that shoebox?
Peyton: Yeah, why?
Madilynne: Go outside for a minute.
Peyton: Why?
Madilynne: Just do it!

Groaning out, Peyton set her phone down on the small table and walked to the door. She pulled on it twice, trying to get it unjammed. On the third try, she managed to get it open, surprised to see the person standing in front of her.

"Mayor," she breathed.

Madilynne's father gave her a smile just visible from the light above the door. Her best friend's father was not the person she had been expecting to see.

"Hello, Peyton. How are you?" he asked.

"Ah, fine. And you, sir?" she asked nervously. Peyton had always liked the mayor, but his authority scared her.

He nodded. "That's good. Listen, Peyton, I just wanted to express my apologies for the recent behaviour of this town towards you and the hotel. I do not know the details except for what Madilynne has told me. It saddens me to see such a lovely person like you be subjected to mistreatment, especially from our volunteer firefighters."

Peyton flinched in surprise. An apology was something she hadn't considered. "It's okay, Mayor Woodside. I love this town. My parents loved this town. I wouldn't be standing here today if I didn't believe in the hotel."

His smile grew larger. "As the mayor and not your best friend's father, it fills me with joy to hear a business owner love this town. That is why I stopped by to give you this," he said, handing her a letter.

Peyton unfolded it and started reading. Her breath fled the moment she read the words: *building permits granted.*

"This is impossible. I just submitted these recently," Peyton uttered breathlessly. When she looked up from the letter, she saw the glint in his eyes.

"I was able to put them ahead of the pack as the father of your friend. But as the major of Daylesford, I was able to lobby and support your plans. The scale and design are beautiful. I have always believed in your parents, but you, Peyton... You are the image of sheer belief and determination. You are my inspiration to make this town better. I believe in you and your plans for The Spencer."

As a friend of his daughter, Peyton threw her arms around him and graciously thanked him. Tears of relief ran down her face when she pulled away from Mayor Woodside.

"Thank you. Thank you so much." She wiped her cheeks. "I can start building my hotel next week."

Mayor Woodside adjusted his suit jacket and said, "You may not believe what I'm about to say, but I am proud of you, Peyton. The things you have done in the last four years? It's incredible, and I know your parents would be proud of you, too."

"I appreciate that so much, sir."

"You go on home now, Peyton. Tomorrow is a brand-new day," he said before he turned and walked to his car.

Peyton looked back at the letter and kissed it before she whispered, "Thank you," to the cold night.

She quickly grabbed her keys, her phone, and her bag. She couldn't wipe the smile off her face as she locked the door behind her—the first smile she wore since Callum. After unlocking her phone as she walked down the path, Peyton quickly messaged Madilynne.

> **Peyton**: Thank you for what you did with your dad and the town council.
> **Madilynne**: I did it because I believe in you and

your dreams, Peyton. My father does, too. Make us proud.
Peyton: I will do my best. This is for us.
Madilynne: No. This is for you. Do this for you. Goodnight, Peyton.

Peyton placed her phone in her bag and nodded to herself. *This is for me.*

The moment she got home, she was too excited for sleep. She worked through the estimated quotes and made a list of all the things she had to prepare and the people she would have to call in the morning. She also would have to call June about next week's album release party. She'd wanted the singer to stay, but June had insisted that she return to the city to make sure the record company agreed and the right promotions was done.

Peyton sat in bed as she stared at Callum's blueprints for The Spencer. Her fingers ran across the way he had written her last name. It was all she had of him—a blueprint of her future. No matter how sad she was that she couldn't be with him, she was thankful for their sometimes moments. They were the most beautiful description of the short amount of time they'd loved again. When she had thanked the stars earlier in the night, she had been thanking him, too, hoping that, wherever he was, he'd heard.

Tap. Tap. Tap.

Peyton froze. She missed him so much that her heart had decided she would hear things. Shaking her head, she breathed out and began to relax in bed, looking over the newly designed hotel.

Tap. Tap.

Peyton held her breath as she turned to face her bedroom window.

Tap.

The final tap drew out the air from her lungs. Then suddenly, on her bedside table, her phone buzzed. Without taking her eyes off the window, she picked up her phone and answered it.

"Tell me it's you outside my window," she said into the speaker, reciting the words she had told him when she was seventeen.

There a long and slow silence that had her heart accelerating.

"It's me, Pey. Go to the window," Callum said, also repeating what he had said over four and a half years ago.

Peyton's heart relaxed after two days of being twisted. She didn't hang up as she pulled the covers off her and got out of bed. Then she quickly made her way to the curtains and pushed them back to see him on the other side with his phone to his ear.

"Thank God," she breathed out before she threw her phone on the bed behind her and opened the window.

Callum put his phone in his pocket and looked up at her. "I couldn't take it anymore. I can't be without you, Peyton. I want to stay with you for as long as I can."

Heavy tears flowed without care. Reaching out, she placed her hands on his cheeks and brought his lips to hers. Meeting, moulding, and mending.

"God, I've missed you," she said against his mouth and between their kiss. When she drew back, she asked, "Are you really here right now?"

He nodded. "Yes. I knew I'd left behind my reason for living here in Daylesford. I couldn't take it anymore."

He hadn't said that his stay would be forever, but she didn't care. She should. But she didn't. She wanted as much time as humanly possible with this man.

Peyton stroked his cheeks once. He felt real. His lips felt real. He was here with her again.

"Say it," she said.

Callum broke into a beautiful and memorable smile. "I love you, Peyton. I can't leave you again."

Peyton kissed him full on the lips once before she said, "I love you, too, Callum. Now come to bed."

She stepped away from the window and watched him climb through it as easily as he had done many times before. Once

Callum had closed the window, she didn't give him the chance to stand properly before she crashed her lips into his and her fingers were in his hair.

"I've missed you," she mumbled over his lips as she made quick work of the thick jacket he was wearing.

Callum broke their kiss as he dropped the jacket on the floor and pulled his shirt over his head, letting it join his jacket. Callum's naked chest was a sight that left her breathless. His tattoos made him more beautiful since she knew they were for her and about her. Callum stepped towards her when he stopped. The framed pictures of his words caught his attention.

"You kept your promise," he pointed out as he slipped off his shoes. Then his hands were on her waist, pushing his body close to Peyton's.

She grinned. "This is why Jenny wanted to save it?"

"She caught me writing it when I first gave you the frame. Guess she wanted you to see them. I'd meant it then the same way as I meant it a few days ago."

She kissed him once before she took his hand in hers and led him to the bed. "Hold me tonight?" she asked.

It was his turn to kiss her once. "Until my very last breath," he promised.

Her heart ached at those five words, but his mouth on hers had her forgetting the ache and feeling relieved to have him in her arms again. The life and fire in her had returned the moment he had.

Thirty-Five

Almost a week after Callum had returned to her, Peyton stood outside the remains of her hotel. On Monday, they would start the rebuild. Today was June's rehearsal album release party. After a day of setting up the stage and making sure the wiring and electricity were working, they were ready. Those in the town were welcome to stop by to see June. Peyton didn't hate the town or the people. She wanted to be happy with her life and held no grudge on those who had played their part in the demise of The Spencer-Dayle.

Peyton sat on the bench in front of the stage with a smile. The rehearsal concert was perfect. She knew her hotel wasn't the most picturesque place to have a release party, but it was what June wanted. Turning around, she noticed Graham and Callum talking. They looked defeated and worried as they talked. She put it down to their exhaustion over making June's album release at the hotel perfect. In the week since his return, Callum had spent a lot of time with Graham. And in that week, undeniable happiness had been shared with him. The hesitation had still been in his eyes as they'd made love, but she was going to help him move past it. They would find a way.

She watched them hug before she walked over to them both, curious of their interaction. Then they stopped immediately once she approached them and Callum gave her a smile that quickly faded

"Hey," Peyton greeted, stopping in front of them. "What you guys talking about?"

Callum let out a soft groan, so soft that she'd almost missed it. But she didn't miss the way he clenched his fist so tight that his knuckles turned white.

"Nothing," he finally let out in a breathless whisper.

"I'm going to go help Madilynne with the food. I'll give you guys some time together," Graham said, excusing himself.

For a second, she caught a flash of sadness in Graham's eyes as he walked past her.

"Peyton, do you want to go for a walk?" Callum asked.

She nodded. "Okay."

He took her hand, his grip on her not as strong as it had been a few days ago, and the cool touch of his skin almost had her jumping. He raised their joined hands and kissed the back of hers as he led her towards the pier.

Callum's fingers were loosening, and every once in a while, he'd stop and try to hold her hand more firmly. And when he did he gave her a smile. Once they reached the pier, they walked across it to the sight of the setting sun. The sky filled with oranges, purples and reds, just like his photograph. Then Callum leant on the wooden railing as he looked out at the horizon as a sad look consumed his face.

When he let go of her hand and looked back at her, the honest fear in his eyes frightened her.

"Peyton," he said breathlessly.

"Yes?" she asked, not taking her eyes off of him.

"You've always deserved better than me."

She shook her head to object. "That's not—"

He stopped her by taking her hands in his. "We don't have a lot of time left, my love. You still promise to live a good and happy life once I leave?"

He's still leaving...

"No," she confessed, her eyes tearing.

He sighed. "Please don't cry, Peyton. It makes this so hard for me to say."

"Then don't say it. Please don't say it."

Tears ran down his face. They weren't like the ones she had seen him shed before.

"I love you. Don't you ever forget that. I love you so damn much. I've fought hard to try to hold on long enough to grow old with you. I've tried so hard to breathe enough to make tomorrow with you. I'm sorry I'm failing you, Peyton. I'm sorry we don't have a tomorrow within us." He struggled to take a deep breath. "I've been trying to tell you all week. I just…don't know how to tell you."

Peyton's heart ached as tears continued to fall. "I don't understand. You're not making sense. We'll figure out a way to be together. I swear we'll be together. If I have to leave this town, I'll do it. Please let me be with you!" she cried.

Callum let go of her hands and cupped her face. "It's not me that's stopping us. It's the universe. All I want is a lifetime with you. I love you, Peyton. You are my forever, never just my sometimes."

He kissed her, his lips not as strong and firm as before. They were soft and not quite making movement. And that's when Callum let out a groan as his hands slipped. He almost fell on top of her, and Peyton had to hold him up.

"Callum!" she cried.

He shouted in pain as his body started to convulse. Peyton wasn't strong enough to keep him on his feet, so they fell onto the pier, his body shaking violently in her arms.

"Callum! What do I do? Callum!" she screamed, her tears landing on his face.

She wrestled his weight to pull her phone out of her pocket, screaming his name as his body trembled.

"Stay with me, please," she pleaded as she dialled triple zero.

Callum's convulsion started to slow down until he breathed out, "Peyton."

She held him tight. "Please don't leave me. Please stay!"

"I—" he started to stay as his eyes slowly closed.

"No! No!" she shrieked as the operator answered.

"Peyton!" Graham's voice screamed.

She raised her head to see Graham racing towards the pier as Peyton held Callum tightly, trying to stop his thrashing.

"Help me, Graham! Please help me!" she shouted from the top of her lungs. Then she looked back down at Callum as his hands trembled.

When Graham reached them, he took the phone from her and started talking into the speaker, Peyton unable to hear a word he said.

"Tell me you love me again," she whispered as she stroked his face.

Callum's shaky hand reached up and rested on top of hers. "I love you forever," he said. Then his breathing became shallow.

"Just know you found redemption the moment you walked back into my life. I love you, Callum," she sobbed.

"Peyton, the ambulance will be here in seconds," Graham said.

Callum's hand fell away from hers, landing against his body. His body relaxed in her arms, and she felt him inhale one last final breath before he breathed it out.

"No!" she cried and placed her hand over his chest.

No heartbeat.

"No!" she cried again. "Come back to me."

She wailed harder than she had ever before as her grasp on him tightened. Then she whimpered into the top of his head, her tears wetting his hair.

"I love you. Come back," she begged softly. "Come back to me, Callum."

Tears dragged themselves across her face as she looked at his pale face. She felt it. Every last Callum Reid breath experienced, she felt.

I watched and felt the love of my life die.

Thirty-Six

Peyton stood by and watched his loved ones gather around his grave. No matter how much she tried, she couldn't convince herself to witness his wake. She had experienced his death in her hands. She had watched him die. No amount of happy pictures of Callum Reid could ever make her forget the last moments of his life.

The pain inside her was unbearable. She wasn't sure how she had made it through the last three days, but she had. Her aunt and uncle had returned to Daylesford, having ignored Peyton's objections. June's album release had been cancelled and moved to the Docklands in the city. Life and the hotel had stalled.

She couldn't will herself out of bed. Callum's funeral was what had gotten her up. Jenny had driven her and attended the service while Peyton had stood outside, crying. Callum's mother had been the one to contact Peyton to ask if she wanted to speak, but Peyton had refused. She couldn't speak of their love. No one had understood when he was alive, so they wouldn't now that he was dead.

Brain tumour.

That's what Graham had told her moments after the ambulance had taken Callum to the hospital to await an autopsy. The first thing Peyton had done was slap Graham in the face for keeping it from her. Never had she believed that Callum was dying. If only she had seen the signs: his headaches, and his recent dizziness, and tiredness. She could have done something. After some struggle, Graham had held her and told her the truth. Peyton had cried and called her best friend a liar. It had taken Madilynne and Jenny talking to her before Peyton settled down.

The front door was always knocked on. But Aunt Brenda would answer and ask them to give Peyton some time. Jay had knocked on the door, too, but he was the last person she wanted to see. Callum dying had made Peyton hate Jay with more ferociousness than necessary.

Now, three days after his death, Peyton stood at a distance. Those who grieved him stood in her way of saying goodbye. She didn't want to say goodbye. She still held hope that he'd be outside her window or at the pier or at their spot in the forest, but he wasn't. Not a day went by where she didn't cry.

"Cherry blossoms," Graham said as he stood next to her.

She noticed the flowers in his hand and laughed. She actually laughed. "Lavender?" she asked.

He shrugged with a grin. "There's that smile. He always did call me lavender boy. Why not get the last laugh?"

That smile he'd noticed faded as she looked down at the cherry blossoms in her hands. "I miss him. I can feel him with me, but I turn around and I'm alone."

"I'm sorry he didn't get the chance to tell you, Peyton."

She picked up a loose cherry blossom and threw it with the wind, watching it fly. "He tried to tell me," she said. "He also left me, thinking it was going to be better."

"I know it sounds kind of cliché to say this, but I know he'll always be with you, Peyton. He loved you more than you realise," Graham said.

She only nodded in agreement.

Peyton gazed at the sight of people starting to make their way to the car park to head off to the lunch Mrs Reid had planned. Peyton wouldn't attend, and the Reids knew that. She had seen them when she'd first arrived at the funeral house. The look on

Mrs Reid's face had broken Peyton's heart. It hadn't just been the look of a mother who had lost her only child. It had been the look of knowing that someone who had loved her son had lost him, too. His parents had arrived in Daylesford in a matter of hours the day he'd died, but they'd never crossed paths. They had been quick to take their son back home to the city.

"It's time you left Daylesford, Graham," Peyton finally said.

"What?"

"It's time. One of us has to make it out of this town. Callum was right. There is something beautiful outside of our town, and for you, it's Mads. You have to leave that farm and be with her. Your dad will be okay. I will visit him daily if I have to."

This time, Peyton saw understanding flash in his eyes, and then he nodded.

"Give me some time to find someone who can mind the farm while I'm in the city. I can work from home, but I need someone to do the manual work. This goes two ways, Peyton. It's time you left Daylesford, too," Graham said.

It was her turn to nod. "Once the hotel is built and I get things on track, I'm going to see the world."

A proud smile developed on her best friend's face. "Where first?"

Peyton glanced at Callum's grave before she looked back at Graham. "Austria. I'm going for the both of us."

"That's beautiful, Peyton." Graham looped his arm around hers. "Ready to say goodbye?"

Peyton shook her head. "Never, but I'll try."

She took a shaky step towards the freshly covered grave. Then she swallowed hard at the sight of his headstone, his name carved into the stone.

When she reached Callum's final resting place, Graham set the lavender on a clear spot, the countless flowers proving that he was a man loved by many.

"You loved her right, Callum. I'll take care of her for you and I'll keep her out of trouble. You'll be missed, mate. Thank you for Madilynne. Thank you for making Peyton smile and laugh again. And thank you for coming back for her," Graham said before he took a few steps back to give her some time with him.

Peyton set the bundle of cherry blossoms on top of his headstone and sat on the wet grass. As she stared at his name, her heart ached to see it mark his grave.

"I miss you. Words can't express the pain and misery I feel. I love you, and saying it over and over again will never bring you back. I get why you didn't tell me. I hated and loved that you didn't. I get why you left the first time. Your mother said you wanted to leave once you found out about your tumour because you didn't want me to see you suffer. And I also get why you left the second time. Graham's right—you loved me right, Callum Reid. I promise to live a good and happy life for the both of us. Life is never fair, but you taught me it's what you do with it because life is purely a cluster of sometimes moments. When they're grouped together, they are the beautiful forever moments of your life.

"Thank you for our sometimes moments, Callum. They were beautiful and unforgettable. They are my forever moments. I like to believe that we were living the forever the universe was depriving us of. We made it to forever, Callum. And forever had never been so beautiful than when it was you."

There were no tears. The reflection of their love and time together had her smiling lightly.

"I made it out of Daylesford. I didn't get far, but I got past the signs thanks to Jenny. She misses you. So does Mads and Graham. But I miss you the most. I'm trying to live a happy life, but it's been hard since you left. But you left behind reasons for me to keep going and find happiness in what I have. We had a love that most people will never experience. I'll visit you in my dreams when I'm not in the city. I love you always. This isn't me saying goodbye forever, not when I can see you and feel you in our sometimes moments," Peyton said as she stood up.

She stared at the cherry blossoms her uncle had helped pick from her tree. They were beautiful and bright pink, a symbolism of him.

"Goodbye, Callum, my love."

Peyton spun around to see Madilynne and Jenny talking to Graham. When they looked at her, Peyton smiled. They were her family. People who supported her through every loss and every pain she experienced. What she did from now on was for them and Callum.

"There's somewhere I want to go before we head back to town if that's okay?" Peyton asked once she walked to them.

"Wherever you want to go today and any day of your life, we'll get you there," Jenny said, a tear running down her cheek.

Looking down at her left hand and then her wrist, she nodded to herself. She glanced up at the clearing sky and breathed out.

God, if you're listening, thank you for him. Thank you for Callum Reid.

Thirty-Seven

"Six days, Callum. That's how many days it's been since I felt your last breath."

Peyton sat at the end of her bed, holding the framed picture of his written love. Some days, she cried, and some days, she didn't. On the rare occasion that she didn't cry, she felt guilty that she wasn't crying. People from the town still stopped by, but Peyton never answered the door. Her aunt still sent them away, asking for more time. Her uncle would stop by for a daily joke that would actually make her laugh, but then Peyton would stay in bed.

The feel of him was starting to disappear. He was becoming just a memory, and she hated it. She wanted to physically feel him breathe and move. She wished she had seen the signs of his failing health sooner; then she wouldn't have had him work on the hotel. They'd have spent his last days together with no care. But Peyton knew Callum hadn't wanted her to put her life on hold for him. She believed that was why he'd left town at seventeen, when he was first diagnosed.

Peyton placed the picture on her bed and turned her wrist over, following the letters she'd had tattooed on her skin.

Callum.

In her own handwriting, his name branded her skin just like her heart. The night after the funeral, she'd held her bandaged wrist to her chest, hoping somewhere he'd felt her love for him.

Suddenly, a knock on the front door had Peyton looking up. In the last two days, no one had knocked on the door, finally getting the hint that she wasn't interested in talking to anyone. Peyton walked out of her room and towards the front door.

If it were Jay again, she'd do what she had done to Graham moments after Callum died and slap him. No amount of apologetic voicemails and text messages could persuade her to forgive him anytime soon. She just needed time.

She opened the front door and was surprised to see Callum's best friend in a suit, holding a box.

"Hello, Peyton," he said. The life and joy in his eyes had been replaced with a miserable cloud—one Peyton knew well.

"Oliver, this is a surprise. How are you?"

His mouth tugged into a frown. "Like shit. I miss him, but I know it's nothing compared to what you're going through."

"I miss him, too. Would you like to come in for cuppa?" she asked, but Oliver shook his head.

"No. Unfortunately, I have to get back to the city. I drove to drop these off for you," he said, holding the box out to her.

Confused, she took the small, pink box in her hand and looked up at him. "What is it?"

"Callum left it behind. The day before his... The day before he called me to say goodbye. Told me that he left a box in his parents' house and, after the funeral, I had to come by and give it to you," Oliver explained and quickly wiped his eyes. It was evident that he had never experienced losing someone who he loved.

Peyton took a step forward and hugged him tight. Then Oliver let out a mumbling sob over her shoulder. After a minute, she untangled her arms and stared at the box she held in her hands.

"Every birthday or anniversary, he'd say, 'I'm going to see here today. Today is the day I win her forgiveness.' But each time he left to see you, he'd call and say he couldn't do it. The first year of chemo he was a mess. When your parents died, he cried, and I had never seen him cry. He just said to me that you would never want to see him after their funeral. You see, Peyton, his last hope of being with you died when your parents did. Your father informed him on how you were doing and kept telling him of when it was a good day to visit. Your dad was the link Callum needed, and it got him through chemo. When they died, he knew he'd never get you back, so he tried less and less. When he found out that the tumour had returned, the first thing he did was call me and tell me that, this time, he had to do it. That's when I told him that Marissa and I would get married in Daylesford like he had suggested."

For the first time today, tears welled and then fell. Hearing that her father had kept Callum informed of her made her heart ache. Hearing that he had gone through chemo alone hurt her more. She wished she had been there to support him. For four years, she'd believed he was living the city lifestyle, but in reality, he had been just as lonely as she had.

"He loved you, Peyton. He never wanted you to see the sick side of him. Knowing him, he'll never stop loving you. I know you were angry with him for a long time, but I hope you can see that he did it all to save you from a life he believed you weren't suited for. He believed his tumour would hold you back," Oliver explained.

"I'm not angry, Oliver. I was lonely. I missed him and I will always miss him. He claimed and took my heart. I understand why he did it," Peyton said, looking up to meet his eyes.

Oliver smiled and nodded. "We'll keep in touch, Peyton. You deserved a life together. I'm sorry it was taken from you both."

Me, too.

"I'll see you around, Oliver." Peyton bid farewell as she watched him walk down the steps.

Oliver stared at the Reid's house before he got into his car and drove towards the town's exit. She too gazed over it. It would no longer be the Reid's as they had placed it on the market after Callum's funeral. Peyton never found out why the Reid's had kept it vacant for over four years but she believed it was so they had another reason to return to Daylesford.

After closing the front door, Peyton stared at the pink box. She went into the kitchen and out onto the veranda. Then she made her way down the steps to the backyard and around the house until she stood under their cherry blossom tree. Taking in the beautiful pink flowers, they reminded her of him. She walked up to the base of the tree and placed her hand on the bark as though she could feel his heartbeat within the wood.

Peyton turned around and sat on the grass, leaning on the tree. Then she peeked at the tree branches to see the light thread through the spaces. She closed her eyes, and in that moment, she felt him with her. And felt his love within her. When she closed her eyes, he was alive with her.

After she breathed out, she stared at the box. She took off the lid to see an envelope. Then proceeded to pick it up and find that, under it, there was a camera and Polaroids in the bottom of the box. Her heart froze at the sight of them. Some looked years old while some appeared to be fairly recent. Placing the box in her lap, she looked at the envelope.

Her name was written in black ink, the same way he'd tattooed it on his wrist. Her heart jerked at seeing his handwriting, missing him even more so. For the second time today, she wiped the tears from her cheeks.

With a shaky hand, Peyton ripped the back of the envelope and pulled out several pieces of folded paper. Then she gave herself a second to prepare her heart before she read his final words to her.

Dear Peyton,

I'm not sure what I can say to make this easier for you and for me. But I am sorry. I never wanted this. I guess I didn't get the chance to tell you. Maybe I avoided telling you because I was scared to watch you die in front of my eyes. It was selfish of me, I know. So give me a second. Right now, you're asleep next to me. And I'm sure this is the last time I'll hold you. As I write this, I'm saying these three words out loud

to you:
Peyton, I'm dying.
I think I only have days left in me.
I'm hoping I still have days left.
Today, you smiled and I almost told you right there. I almost ripped your heart out with two words:
I'm dying.
You laughed today and I almost said: I'm dying.
You cried today and I almost said: I'm dying.
You held me today and I almost said: I'm dying.
You kissed me today and I almost said: I'm dying.
You made love to me today and I almost said: I'm dying.
You told me you loved me today and I said: I love you, too.
You slept today and I almost said: I'm dying.
You told me you loved me again today and I almost said: I'm dying.
You rested your head in my lap under the cherry blossoms today and I said: I love you forever, Peyton.
We sat in our spot today and I almost said: I'm dying.
I almost said goodbye today, but you said: I'll love you more than each breath I take and each moment I live after you. I love you like the waves hug the shores, only apart for so long, always together by nature. I'll love you even after every star burns out in our galaxy. I'll love you even after the last breaths of forever are made.
You broke my heart today and I said: You'll live a happy life.
You let me hold your hand today and I thought: You are my forever, Peyton. Never just my sometimes.
You woke up in my arms today and I almost said: I'm dying, Peyton. Please forgive me today.
I've mentally thought of the words I'd say to you. But how do you tell the love of your life that you're dying? How do you willingly kill yourself before the

tumour does? How do you watch the hope and love die in her eyes? How do you keep from telling her that you'll never see her again, hear her heartbeat, hear her breathe, and hear her tell you she loves you? How? The answer is: I don't know how to and I didn't want to.

There was never a good time to tell you. My plan was never to walk back into Daylesford with you telling me that you loved me back. I never planned to finally tell you that I loved you. I never planned on kissing you, holding you, making love to you, or seeing you smile at me. I never planned, but I hoped – no, I dreamed – for all of those. You, Peyton Olivia, are my biggest dream. I'm sorry I couldn't be there to witness all of life's firsts you have yet to discover. You will make a beautiful fiancée, a beautiful wife, a beautiful soul mate, a beautiful mother, and a beautiful lover.

I want you to be all those for me. I've begged and tried to negotiate with the world. I never wanted a future more than after the tumour came back. If I could marry you right now, I'd do it. I'd kill for it. I'd give up an extra day of my life for you to be Peyton Reid, my wife, my soul mate, the mother of my child, and my ever-so-beautiful lover. If God gave me more time, I would make it all happen. But God gave me limited time and I wasted four years of it away from you. I didn't want you to see me go through chemo. I didn't want you to see me want to give up on life. I didn't want you to think of me dying. I wanted you to live. I wanted you to find happiness and be free from me. I wanted you to be saved from me.

Weeks before I saw you again, the doctor told me that, this time, chemo didn't work. My first thought was of you, not of my life. I needed to come back for you. This time, I had to make it past the sign. I had to be in breathing distance of you. I needed to feel your pain. I needed to know that being away was the best for you.

I needed to remember why I left the first time. I love you, I have loved you, and I will always love you.

I don't remember how we met. We were just in each other's lives. But I'll tell you about the moment that I wanted more from you. The moment that I knew I was in love with you.

I was walking home from town. Mum had me drop off some cakes for some of the businesses. I walked around the lake to see you sitting on the pier. You were watching the sun set. You watched it with this wonder and beauty. You were sixteen. You were beautiful. You had my heart in that moment. I had held your hand at thirteen, but at sixteen, you had my existence. I walked up to you and sat next to you. We were best friends, but this moment was magical. I knew that I loved you in that moment. You made my heart beat for a purpose. I asked you all the time, but this time, it was different. I asked you if you wanted me to walk you home with all my love and with all of my heart. Not because you were my best friend but because I was in love with you. I have been in love with you unconditionally. I have been in love with you for more than forever. You are my one and only love. I will always love you more than the last breath I take in life. I will love you more than the waves hug the shore. I will love you more and more with every day that passes us. I will love you after every star in existence burns out.

My last breath will be of my lungs exhaling my love for you. I will wait for you until I see you again, maybe in heaven or maybe in another life. Heaven may be out of my reach, so I will see you in another life. I will be looking for you. I may not know it, but each breath I take and each step I take will lead me closer to you. My favourite flower will be the cherry blossom. That'll be our code. And maybe in this other life, I get to grow old with you and love you the way

I should have.

No matter what life we live after this one, I will love you in every life we live until the end of time. I will find you again, Peyton. I will find you and I will love you, and it will be right for us. You are the most important person in my universe. You were everything in existence that made sense. You made me love so much that it terrified me to stay when I found out I was sick.

I never want you to be lonely, Peyton. Find him. He's out there waiting for you. He will love you the way I couldn't. He will love you until forever. Unlike me, he is capable of doing so. Find happiness, Peyton. Never be lonely. I will be watching over you. I will make sure you find him and happiness. I want you to have a life that gives you everything. Have kids. Have forever moments. Have a lifetime of memories. Love someone more than you loved me. Love him because he will love you through the pain I caused you. He will heal your heart and make you better. Introduce him to your mother's French toast and make him fall in love with them.

I was your first love, Peyton. But I am not your last. Your heart will heal and your belief in love will mend. You will be stronger and you will live a life without regrets.

You are the most beautiful and awe-inspiring woman, who deserves to have the universe at her feet. I've left you a box of all of our sometimes moments. I know some people give the love of their life diamonds or jewellery, but they don't mean as much as the Polaroids that proved our love. I've also left you my camera to take Polaroids of your forever moments. I want you to take a countless amount of pictures.

Peyton Olivia Spencer, our sometimes moments were my forever moments. We didn't have an end; we just had a goodbye until I see you again.

You were the cherry blossom of my life, the bright light that made me great.
But it's time it was said:
Supercalifragilisticexpialidocious.
Thank you for your love and for letting me fall in love with you. It has been a privilege.
It was never just a kiss.

You have my heart forever,
Callum

Peyton held his letter against her chest as she leant her head back on the tree and stared at their cherry blossoms. Tears ran down her face as she smiled and thought of all the times they'd sat under this tree and forgotten the world. This was their safe haven and the one place in the world where one kiss had changed them.

It wasn't just a kiss. It was a kiss that started our sometimes. And our sometimes is our forever.

Nine months later.

"Come on, Peyton!" Graham yelled out to her.

Peyton and her best friend, Madilynne, walked up the path together, as Peyton shook her head. "Mads, you are marrying an impatient man," she pointed out.

The moment Peyton reached the end of the path, Madilynne was grinning like a fool. "We both know he's excited about today. We all are. This man has the patience of a mountain."

Peyton made a gagging noise. Graham had spent his time between the city and the town. But now that Madilynne had finished her degree, she was moving back to work for the hotel, and with the lavender farm expanding, Graham needed to be onsite more often. Madilynne didn't mind. She'd admitted that she was tired of the city, and the moment Graham had proposed, she'd said that they were moving back to Daylesford.

Graham took his fiancée in his arms and kissed her. Not wanting to see anymore of her best friends' public display, Peyton took a step away from them and walked towards Jenny, who was standing just in front of the hotel. Peyton stood next to her and looked over the building. The cream-coloured stones were vibrant and beautiful against the lavender. Callum had designed her the most stunning hotel, and she couldn't wait for it to open for business in a few weeks' time.

"He'd be so proud of you," Jenny said, wiping her face.

Peyton wrapped her arm around Jenny's back and nodded. "I know."

"Are you all packed for your trip?"

"Yeah. Aunt Brenda has made sure that the Austria tour guide is safely in my carryon," Peyton said.

"We'll be here waiting for you," Jenny said.

Peyton smiled. Life had its moments of sheer pain and misery, but it also had its beautiful and pure moments. Right now, it was one of the beautiful ones. Peyton unwrapped her arm from around Jenny and stood straight before pulling out Callum's Polaroid camera from her bag.

"Wait for us," Aunt Brenda called, carrying a tray of drinks and placing them on the small table they set up.

Madilynne's father and mother walked from around the back of the hotel with plates of sandwiches and set them on the table, too.

"I'm proud of you, love," Uncle John said as he kissed her cheek. "Any words before the sign is bolted up and unveiled?"

Peyton looked around at the people who surrounded her. The people she loved. She didn't want this to be a big town celebration. This was about them—her family.

"Thank you all so much for being here and believing in me and the hotel. I wouldn't be standing here today without your support." When Peyton reached for a glass, everyone else followed. "And I wouldn't be here without Callum. He is my bright light that led me to this moment. I love and miss him like you do. He is the heart of this hotel by the lake. To Callum," she said, holding her cup in the air.

"To Callum!" they all cheered and clinked their glasses.

"Honey, you ready?" Jenny asked her husband.

Constable Fields nodded and looked at Nigel, the tradie who was once her dance floor builder and now friend.

"Ready, mate?"

Nigel nodded as he bolted up the sign in place. "We're ready," he said from the ladder.

"Do it!" Madilynne shouted.

Peyton held her breath as she felt Jenny and Graham's hands on her shoulders, supporting her. She was about to experience what her parents had when the first sign for The Spencer-Dayle had been put up. But this time, it was Peyton's hotel sign that was going up.

When Nigel and Constable Fields pulled off the sheet that covered the sign, Peyton's eyes watered at the beauty of it. It was perfect and it was theirs.

She finally understood this moment for her parents. It was unforgettable and awe inspiring.

"The Spencer-Reid," she read out loud.

Peyton lips tugged into a smile as the happy tears ran down her cheeks. Then she heard everyone clap as they took in the sign.

This is ours, Callum.

Peyton held up the Polaroid and took a picture of the hotel. Neither parents nor the town had built The Spencer-Reid. It had been built by her and those who supported her.

Handing Graham the Polaroid, Peyton spun around and slowly walked over to the edge of the path. She paused for a moment before she held up the camera so she could see the pier in the small, glass square. After taking a deep breath, she proceeded to take the picture. The Polaroid developed and she looked at it—a structure that held so many of their memories.

She took the permanent marker from the pocket of her bag, uncapped it, and held the tip to the white frame of the picture. Then she glanced up at the pier one more time before she started to write. The moment she lifted the pen off the picture, she held it up against the pier.

Sometimes moments defined our forever moments.

"Their wedding was beautiful," Jenny beamed as she looked through the Polaroids Peyton had taken.

Peyton smiled. "I can't believe two of my best friends got married. I can't believe how long they stayed apart because of me."

Jenny sighed and placed the photographs on the front desk. "And you brought them together."

She waved the Polaroids at Jenny, dismissing her. "Yeah, yeah."

After picking up the picture of Madilynne in her tulle mermaid wedding dress, she put it in the black frame, ready to be placed on the wall of sometimes moments. Then she held another stack of pictures from her trip from Austria and smiled. It was a trip she'd never forget. She had done it all. Everything she couldn't do with Callum, she had done for them.

The day she'd come home, Jay had been at her door. They sat on the step and stared at the Reid house together. Then he apologised and Peyton listened. In the end, she'd forgiven Jay just to keep peace. She wanted to live a life with no burdens, and Jay had been one. The moment she'd forgiven him, she'd felt free, ready to live every day like her last. After that day, when they walked past each other in town, they would turn and smile but never stop.

"I'll grab some of the frames from the office," Jenny said.

Peyton nodded and opened the lid of the pink box Oliver had delivered to her almost a year ago. Then she pulled out a stack of their Polaroids and smiled. She no longer cried as often as she had when Callum had died. She'd learned to appreciate their time together. And he'd been right—she did reflect on their time together.

She picked up the instant picture of him that she had taken and placed the rest in the box. The sight of him had her heat aching. It still did that. Peyton ran her finger down his beautiful face and smiled. She missed him. Her love still burned brightly and it always would.

When the doorbell rung, she set Callum's picture down. Peyton looked up, expecting a guest. Instead, a man holding a large bundle of lavender walked through the door. The first things she noticed were his plaid flannelette shirt and his work boots. Then she frowned at the muddy boots, which would leave dirt on her floorboards. She noticed that he held a clipboard, staring at it.

"I'm looking for Peyton Spencer," he said the moment he reached the desk.

When he lifted his chin, their eyes met. His light-brown ones had her breath catching. And for a moment, she swore her heart stopped. It was brief, but she felt it. Her heart hadn't done that for quite some time.

Since…

Peyton stopped her train of thought and focused on the surprised look on his face. The way his eyes twinkled and his lips parted had her breath catching. The unnamed man placed the lavender and clipboard on the desk before he rubbed his short beard.

"I'm Peyton Spencer," she said as her palms started sweating, which wasn't something she was familiar with.

"I have a delivery for you. Just need a signature here," he said, picking up the clipboard and handing it to her.

She let out a laugh, but she wasn't sure why.

"Is something funny?" he asked, raising his brow.

She shook her head, getting some control over herself. "I don't know. I'm sorry. That was rude." Peyton grabbed a pen and signed her name on the line. Then she took off the small envelope from the bundled lavender. After removing the card, she read it.

Have a great first day.

Love,
Mr & Mrs Scott.

"Thank you," she said, looking up at him. As she noticed the curiosity in his eyes, a blush reddened her cheeks.

"Cooper Hepburn. I'm the new operations manager while Graham and Mads are on their honeymoon," he said, introducing himself.

She nodded. "And I'm *still* Peyton Spencer. I'm the owner of The Spencer-Reid."

She handed over the clipboard, his hands gazing over hers. Her heart stopped once more and she became a little breathless. It was the smile he wore. It was beautiful and genuine.

"Well, maybe I'll see you around town, hotel girl." He grinned.

She shook her head. "Maybe I'll see you around…"

Cooper nodded at her before he turned and walked towards the exit.

The moment he reached the door, Peyton breathed out and said, "Lavender boy."

He stopped and quickly spun around, smiling at her. "Lavender boy?" he asked. The playful grin had her heart racing.

Callum's words ran through her head. *"I always knew you'd marry lavender boy."*

The twinkle in Cooper's eyes had Peyton swallowing hard. She knew that look. He might not know it, but she might have just seen forever in Cooper Hepburn's eyes.

She nodded. "Yes. Lavender boy."

"I'm glad I made this delivery today. It was nice meeting you, Peyton Spencer."

"You, too, Cooper Hepburn."

Cooper nodded once with a smile before he walked out of her hotel. When she felt the butterflies soar in her stomach, she knew. Pulling out the picture of her and Callum, her heart warmed at the look in Callum's eyes. It was the same look she'd seen in Cooper's.

"Thank you for sometimes, Callum. I think I may have found my forever with lavender boy."

Epilogue

Dear Callum Reid,

You don't know who I am, but I like to think you had an idea of me. My name's Cooper Hepburn, the husband to Peyton Hepburn and father to our child, Callum Stuart Hepburn. I've been meaning to write this for a while, but when Peyton got pregnant, my focus was on her and getting ready to welcome our son into our lives.

I feel like I know you. I've heard enough stories to know I would have liked you… Actually, that's probably a lie. I would have respected you, but I think if I had met you, I would have hated you. At the time, you had my wife's heart. And that would have killed me. You still have a place in her heart, and that's something I would never want to have. Her love for you will be something I can never try to claim.

I want to say that we've had the easiest of loves, but I would be lying. We've had an adventure, and adventures come with a lot of complications and a lot of successes. Peyton claims that I'm perfect, but I'm far from it. I try my best to be for her. But I want to tell you the two worst days of my life. They were the times I thought I had lost her. I will never forget those days.

The first day was when we were dating. I didn't know of you very well then. I was still trying my best to get her to trust me. It was the day after we'd first been intimate. She had cried, and I hated myself for making the woman I love cry. I didn't understand why she had cried. I didn't know. Peyton made me leave and she didn't talk to me for almost a week. When I couldn't take it anymore, I stormed to her house and demanded to know what I had done. She wouldn't answer me, and that's when I yelled at her. It was the first and last time I ever yelled at her. From the top of my lungs, I screamed, "You'd rather me dead and Callum alive, don't you? You hate that I'm alive and he's dead! You hate that you slept with me. You wish it were him and not me! Well guess what, Peyton? He's dead! And right now, the way you look at me, I'd rather I were the dead one. Maybe you'd love me more."

I'm not proud of those words. I'll always regret saying them. Peyton didn't speak to me for three weeks. I deserved it. I had accused her of not loving me because I wasn't dead. I was scared to lose her, but I had said everything that ensured that I would. I was jealous of you. I have never been jealous of anyone until I was of you, Callum. I wanted Peyton to love me. I wanted Peyton's heart. I believed there wasn't room for her to love me after you. I had planned to work the last few months off my contract and return to the suburbs. But I needed to leave quickly. I wasn't needed in town anymore. It was the night before I was going to leave when Peyton was at my door, crying. She apologised, saying that she was being selfish and that she should have told me. Graham had told her of my plans of leaving. She begged me not to go. She begged me to listen to her. When I agreed, she said only three words, and they were 'I love you.'

I have no explanation for how I felt when I heard those three words. But I think you know what it's like to be loved by Peyton Spencer. When I confessed that I loved her, too, she cried and kissed me. That night, she told me everything about you. She told me that she'd cried because she'd realised she felt guilty for loving me more than she loved you. That, in some way, she felt like she was cheating on you by loving me. I had never felt like more of an asshole than those weeks of my life. I almost lost Peyton and I didn't want that to have ever happen again.

The second worst day of my life was when our son was born. It's a terrible thing for a father to say, but just listen. You'll understand. Peyton went into labour and we rushed to the hospital. Everything went to plan until after my son screamed and Peyton's hand fell from mine. Our son was too big to be born naturally and a Caesarean was performed. Peyton didn't even see him before her eyes shut. She was haemorrhaging and losing a lot of blood. The helpless feeling of knowing my wife was about to die was surreal. I had never felt so lost in my life. In that moment, I was blessed with a beautiful son, but I was close to losing the love of my life.

I also knew what it must have been like in the last moments of your life. I felt like I was you, Callum. I didn't know how to say goodbye. I didn't want to believe what was happening. I thought of my life without Peyton and it was impossible. I was scared. The jealously I held for you disappeared and every self-doubt I had left me. The only thing that mattered in my life was ensuring my son grew up with his mother by his side. Peyton doesn't know why I named my son after you. Why? Because while the doctor was trying to save her, she called out your name and reached out in the direction the nurse had taken our son. I wasn't envious or jealous that she hadn't called out for me. Peyton had named our son and I was proud.

I'd never thought the feeling of being Peyton's husband could be surpassed. I was wrong. Being the father of her child did it. The relief of knowing we were going to raise our son together comes close. I prayed to God to save her, but I also prayed to you, hoping you'd influence Fate.

Peyton showed me your last letter to her. You spoke of her experiencing life's firsts after you, Callum. Those life's firsts she shared with me. And they have been the best moments of my life. (I also fell in love with her mother's French toast the moment Peyton introduced me to them!)

Everything you wanted her to achieve, she has. She became someone's fiancée, someone's wife, and the mother of someone's child.

For whatever reason, I was blessed to be that someone. And for that, I thank you. You played your part in our forever. You brought Graham and Madilynne together. If they had never married, I would have never taken over the farm, never met Peyton, never fallen in love with Peyton, never asked her to marry me, never married her, and never held and loved our son.

She tells me that I am her forever moments and that you were her sometimes. But I think that's where she's wrong. In some stages of her life, Peyton never had sometimes. In those moments, she lived and she had forever.

I hope that the man you wrote of was me. I hope I do justice to the man you envisioned for Peyton. I hope you can see that I've done my best to be enough for her. I hope that you approve of my love. If not, I'll love her harder than I already do, although I'm not sure that's possible.

Thank you for loving Peyton the way you did. I know

that she will always love you and I hope one day she tells our son of you.
Thank you for Peyton. Until the day I die, I will never stop thanking you, Callum Reid.
My happiness, my wife, and my son are because of you.

Cooper Hepburn.

THE END

Remember me and smile, for its better to forget than to remember me and cry.

~Dr Seuss

A message from **LEN**

Sometimes Moments has been a very special book for me. Being my first standalone, it allowed me to write freely. I loved the concept of this book and what 'sometimes moments' meant. I'm not going to lie, I was worried and scared. And there were times where I didn't want to publish it at all. The ending was something I had never written before. But when I sat in class back in my final year of university in 2014, this story began and I knew how it ended from the moment I wanted to write it. I wanted Sometimes Moments to not be about a 'sad' story. I wanted it to be about a beautiful story. The story of Peyton. The story of Callum. The story of them. I wanted it to show people the beauty of hope and of there being *more*. The beauty that 'The End' wasn't something to cause pain. There is always a forever—even if it wasn't the ideal or wanted forever. Because well, life is a cluster of sometimes moments.

If anything, I hope this story showed you the beauty of the little moments in your life. Appreciate them. Love them. They'll be the times you reflect on later in life. They will be the times that make you smile or laugh or maybe even cry. They will be the times in your life that you look back on and *feel*.

Live life one sometimes moment at a time.

Until you have two.

Then three.

Then four.

And then you have a cluster.

That's when you're making forever moments.

Sometimes moments are what make your forever memorable and beautiful.

Acknowledgements

Writing this book was tough but it was also something I loved writing. When I sat and thought about who to thank, I wasn't sure who to *truly* thank. In all my books I thank a wide range of people. But for this book, I will thank the ones that made Sometimes Moments what it is.

First and foremost, Jaycee Ford and Alex Rosa. The very first to read Sometimes Moments. They happen to be the people who this book is dedicated to. My best friends. I wouldn't be the author that I am without you both. I love you both so greatly. Two of the greatest and most important people in my life.

My cover designer, Najla Qamber. You took so many different pictures and made me the most beautiful and perfect cover. Everything I envisioned you made it all the more breathtaking. Thank you for your hard work and the for the love you put into making my covers.

My editor, Michelle Kampmeier. You took this crazy draft and made it beautiful. You added a lot more soul into it than I could. Thank you for not laughing at all my silly mistakes and for the changes. You made this book flow beautifully. And thank you for your friendship and for agreeing to edit Sometimes Moments.

My proofreader, Jenny Carlsrud Sim. You have been vital in publishing this book. You took proofreading to beyond what it is. You gave it love and attention. Thank you for squeezing Sometimes Moments in. Thank you for your changes and suggestions. Thank you for your updates and your enthusiasm and love. Thank you for pointing out teasers and for making this book *perfect*. I have loved every minute we have worked together.

My beta readers, Danielle, Michal and Veronica. Thank you for reading this story in its first draft stages. Thank you for being there at its weakest and for believing in the story. You've all been amazing.

There is someone special I need to thank, Erin Spencer from *Southern Belle Book Blog*. Erin, thank you for listening to Jenny talk up Sometimes Moments. Thank you for giving it a chance and your time. When I first got into contact with you, you blew me away with you enthusiasm and want to read a book by someone you have never come across. I wanted to be your friend the moment you said that you'd *beg* to read Sometimes Moments. Your voice message still makes me smile. Has anyone ever told you your accent is the most sweetest thing? I loved it. Thank you for loving Sometimes Moments and for believing in it.

As always, thank you to my family and close friends. For having to put up with me in this whole writing-shin-dig affair. I love you all.

And my readers, thank you for believing me. For *still* believing me. Third book I've published and you're still here. If this is the first book you've ever read by me, thank you for giving me the chance to let my story take up your time. Thank you for the chance to let me enter your lives. Thank you for loving my books enough to let me continue to write more. Your love gives me the confidence and hope I need to continue. I strive to be my best to give you all the best. I'm where I am because of you.

Also, to the many blogs that have supported me. Thank you for writing a status or a post about me and my books. You have no idea how important you are to me. To all the authors I've met along the way, friends until the very end!

To Penny Rudge, lonely island FOREVER! Thank you for being my friend in all of this. Our random chats and loves. I just needed to thank you for all your love and support.

You are all never my sometimes—always my forever.

Thank you <3

Your Sometimes Moments

Last year I asked the public to share their own sometimes moments. The responses have been absolutely beautiful. It is a privilege to be able to read the moments in my readers and fellow authors' lives.

These are your sometimes moments…

When you held my hand for the first time. You hesitated at first and then you exhaled. It was like a 'screw it! Now or never' kind of exhale. And then, you grazed my pinkie and then went for it. You held my hand. And then you started the story of us. And then somewhere along the lines it was no longer us. It was you. And then it was me. We were no longer a we. But I still love that moment and will always treasure that exhale you made.

Len Webster, author of *Sometimes Moments.*

I asked him when he knew I was the one, and he replied with, "The moment I laid eyes on you." I was speechless, so he came closer to my ear and whispered, "And I fell in love with you the moment you said your first words to me.

Marcella Williams

My husband and I have been together for ten years and married for almost eight. We have our ups and downs, but mostly downs as of late. Exactly two days before our ten year anniversary, I was rushed to the hospital. After surgery and suffering from complications, we were told that I might have a bloodclot in my lung. We don't pray as much anymore but he and I prayed before the test. The doctor came in after the test and my husband gripped my hand. The doctor then said no bloodclot. I smiled and turned toward my husband as I saw a tear roll down his cheek. That was the moment that I knew that we were

stronger than illness and petty arguments, and we would have a lot more sometimes moments in our future.
Jaycee Ford, author of the bestselling series, *The Love Bug series*

I roll the car window down and inhaled deeply.
"What are you doing?"
"I love the smell of wet pavement after it's been hot."
"... me, too."

- Renee Roy

One beautiful day I was cleaning my boyfriend's and my room. I was listening to music not really paying attention. For some reasons I happened to look out the window and see my boyfriend in the yard with his son. At that moment 'So small' by Carrie Underwood happened to start playing on the radio. I sat down and cried because then I realized I loved those two men in my life, no matter what problems we faced. Unfortunately, we ended up not making it together but that moment is forever with me and until the day I die, I will most likely love them.

- Tabitha Borger

About the Author

The truth is, Len Webster is a romance-loving Melbournian with dreams of finding her version of 'The One.' She calls Australia home, but secretly wishes a man with a beautiful accent would whisk her away. She's been called a hopeless romantic and a firm believer of happily ever afters, which she doesn't object to.

Having just completed her Bachelor in Business and Commerce, Len can be found daydreaming of her next Europe adventure or swooning over Mr Darcy. Her best friends are a hot cup of tea, red velvet cupcakes, a warm jumper and her MacBook, ready to write to her heart's content.

Connect with Len

Facebook: https://www.facebook.com/lennwebster

Twitter: https://twitter.com/lennwebster

Goodreads: https://www.goodreads.com/author/show/7502135.Len_Webster

Amazon: http://www.amazon.com/Len-Webster/e/B00HIFA2GM/ref=ntt_athr_dp_pel_14

Instagram: http://instagram.com/lennwebster

Made in the USA
Charleston, SC
16 January 2015